The Last Day

By
M.M.E. Yoho

For My Husband who provides me with never-failing support and encouragement, my children who bring joy and light into my life, and finally for my mother, I miss you everyday.

Preface

If I had known that May 22nd was going to be the last day I would have been more attentive. My mother had gotten out of bed early to make me a farewell meal, and I would have spent more time lingering over breakfast with my parents and younger sister if I had known. I should have savored each bite of those fluffy pancakes topped with real maple syrup, eaten just one more piece of that crispy applewood bacon. If I just would have spent more time reassuring my mother her startling blue eyes might have lit up with their usual humor rather than the worry that was reflected there when I said goodbye. I definitely would not have let the last words I said to my sister be so harsh and dismissive.

Perhaps if I had known that it was the last day, I would have done more than just glance up to look for rain clouds. I would have also noted that the blue sky looked a little too blue and maybe a bit too perfect. I should have realized that the clouds seemed very uniform, all shaped and sized the same. The birds weren't chirping and singing their usual springtime songs of joy. I realize that now.

Sampson, our black and white cocker spaniel, wasn't his happy-go-lucky self that morning either. I wish that I hadn't been so frustrated with him, that I had taken just a few extra minutes from my day to pet him and scratch that particular spot just behind his left ear that always made him so happy. Instead, I just yelled at him to hurry up and stop staring at the sky like an alien was going to appear. However, I was in a complete state of oblivion. I could hear Mrs. Trible next door in her backyard yelling at her dog, Petey, in frustration.

Looking back now, it all seems so obvious, but at that moment in time, it just seemed like a typical day. The Sunday morning paper had been waiting for my father, as usual, on the doorstep. Lucy, my sister, had seemed annoying as she complained because I was getting to go to the beach with friends a week before the family headed there. She was stuck at home finishing up her last week of school while I was getting to enjoy a graduation celebration with my friends.

Sometimes perfection precedes anarchy and normal precedes chaos. On that day I didn't notice the perfection in the sky, and I also didn't know that anarchy would soon rule. Life seemed exciting and new, yet ordinary. I didn't know how the day would end and couldn't even imagine the struggles that were headed my way. All I saw was a brand new sunny day that was going to lead me into the best summer of my life. If only I had known that it was going to be the last day I would have done things so very differently.

Chapter One

I opened my eyes with excitement when I heard the phone alarm chime out my wake up tone. Today is going to be a great day, I thought as I completed my morning ritual of a few quick stretches, followed by a quick check of my phone to see which of my friends had been trying to contact me. I glanced around my large room and smiled at the sight of the packed luggage waiting by the door.

I love this room, I thought as I rolled out of my queen sized bed. I had carefully chosen every picture on the wall and the grey paint, with scarlet accents, reflected my love of all things from The Ohio State University. Today was the last time I would see my Ohio bedroom for a while. My parent's business let us have the flexibility and luxury of living in the upper-class suburbs of Columbus, Ohio during the school year and spending summer months at our beach house in North Carolina. Today my friends and I would head to North Carolina, a week before my family, to open the beach house and celebrate our recent high school graduation. After a summer filled with rest and relaxation, I was planning to return to Columbus and move onto campus to start college. That is when adulting would begin, but for now, I was going to take some time to have fun and get a great tan.

I heard my mother moving around in the kitchen downstairs as I stepped into the shower and realized that I needed to pick up my pace or Ty would be here to pick me up before I even had the chance to eat breakfast. I let myself daydream about Ty as I quickly washed my hair and finished up all necessary shower tasks. Ty, also known as Tyler Robins, was my beautiful rebel. My parents weren't big fans of my relationship with Ty, even though they had known him since birth and his parents for longer. They just thought that we were just too young to be as serious as we were. Ty's father and mine had been friends throughout high school and college, and although my father was fond of Tom Robins, he didn't understand what he called his "unconventional, doomsday thinking." Mr. Robins was sure that sooner, rather than later, there would be some sort of catastrophic event which would lead to either complete annihilation of the human race or, at the very least, a drastic change in life as we know it. The Robins family had a bunker in their backyard, and Ty's mother had a year's worth of food stockpiled. They were definitely preppers like you saw on the doomsday television shows, and although Ty made jokes about it, I knew he was prepared just in case his father happened to be right. He always seemed to be more aware of what was going on around him than the rest of our group. Ty's father had made sure that the truck that Ty drove was equipped to handle anything that might happen and, instead of tools in the shiny silver toolbox that sat in the back, one could find any supplies that they might need if the world went crazy. Mr. Robins made a good living helping others prepare for imminent doom, and there was no way that his son wouldn't be ready as well.

I would say that I fell in love with Ty despite his prepper tendencies. To be honest, I fell in love with him when I was five years old, and he was six. He wouldn't stop making fun of my name and pulling my hair. His hair was too long, and his smile was crooked, but he made me laugh and pushed me to step beyond my comfort zone and try new things in life. He goaded me into climbing a tree when I was six, and boy was my mother angry about the ruined Easter dress and scraped knees that came along with that adventure. From camping, which I have grown to love, to eating a cricket, which I will never forgive him for making me do, Ty had been with me through it all. When I was about ten, his father began talking about a catastrophic event being imminent, and he believed that everyone should be preparing for it. Ty idolized his father, and I knew that, even though he made jokes with our group of friends when his father's prepping practices came up, or someone made what they thought was a funny end of the world joke, he really did believe what his father had always told him. Sometimes when he held me close, he would whisper in my ear, "I've got you, Elli. No matter what I will always keep you safe."

After a shortened version of my usual morning rituals, I threw on the clothes that I had so carefully chosen the night before. The hours that we would be spending in the car required that I wear something comfortable, but I wanted to look good too. I always tried to look good for Ty. As far as I am concerned, I'm average looking at best. My brown hair might shine, but it usually had its own idea about what it wanted to do unless I was willing to spend over an hour taming it with a straightener. My eyes couldn't decide if they wanted to be blue or green and there was nothing special about my face. It was just an average shape, and I was just average looking Eloise. Even my name wasn't impressive. Eloise is so old-fashioned, as my parents had intended my name to be. My sister suffered the same fate. Lucy was really Lucille. At least my friends all called me Elli, which I love, but Lucy is stuck with Lucy like the annoying Charlie Brown character. Lucy had at least gotten my mother's flawless beauty. She was long-legged and thin. Her blonde hair always stayed in place, and her eyes were so light blue that they almost appeared translucent. I was shorter and curvier than both my mother and my twelve-year-old sister. Ty always told me that I was too self-conscious because, according to him, I am the most beautiful and perfect creature on the planet. When he said it, I always responded that love is blind, and so he must really love me. I see the way all the other girls look at him and then at me. They are obviously trying to figure out how someone as attractive as him could choose to be with someone as mousy as me. I often ask myself the same thing so I can't blame them for wondering.

The smell of bacon emanating from the kitchen made my stomach growl and reminded me to stop contemplating Ty and get down to the breakfast which Mom was working so hard to create. I was struggling to get the biggest of my suitcases down the steps to the foyer when a strong arm reached over me, lifting it as easily as a pillow. Startled, I jumped before looking up to see the smiling face of my father.

"Good morning El. Did you pack everything you own or have you got some rocks in here too?" Although Dad's eyes were smiling, I could see the worry there as well. I knew that he and my mother were worried about me taking off on this trip without them. It would be the first time that I had traveled without the family, and they had always been very protective of me. I think the worry and protectiveness came from the fact that I was always sick as a child. Even at birth, I had been too small to come home from the hospital for a month. Of course, that could have been because I was born eight weeks early. My mother always calls me her miracle baby and a fighter, but deep down I know that I'm really not a miracle or a fighter. I'm afraid of everything. Strangers make me nervous. Crowds and parties are enough to send me into a panic attack. Without Ty and my friends, who know me so well, I think I would probably live life like a hermit crab. Instead of a shell though, I would curl up in a blanket with a hot chocolate and a good book.

I released the suitcase as Dad grabbed it. Before he could leave, I turned to kiss his cheek. I would always be daddy's girl, no matter how old I was. "Good morning Dad. I think I left a few things behind, but I have another few suitcases to grab. I was going to let Ty have the honor of going up to get them for me when he gets here. I just don't want to forget anything. I want to relax and enjoy this summer, and maybe shop a little because I am sure that even with all of these suitcases there is something that I am forgetting."

My dad chuckled as he picked up the heavy suitcase and headed down the stairs. For a brief moment, I considered going back to my room to grab another suitcase but the smell of the bacon was like a siren's song to my stomach, and I quickly bounced down the stairs and towards the kitchen. I passed Dad about halfway down and called out, "I'll try to leave some bacon for you, but if I were you I wouldn't expect to find any left!"

I saw Dad pick up his pace a bit as I rounded the corner into the kitchen. Mom was standing by the stove looking more like a cover girl model than a mother of two in her early 40s. She was dressed in a cami top with some pink lounge pants. Her blonde hair was piled in a messy bun, and there was a natural pink glow to her cheeks and on her lips. She looked like her name, Barbie. She hated her name, and, in fact, chose to go by her middle name, Marie. Her hate of her name is the main reason that Lucy and I had such old-fashioned names.

A mound of bacon sat on the counter beside the stove, and I could see that she had been mixing what appeared to be pancake batter. She quickly sat the bowl aside, walked over, and hugged me. I could see the worry in her eyes but chose to ignore it as I returned her hug. I wasn't sure that she was going to let go, but she finally did and went back to her bowl.

"Good morning, Mom. Those wouldn't happen to be banana pancakes would they?" Mom gave me a wink and a half smile as she started to pour the batter onto the griddle. "Are you spoiling me? Or trying to make me look bad in a bikini?"

"Oh my dear, you would look beautiful wrapped in rags, when will you learn this? I just thought you might like a few of your favorites to get a good start to this morning. We will miss you, and you must promise me that you and Ty will be careful. Just because Ty is eighteen doesn't mean that he is mature enough to be responsible for one of my babies. What if there is a car accident?"

"Mom, come on. You know better than to worry about how well Ty can take care of me. I also think that I do a pretty good job of making my own decisions and taking care of myself. Now let me stuff myself with your delicious cooking before I am stuck eating fast food for a week."

Lucy stumbled into the kitchen just as the first pancakes were coming off the griddle. Her complaining began immediately, as had become the pattern in the past few months. She used to be happy and, well, pleasant most of the time but as my graduation had neared she had become increasingly difficult to coexist with peacefully. She had been getting progressively more annoyed at my growing independence while she was still expected to be in the house by 9 pm, even on weekends, to her utter embarrassment. Lucy and her friends abused the lifestyle of privilege that my parents both worked hard to provide us. Lucy was too young to remember any of those years when my parents struggled to keep food on the table and the heat on, but I remembered them all too well. I don't take for granted all of the comforts and conveniences that we had. I was shocked when I had gotten a car for a Christmas gift the year before, but Lucy believed that she was entitled to have everything that she wanted and do anything that she wanted without limit. A giant sigh preceded her bored, annoyed opening complaint.

"It's Sunday! I don't know why I have to get up early just because Eloise is getting to leave for the beach." She always called me Eloise when she was annoyed. "It's not like I am getting to go off with my friends to have a good time. I could have slept in for hours!"

"Good morning to you too, Lucille." I returned with a bright smile in her direction. Her glare at me gave me a bit of satisfaction. I knew that she wanted more freedom from my parents but taking her frustration out on me wasn't going to fly. I had spent years taking her places with me and including her with my friends, but she was just too young to do the things that we did now. I was almost an adult, and she needed to understand that. "I am sure that you will have a great last week of school without me. You can follow Jason Dean around like you always do, all doe-eyed, hoping that he will pay attention to you."

I could see the hurt in Lucy's eyes, as well as disproval in my mother's, as soon as the words left my mouth. I felt immediately guilty. I knew I shouldn't have said anything, but she just annoyed me so much sometimes. I opened my mouth to apologize, but Lucy jumped up from the table, called me a jerk and left the kitchen. I didn't look up as my mother sat a plate of bacon and pancakes in front of me.

"I'm sorry," I said quietly. "I'll go apologize."

Dad gently patted my hand and Mom patted my back as she walked away.

"She won't listen to you right now. You know that. You have to give her some time. I know that she pushes your buttons on purpose, but you have to not let her bait you into responses like that. Don't let it ruin your day. Call her later with an apology, but for now, eat your food before it gets cold." Mom said as she sat the heated maple syrup in front of me. I noticed that the plate she sat down for Dad had a heaping serving of bacon and a large stack of pancakes, but her plate contained some fruit and just one piece of bacon, a treat for her.

"Mom, why don't you have some pancakes? They are so good!" I muttered as I placed a fork full in my mouth.

"I have to watch my figure," she replied as she daintily speared a fresh strawberry and placed it gently in her mouth. My mother was the last person who needed to watch her figure or count calories, but she always seemed to be on some fad diet. I always wondered why she worried about it so much, but she worried about every calorie and even an ounce of weight gain. I knew it wasn't caused by pressure from my father. He was always telling her that she was stunning and didn't need to worry about diets and calories, while he was trying to get her to taste his cheesecake. She had worked as a model before she married my dad and she once told me about how much pressure there was for models to maintain excessively thin figures. In one of her modeling pictures that I had found hidden away, she looked like skin and bones. It just looked very unhealthy, in my opinion. She must have sensed my disappointment in the fact that she wouldn't join us for pancakes because she took a bite of her bacon and reached with her fork to my plate. I smiled when she stole a tiny piece of my pancake. It was somewhat bittersweet that she seemed to savor it so much.

Talk at the table turned to a discussion of the route that my friends and I would take for the trip, as well as our plans to camp for the night in the mountains along the way. I knew my parents were very nervous to send me off with a group of teenagers, but, for the most part, my friends and I were very responsible. Ty was always ready for anything that might go wrong, and he always made sure that I was safe. You would think that his prepping tendencies would make my parents more comfortable, I thought to myself. It wasn't Ty that they disliked, it was just the idea of me being so entirely devoted to someone at my age. They thought that we were too young. My mother always told me that I didn't know who else was out there, and my response was still the same. I didn't need to know who else was out there because Ty is the perfect human for me. He makes me a better person, and I do the same for him. That is all that matters. Life isn't about trying every piece of chocolate, I told her, just finding your favorite flavor. Once you have that, you don't need to taste every other one.

After having been cautioned about the danger of strangers, what to do in the case of an accident, and how to avoid all the other common pitfalls that naïve teenagers succumb to, my parents moved on to discussing all the responsibilities that we would have once we got to the beach house.

My mother started. "You know that it can't be ALL days of lying on the beach when you get there. The house has been shut up for months. You will need to get everything back to living condition. I added funds to your bank account, so you should go to the grocery and get everything that you will need for the week, as well as the basics that we can use for a while. Make sure you call Bill. You remember Bill, Mr. Dugan, the property manager? Yes. Call him when you arrive so he knows that you made it there and he can help you if there is an issue that needs immediate attention."

"If you get there and find damage," Dad continued, "and it is not something that you need Bill to take care of right away call me. I will get someone to take care of it. If you find anything else awry call me and I will tell you what to do from there."

"And absolutely no alcohol and no big parties," Mom added. "Just you and the friends that you have told us are going. Relaxing and having fun is good, but partying and damaging is not."

I rolled my eyes a bit at the last comment. Mom knew me and my friends better than that. We did not drink or party. Yes, we liked to go out and have fun, but my core group of friends did not participate in the activities that get most teenagers into trouble. My mind momentarily went to Gary. Gary had been a part of our group from elementary school. He was the kind of kid who worried about everyone being included, and he would go out of his way to comfort anyone who he thought was unhappy. He'd stuck with us until about the eighth grade when his parents divorced. He took the break up poorly and started hanging out with a different crowd of friends. They partied, a lot. I had heard that drinking and drugs were always prevalent at Gary's events, but I had no firsthand knowledge because I hadn't gone to any of that kind of his parties. He and his mother still lived in the big, extravagant house two streets over, while his father had bought, and married, up according to Gary. He was bitter, and he took it out on his mother, his girlfriends, and himself.

Gary had been the talk of the town for the past few months. At his last big party, Gary's girlfriend had been found floating face down in the pool. Although the partygoers pulled her out of the pool and tried to revive her, they hadn't called 9-1-1 for fifteen minutes. By the time they arrived there was nothing that they could do for her. I'd heard rumors that Gary was responsible for her being found in the pool in that condition but rumors are just that, rumors, and I didn't know what to think. All I knew is that Gary was sitting in the county jail because he had been eighteen at the time and the sweet, considerate boy I knew from elementary school was gone.

"Mom, you know we don't do that. We aren't like Gary. We will take care of everything we need to, and then we will hang out on the beach perfecting our tans. I have no desire to hang out with a bunch of drunken teenage idiots. Where's the fun in that for me? I would end up taking care of everyone and feeling responsible for making sure they stay safe."

"I'm sorry sweetie. I worry about you. I'm your mother; it's my job."

I pushed away from the table and gave her a quick hug before grabbing my plate. "I have a little bit of time before Ty is supposed to be here. Do you want me to clean up?"

"Oh, that's sweet but don't worry about that. Clean up will be a great distraction for your father after you've left." We all laughed at that. Dad hadn't touched a dirty dish with the purpose of cleaning it since longer than I could remember. As much as I love my father, he has very traditional roles about what "the woman" does around the house and what "the man" should do. Luckily those beliefs didn't extend to the business he and my mother had built because there they were completely equal in all ways. I think that my dad says that cleaning the house is "woman's work" because he hates to clean. He is happiest when he is outside, working in the yard or working on the cars. He also knows that my mother doesn't mind all of the domestic chores. Of course, there is also the fact that, for her birthday a few years ago, he hired someone to come in and clean two days a week, so the domestic chores do not include icky things like bathroom scrubbing or, my least favorite, dusting. The inevitable floating dust particles always gave me sneezing fits. Mom said I was probably allergic to dust, but I refused to go to the allergist to get poked by needles to find out. My solution was better, I thought, I just didn't dust.

After I cleaned up my place at the table and placed all of the dirty dishes in the sink, I heard Sampson whining at the back door. I went over and knelt to pet him, but he looked up at me like he couldn't figure out what was going on. I opened the door so that he could go out, and he slowly made his way into the backyard. Usually, he was full of energy and happiness in the morning. I guess he is as upset with me as Lucy is, I thought to myself. I bent down to quickly scratch his favorite spot just behind his ear and told him that he would be coming to the beach to join me in just a week. His eyes were sad as he stood on the deck looking up at the sky. After giving him a minute or two to go out and do whatever it was that he needed to do, I started to get a little frustrated with him.

"Sampson, go out and go potty!" I said to him sternly. Usually, he didn't have any issues with heading out to explore the yard. He liked to make sure that there weren't any creatures hiding in it that didn't belong. Today, however, he would not leave the deck or stop staring up at the clear blue sky. I glanced up myself, trying to figure out what the heck was so interesting but all I saw were blue skies and fluffy clouds. I heard our neighbor, Mrs. Trible yelling at Petey. Apparently, Petey didn't want to go potty either, I thought. At least I wasn't the only one dealing with a contrary dog this morning. After a few more minutes of trying to coax the dog to go out to the yard, I gave up and had to practically drag him back into the house.

My dad was sitting in the living room watching his Sunday morning news show but looked up to the ruckus that the dog and I created as I dragged him back inside. "There is something wrong with this dog!" I exclaimed while Sampson sat at my feet whining. "He won't even go out into the yard. He just sits on the deck and stares up at the sky. There's nothing in the sky but clouds!"

Dad turned towards us and called the dog, who refused to stop whining at the back door. "That is really strange. Maybe there was some big creature in the backyard last night, and Sampson can smell it. I'll go out in a bit to look around. Don't worry too much about it pumpkin. I'm sure that he's fine. He's probably just having a bad day. If he senses that you are leaving him behind and thinks that if he acts weird, you will stay here to take care of him."

I bent down to give him Sampson a hug. The sound of someone pulling into the driveway caught my attention and I quickly headed to the front door. By the time I got there and opened it Ty was stepping onto the porch. He immediately scooped me up into a big hug and placed a tiny kiss on the spot just below my right ear that always sent tingles emanating in all directions. He gently sat me back down on my feet, and I heard his quiet chuckle as he looked into my eyes.

"Good morning beautiful. I'm happy to see that I can still make you blush babe."

Looking into Ty's eyes always made me feel as if I was the most special girl in the world. He eyes shined with love and acceptance. The only problem was that they were too far away. Where I was small, soft and curvy, Ty was all hard muscles and angles. There was also the fact that he was a full foot taller than me. Our friends all made fun of us, but, in my mind, we fit perfectly, well except for that pesky fact that he is beautiful and I am a plain as unbuttered toast. Blech!

This morning his hair was as wild and unruly as his spirit for adventure. Just looking at him I knew that we would have the best summer of our lives. I knew that he would keep me safe, no matter what went wrong, and I knew that he would do everything in his power to make sure I enjoyed every moment of the time that we had. The best part was that Ty would not be leaving at the end of the week like the rest of my friends. He was planning to stay with us for at least the month, maybe longer if I could talk my parents into it. Nothing sounded better to me than sitting on a beach with Ty by my side. I mean, I love my family but Lucy was getting annoying, and my parents were so busy, even when we were at the beach, that they often didn't have a lot of downtimes to devote to the simple task of relaxing. Sundays were the only exception. When Lucy was born, and their business started to take off, they had made a rule that there would be no business on Sundays. They didn't even make a simple offhand comment about the business on Sundays. Once they were done on Saturday, there was no more talk of J & M Inc. until Monday morning at 8 a.m.

I grabbed Ty's hand and pulled him into the house. I was ready to get going on this adventure, and I was sure that he was too. He chuckled again when he saw my big suitcase at the bottom of the stairs, and I lightly slapped him in response.

"Just so you know, I have two more upstairs waiting for you to go bring them down for me."

"Did you pack everything you own?"

"No! Just everything I need," I laughed back at him, smiling my most angelic smile.

He leaned down and whispered in my ear, "Oh? So you have some cute, short, lacy nighties in there?"

I could tell that the blush was back. I refused to look at him as he once again chuckled and straightened back to full height. These suggestive comments were not unusual from him. He's a guy; I get that. I knew that most of our friends were having sex and, it wasn't that I didn't want to be with Ty in that way, but I didn't want to rush into anything simply because everyone else was. He and I had sat down about a year ago and had a serious conversation about it. I told him that I just wasn't ready and that I didn't think that we had any reason to rush because I believed that we would have a lifetime together. He hadn't pressured me at all, either before or after our conversation. However, making me blush remained one of his favorite pastimes. I was used to his little teasing comments, and I knew that if he thought that he was truly making me uncomfortable, he wouldn't make them. Uncomfortable in a negative way wasn't even close to how I would describe the way that his comments made me feel.

"Mr. Randalls, good morning sir." Dad had walked in from the living room when he heard Ty's voice.

"Good morning, Tyler. How are your parents?"

"They are good, sir. Dad has been working on some new defensive systems that he wants to market. They are very innovative. Mom is thinking of starting to teach some classes on some of the old-fashioned methods for canning and preserving food, as well as other pre-industrial ways of household life. I think one of these days I'm going to go home to find she has made my clothes out of cloth she wove herself. I'm not quite sure I'm ready for the American settler look yet. How are you this morning, sir?"

"It's just another lazy Sunday morning here. Nothing out of the ordinary, except for the fact that my oldest daughter is taking off with her boyfriend for her first independent vacation. No reason to stress at all. We also have a dog that is a bit weird today. Don't we El? I was just going to grab my shoes to go check around outside to see if something unusual is going on in the backyard."

"Anything I can help you with sir?"

"No, I think El has some manual labor for you to do. Just don't leave until I get my goodbyes you two." Dad patted Ty on the back and headed to the hall closet to get his shoes. Ty and I turned and headed up the stairs to grab my remaining bags. I saw Lucy stick her head out of her door as we reached the top of the staircase but when she saw me looking she quickly pulled it back in and shut the door. Still mad at me, I thought. I guess I'll have to wait to apologize by phone later.

At the top of the stairway, Ty paused, unsure where to go. My parents' rules were quite strict when it came to boys upstairs, they weren't allowed to be there. I had mentioned earlier that I was going to have Ty get my suitcases and, since he was just going to get them, I knew him being there would not be an issue. As he had not been allowed in my room before, Ty had no clue where my room actually was. I turned to the right and tugged his hand to lead him to my room. I don't know why, but I felt very nervous about Ty seeing my bedroom. It seemed very intimate to me as most of my private moments, both good and bad, had occurred in my bedroom. I had lied in bed and cried myself to sleep every night during the six days we had been broken up two years ago, and the realization that I loved him had occurred early in the morning on the seventh day. We hadn't even had the slightest of arguments since that week. I think that the week had been an intense learning experience for both of us. The cause had been such a stupid disagreement over friend's actions anyway, but we learned a lot about ourselves and each other. We were now a stronger couple, all because of the torment of those seven very long days.

Ty paused at the doorway to my room, and I could see his eyes sweeping from one side of the room to the other. When his eyes landed on the bed, they paused for a moment, and I saw him swallow before he scanned on. The door to the closet was open, and his eyes paused again at my closet where my clothes were all neatly hung and color coordinated by type.

"You know," he commented, "once we are so happily married and living in our little cottage on the beach our closet will not be nearly so neat."

As Ty walked further into the room to pick up the suitcases that I had left on the bed, his eyes caught on the door to the attached bathroom that was slightly ajar. Again I noticed the swallow. "So, you have your own bathroom? This is where you shower, maybe take bubble baths? Where you complete all of those secret grooming rituals that girls have?"

Once again the blush was back. The difference this time was that Ty didn't seem to be doing it on purpose. It was like his mind was providing him glimpses of my private moments, and it seemed more intimate than was comfortable for me. I casually walked over and closed the bathroom door. I decided it was time to try to lighten the mood a bit between us, so I made my way to the suitcases.

Teasingly I said, "Do you think you are strong enough to carry these suitcases downstairs for me?"

After making the statement and not getting a reply I casually glanced at Ty, trying to not let him see how his earlier comments had affected me. My mistake, I realized, was twofold. First, I should have never come to stand by the bed, which drew his attention to me standing by the bed. Second, I should never have looked up into his eyes after I had done so. The space between us seemed to be filled with an electrical charge. The look in his eyes was hungry, for lack of a better word. He started to slowly walk towards me, and, if my mother's voice hadn't rung out as she came up the stairs, I'm not sure what would have happened.

"Hey kids, are you guys up here getting the suitcases?"

At the sound of her voice, Ty gave his head a small shake, as if to rid himself of a thought, and stopped mid-stride. "Hey, Mrs. Randalls. Yeah, we're in here. I was just about to carry these bags downstairs for Elli."

Ty walked over and easily picked up my two suitcases just as my mother poked her head into the room. It was impossible to not see the wink and sly grin that Ty sent my way before he turned to face my mother, who seemed to be utterly oblivious to the teenage tension that was in the air.

"So how long do you two have before you need to leave?"

"Well, we are supposed to meet Jules, Ben, Kenny, and Mandy in the parking lot at the high school at 10, so I guess that leaves us about 30 minutes. Something you need help with before we take off?"

"Oh no, but I do happen to have some bacon and banana pancake mix left and would be happy to feed you. That is if you and my daughter would like to come to keep me company in the kitchen while I clean up from breakfast."

"Sure mom. We'll just take the suitcases to Ty's truck and be right in." I was relieved to see that Ty went ahead with my mom so I could take a minute to get my wandering thoughts under control. I called after them, "I'll be down in just a sec. I want to make sure that I didn't leave anything behind."

"I can't imagine that you don't have everything you own packed into these suitcases." Ty laughingly called back up to me.

I took a final look around my room and found nothing that I thought I would need over the summer. I went into the bathroom and gave it a quick once-over as well. When I looked into the mirror, I realized that my face was a bit flushed and hoped that my mother hadn't noticed, or if she had noticed I hoped that she just thought that it was the excitement of our upcoming adventure that was making my cheeks rosy.

When I made it downstairs, Ty had all three of my suitcases out by his truck and seemed to be pondering the truck bed as if it were a puzzle he needed to figure out. "Please tell me you didn't pack another suitcase while you were up there."

"Ha-ha funny man! What's wrong? Do you have too many fire starters and prepackaged meals in your truck for my suitcases to fit?"

"Really? Everything I have back here we will need, I guarantee it." Ty stalked towards me and leaned down to whisper in my ear. "It's my job to keep you safe, and I will do so until I draw my last breath if necessary."

I gently caressed his cheek as he continued. "Do I necessarily think that something will happen while we are on this trip? No, not really. However, on the off chance that I'm wrong I am well prepared. My father has been a bit more worried than usual lately, and I think that it doesn't hurt us to have what we will need if something does go wrong. You know that I will take care of you. I make you feel safe, that's my job, and that is why you love me. Just admit it."

I smiled up at Ty and replied, "Well, that would be one of the reasons. There are so many others though that I'm not sure that it even ranks in the top ten."

I quickly kissed him. "Now let's figure out how to get these suitcases in here, so my mother doesn't think we ran off without telling her goodbye. Besides, I bet your pancakes are getting cold, and if there really is bacon just sitting in the kitchen, Dad will eat it if he comes back inside before you get there."

Ty and I walked over to the truck to take a look in the back. After a little discussion and collaboration, we were able to get my suitcases securely situated. Ty secured and locked the bed cover, and we headed back into the house. Our timing must have been perfect because Mom was just sitting a plate on the table for Ty and Dad was just walking in the back door. I laughed as Dad grabbed a piece of bacon off of Ty's plate as he sat down at the table to join us. Mom continued working on the dishes, and I started gathering up anything dirty that I saw and taking it to the sink for her. Mom was old-fashioned in some ways and preferred to wash the dishes by hand, so I picked up a dishcloth to dry for her.

"So, Tyler, I trust that you are going to be taking good care of our girl? We are placing something precious in your hands for safe keeping. You will keep her safe won't you?"

"Dad!" I exclaimed at the same time that Ty replied, "Of course sir."

"Elli, it's okay," Ty reassured me. "It's understandable that your parents are concerned. Mr. and Mrs. Randalls, let me assure you that I will do everything within my power to ensure that Elli is completely safe at all times until we see you in a week. I will drive carefully and be vigilant while watching other drivers. I will make sure that she is safe in the ocean. Heck, err sorry.... I'll even make sure that she is applying sunscreen every hour. You know my father, and I know that you don't really agree with his, ummmm, tendency to want to be ultra-prepared, but he has made sure that we have everything that we could possibly need for this trip. She will be more than fine, and she has her phone and can stay in contact with you at all times. I know there are a few spots in the mountains that do not have cell service but I will do my best to ensure that we have service tonight. I will also remind her to text you before we go up into the mountains. Is there anything else that I can possibly do to reassure you?"

Ty paused to dig into the plate of food my mother had sat on the table in front of him. After a moment of silence, she responded. "It's not that we don't trust you Tyler. Yes, you are eighteen, but you are still not really an adult. Adam and I were both young once, and we know how it is to feel so alive and invincible. When teenagers get together there is often drinking and partying and, yes I know, you two have not been involved in these things before, but I fear it is inevitable because every young person wants to try it. When you are under the influence things happen. You aren't safe, you aren't responsible, and you make bad decisions. I've been there. It's happened to me. I don't want that for El. I don't want her to have to live with guilt because of a stupid choice."

Ty started to answer my mother, but I put my hand up to stop him. I paused in my drying to provide her an answer myself. "Mom, this isn't about Ty. This is about me and whether or not you trust me and the choices I make. Do you? Have I ever done anything to make you doubt my decision-making abilities?"

Mom looked into my eyes and then sighed as she looked away. I could still see the worry there, but she said, "No my love, you have not. Please just be safe."

Once that was settled, the conversation turned to safer subjects, such as our planned route and proposed timeline. Dad and Ty got into a discussion about edible plants that his mother had been studying, while Mom and I continued to work on the breakfast dishes. Sampson was still whining at the back door, and I asked Dad if he had found anything in the backyard or figured out what was wrong with the dog.

"No, I went out into the yard and looked around but he wouldn't even come outside with me. I didn't see anything unusual in the yard at a glance, but I will go back out and investigate more in a bit. I wanted to make sure that I got a little more time with you before you leave."

I finished drying the last dish, wiped the water from my hands, and walked over to where Dad was sitting. I leaned down and kissed him on the cheek before taking the seat across from Ty. "The weird thing is Mrs. Trible was outside yelling at Petey about the same thing when I was out there with Sampson. It seems odd to me. I don't understand why they would both be acting that way."

"Maybe it's something in the water," Ty said. "Buster was acting kind of weird this morning too. I mean, he went out into the yard and sniffed around but kept staring up at the sky. He ran back to the door after just a minute or so. I usually have to coax him back into the house with the promise of a treat."

The clock on the microwave caught my attention, and I realized that we had been talking with my parents for so long that we were now fifteen minutes late. "It's 9:45. We are going to be late if we don't get a move on."

Ty glanced quickly at his watch and stood. "Thank you for the wonderful breakfast, Mrs. Randalls. You are an excellent cook."

After lingering hugs from both my parents, I love yous and goodbyes were passed around. As we walked to the front door, my eyes were drawn up to Lucy's room. A little voice in my head told me to go up to try to make amends, but I knew that we were already running late and I hated to be late. I gave my mother another quick hug and ran outside to jump in the passenger seat. As we pulled out of the driveway, for a fleeting moment, it felt as if I was making a huge mistake. I turned to look back at my parents who were still standing on our front porch waving. Mom's smile seemed forced, and I thought I caught a glimpse of tears. I gave a final wave before turning to look ahead. Ty gently grabbed my hand and brought it to his lips for a quick kiss. When he looked at me the sparkle in his eyes promised adventure to come and made me forget the worried look on my mother's face. Worry is what mom's do, I thought as I dismissed the concern. I'm almost eighteen, and it's time for me to be independent. One adventure without her would not be the end of the world for either of us.

Although we were about five minutes late arriving at the designated meeting location, I was unsurprised to see that we were the first ones there. As much as I love my friends, they could never show up anywhere for anything on time. Ty and I sat in his truck in comfortable silence listening to the classic rock station that he loved. I had grown used to it, and some of the songs were growing on me, but it wasn't my first choice. I was humming along to something I thought might be Pink Floyd and letting my mind drift to the rolling waves, sandy beach, and warm North Carolina sunshine that I would be enjoying tomorrow. Ty's voice interrupted my thoughts. He sounded unusually hesitant.

"So," he said somewhat quietly. I shifted to face him, and he continued. "It was, umm, different seeing your room, the place where you sleep and dream. I often lie in bed at night and picture you sleeping beside me. In my mind, you are always so peaceful and beautiful when you sleep. Well, you are always beautiful. I want ..."

The sound of a car pulling into the parking lot stopped Ty from continuing his sentence. It was difficult for me to move my eyes away from his. The sincerity and longing I could see in his eyes and on his face were mesmerizing. I didn't want the moment to end. I wanted to hear where the conversation was going. A knock on Ty's window finally made us break eye contact.

"Come on lovebirds, time to socialize."

Ty sighed and opened his door, giving my hand a quick squeeze first. "Good morning Jules. Ben, you're an asshole. Running a little late, as usual, I see. We were supposed to be here and on the road at 10."

"Talk to Jules about it. She wasn't ready. In fact, she was still packing when I was ready to go. We were up a little late last night, weren't we baby?" Jules blushed, and I rolled my eyes. Ben never missed an opportunity to let anyone and everyone know that he and Jules were having sex. He was just immature like that.

Jules was one of the sweetest girls I knew. She was a petite blonde who came from a situation that was very different from the rest of our group, but she still fit in with our group as if she was born to be there. Jules and I had English together during our freshman year and had become best friends. Mrs. James had forced us to read our poetry aloud in class, and Jules' poetry had touched me in a way that made me want to reach out to her. She wrote such beautiful poetry. It was haunting, full of vivid images of a lost soul. As we had become closer, she had shared tidbits and glances into her home life. In the past three and a half years she had spent many nights, or entire weekends, at my house. However, I had never been to her house. I knew that her father left when she was very young and that she did not ever see or hear from him. Her mother "worked nights" and Jules was often left alone. Over time she had become a part of our group, and last year she and Ben had become a couple. When Ben's mother had found out about Jules dysfunctional home, she had pretty much adopted her as one of her own. So Jules and Ben were together pretty much 24/7. I knew it embarrassed her when Ben was so suggestive about them but I also knew that he made her feel safe and happy.

"So where is your handsome half?" I heard Ty ask Ben. Identical twins, Ben and Ken, were about as opposite as night and day but they both fit into our little clique. Ben was outgoing and often obnoxious while Ken was quiet and introspective.

"I don't know. He was gone by the time we got up and going. I figured that he had already left to get Mandy."

Mandy was the one person in our tight-knit group who I often wished would find a new set of friends. She was often bitchy and always demanding and needy. Mandy had become a part of our group only when Ken began dating her earlier in the year. She often treated Jules and me like she was so much better than us and it always seemed like she thought we should be thankful that she spoke to us. Her family was very wealthy, and she made sure that everyone knew it. They weren't wealthy in the way that mine, Ty's, Ben and Ken's family were though. Mandy came from generations of wealth, old money she always said. She was especially nasty to Jules, and it made me want to slap her. However, I had talked with Jules about it, and she had asked me to just let it go. I did because Jules wanted me to but I found myself biting my tongue often when Mandy was around. I had not wanted to invite her on the trip, but Ty convinced me that it wouldn't be right to ask Ben, Jules, and Ken while explicitly excluding her. I had been so angry when she had said it might be fun to go see how poor people did the beach. I secretly hoped that she had changed her mind and was flying to Paris instead of coming with us, and that was why Ken was so late.

While we waited for Ken and Mandy, the conversation turned to the trip and all of the things that we all wanted to do in the week that we had. My main focus was on relaxing and recovering from my horrendous finals week. I knew that Ty really just wanted to be where I was and Jules was just happy to get away. Ben, however, was worried that there wouldn't be enough excitement just relaxing on the beach and was inquiring if we would be able to find some more exhilarating adventures. I knew that Mandy would want fine dining and expensive shopping, but she wasn't likely to find that where we were going. My parents had searched long and hard before they had chosen the spot on which to build our beach house. It was quite remote and somewhat isolated. I loved it! ... And she would hate it.

After about another half of an hour of waiting Ty finally decided to try to call Ken. Ty walked away to talk when Ken answered. I watched his mannerisms and could hear the tone of his voice. He was nodding his head and frowning, his tone tense and annoyed. He did not look pleased when he walked back towards us.

"Apparently Mandy wanted to sleep in and felt that it didn't matter that we had a plan to meet at 10. She hadn't packed and is currently putting her makeup on. We decided that we would meet up later. Ken knows the route we are planning to take and said that he will call when they finally get on the road. He isn't anticipating seeing us until tonight, but I am guessing that Mandy does not want to camp. We probably won't see them until tomorrow."

"All right, let's hit it then," Ben exclaimed. He and Jules climbed into his truck while Ty and I got back into his. It was time to get this adventure started I thought.

Chapter Two

The beauty of the day filled me with joy as we started south out of Columbus. We were following the path that we had planned in advance, down route 33 through small villages, fields, and forests. Flowers were beginning to bloom, both in groomed flower beds and wild along the sides of the road. We passed many farms and fields where farmers were out working to get their crops planted, fertilized, or whatever they did. I realized that I really had no clue how veggies made it from a farm to my plate, they just always had. I was fascinated by the hard work that these dedicated farmers put into their crops so that other people, lazy people like me or city dwellers, could enjoy a scrumptious ear of sweet corn in the fall. I couldn't imagine living that lifestyle, up with the sun every day and working in the fields in sweltering hot or freezing cold temperatures. I wouldn't mind taking care of animals, I thought, but there were parts of that process that I wouldn't enjoy either.

"Maybe someday we will live on a farm," Ty said thoughtfully.

I laughed because his statement was in such direct opposition to where my own thoughts had gone. "I'm not quite sure how that fits into my career goals. Am I going to psychoanalyze the cows?"

Ty laughed. "Baby, you will be too busy psychoanalyzing me to have any time to help the cows overcome their traumatic childhoods."

Ty knew that I wanted to go into psychology and work with children. He had always talked about joining the marines once we got out of school. However, now that the time had come for him to enlist he seemed to be hesitant. He said that he just wasn't sure anymore, but I thought that he just didn't want to leave me behind. I hoped that he wasn't worried about me finding someone else. He was it, the peanut butter to my jelly. I didn't want to be with anyone else and, unlike other girls my age who said the same thing about their boyfriends, I did not start looking at other guys and flirting as soon as he wasn't with me. I would always love my family, and they would forever be an integral part of my life, but Ty was my future. He was the one who I would share the most important moments in my life with. We would get married, have babies, and be two old crazies rocking in chairs on the front porch together when we were old. Ty was the one. The end!

"Do you really see us as farmers," I laughed. "You want to get up at dawn every day? Plant crops and worry about bugs eating them? Or too much rain? Or not enough rain? Maybe you want to raise pigs and cows? Sorry, I just can't see you spending your day on a tractor or in a barn."

"Well, maybe not but I don't think I would mind it. Besides, I would love seeing you in a farmhouse kitchen making me and our children breakfast. That would make for a good life, no matter what work I was doing."

"Who said I could cook? I thought you were going to be doing all the cooking?" I joked with him.

"Well, I guess we will learn to cook together," he laughed.

The miles passed quickly, and when we crossed into West Virginia, we met up with I-77. Farmland had given way to mountain views, which were beautiful and intriguing to me in an entirely different way. Some of the homes and small towns we flew past were isolated. A quick run to the store would not be an option for those families. However, the quiet solitude and stunning views would probably make a longer trip for groceries worth it. I could imagine that the views in the autumn, when the leaves were changing to fall colors, would be breathtaking.

A few miles before we hit Charleston, West Virginia Ben called to declare that he was starving and wanted to stop for lunch. Stopping for a break seemed agreeable to everyone. We found a little diner, Ty's favorite, and stopped for some food. In true Ben style he started complaining the second he climbed out of his truck.

"Man you drive too slow! What are you, like a ninety-year-old, blind grandpa? And what is this place? Why couldn't you be normal and just stop at the McDonalds a few exits back? I wanted a Big Mac."

"I'm not going to speed through the mountains Benjamin," Ty goaded. Ben hated his full name. "I promised Elli's parents that I would drive safely and even if I hadn't promised them I would still drive safely. There is no reason to drive like a maniac just to get there thirty minutes earlier. Why don't you stop your whiny ass bitching for a change and just relax and enjoy something? And, if you want a friggin Big Mac, get in your truck and go get one. I'm sure that you can find your way by yourself."

Ben sulked into the restaurant while Jules stayed behind.

"I'm sorry, he's been grumpy since we left. I think he's mad that Ken blew us off. It's been happening a lot lately, and he's just not used to being second to anyone, especially when it comes to Ken."

I grabbed both Jules and Ty's hands and pulled them towards the diner after Ben. After we had all settled into a booth, I finally spoke my mind. "Ben, I realize that you are not happy, for whatever reason, but this is supposed to be a fun trip. I really don't want to spend it listening to you bitch about whatever ever pissed you off."

Ben looked a bit hurt at my words, so I continued. "You know I love you. This trip wouldn't be the same without you and Jules here, but can't we just focus on what's good? Yeah, you may not like diners, but look at how huge that cheeseburger is. I don't think even you would be hungry after eating that."

Ben grinned at me, and in an effort to goad Ty replied, "You hear that man? She loves me not you. I'm going to go all polygamous and have two wives, and you are going to be left all sad and alone."

Jules playfully slapped his arm, but the mood was lifted just the same. The rest of the meal was spent talking about mountain views and the life of a farmer. I was surprised when Ben said that he had always loved spending summers on his grandparents' farm and would consider taking it over when his granddad was ready to hang up his hat. I could picture Ben as a farmer even less than I could Ty. However, I could picture Jules taking care of animals and riding horses. She would probably love a quiet life on a farm, I thought.

We didn't rush over lunch, even though I thought that Ty really wanted to make up some of the time that we had lost waiting for Ken and Mandy. It was nice to just sit and chat with my friends without worrying about upcoming tests or grades. We relaxed for a few minutes after the boys had finished ginormous slices of pie topped with ice cream. I told Ty that I was going to go out to try to call Lucy before slipping out of the booth. I still needed to apologize and didn't want it weighing me down all day.

I stepped out into the bright sunlight and took a minute to admire the beautiful day before getting my cell phone out to place the call. As the phone rang, I looked back into the diner and saw Ty at the register paying the bill. He was chatting with the locals and was clearly enjoying the conversation. Ty had a naturally friendly demeanor and could strike up a conversation with anyone at any time. It served him well, and we always seemed to be able to find the best little out of the way restaurants or nature trails that weren't on the maps.

When my call went to voicemail, I felt my irritation with Lucy intensify. It was just like her to push my buttons in an attempt to provoke me to snap back at her. Then she played the martyr until I basically ended up begging her to forgive me. I knew that I had been wrong, but lately she seemed to be always trying to annoy me. I didn't want to apologize in a voicemail, so I disconnected when I heard the beep and quickly dialed my mother.

"Hi, Mom!" She had picked up the phone almost immediately, and I wondered if she had been just sitting beside it waiting for my call.

"Hi, sweetie! I miss you already! How is the drive going?"

"The drive is going great! The only little problem is Mandy, but I figured that she would be a problem."

"Oh no, what happened? I hope she doesn't ruin your week."

"I refuse to let her. Just the usual drama really. She wasn't ready when Ken went to pick her up. When they hadn't shown up by about 10:45 Ty called and discovered that, apparently, she had decided that she wanted to sleep in. They are supposed to meet up with us tonight, but I'm guessing that we won't see them until tomorrow," I explained. "I tried to call Lucy to apologize, but she didn't answer. Is she still in bed?"

"She left with Ginger about an hour and a half ago. How odd that she didn't answer. I'm sorry sweetie. Don't let your sister ruin your trip either. Just try to give her a call later."

"I'll do my best Mom. I'd better get off here. Everyone is ready to get moving again. I'll talk to you soon. Love you!"

I felt Ty put his hand on the small of my back as I disconnected the call. I smiled up at him and looked around to see Ben and Jules walking out of the diner. Ben seemed more relaxed, and Jules had one of the biggest smiles that I had ever seen on her face. It was good to see both of them simply enjoying the moment as lately there had just been too much stress for all of us. I realized that our stresses might seem inconsequential to some, but there was so much pressure to get into the right college and do well on your tests, not to mention the constant pressure to stay out of trouble, especially after the incident with our old friend Gary. It wasn't so bad with my parents because they really did trust me, however, Ben and Ken, and by extension Jules, were constantly being quizzed and questioned about where they were going, what they were doing and who they planned to be with. Maybe we weren't paying bills, going to jobs, and taking care of a family but we were trying to figure out how we were going to do those things in the future. There were two things that the situation with Gary had taught me. First, it was abundantly clear to me now how fleeting life can be. One minute you might be smiling and enjoying a party, and then in the next minute, you could be gone. Second, I understand now, in a very specific way, how one decision can change your life, for better or worse.

Ty leaned down to whisper in my ear, "What's wrong babe? You look lost in thought. Is everything okay with Lucy?"

It had always been impossible to hide anything from Ty. "Lucy won't answer my call. I talked to Mom, and she told me not to let Lucy, or Mandy, ruin my trip. As for what I was thinking, I was thinking that life has been stressful lately and that I am really looking forward to some one-on-one, quality alone time with you."

He turned me around to fully face him and pulled me into his chest. Leaning down, he nuzzled against my neck and then whispered in my ear, his voice more seductive than I had ever heard before, "So you want to be alone with me for some quality time? I can guarantee you that I can make that happen. In fact, if you want we can ditch these losers and spend the entire week playing house. Alone."

I would have laughed if I didn't sense that he was serious. I hugged him close and looked into his eyes. I started to pull his lips to mine, but Ben's voice interrupted the moment. "He has really got to get better timing," Ty muttered under his breath as he separated himself from me. He took my hand and led me back through the parking lot to his truck.

"How long until we get to the campsite," Ben called out.

"If we still want to camp near Pilot Mountain it will be about three and a half hours. That will give us time to explore the park tonight before it gets dark."

"Sounds like a plan my friends. Let's hit the highway."

The chemistry between Ty and I seemed altered in some way when we got in the truck to get back on the road, but I tried to focus on the landscape that flew by our windows. I had always loved nature and taking trips to naturally beautiful locations was one of my favorite things to do. In recent years, to save time, my family had begun to fly to our vacation destinations. Although I loved the sight from high above the earth, I felt like you missed seeing the beauty of the country from the air. We were passing so many different types of landscapes during this trip that it seemed as if one kind of beauty just transformed into another as the miles flew by. We drove past small villages and bigger cities, and I found myself imagining life in each. I had lived on the fringe of a large city for my entire life, although I also knew what a secluded life felt like from the summers spent at the beach house. Smaller towns seemed to have the best of both worlds, in my opinion. They tended to be close enough to conveniences, but if you lived just a bit outside of town, you could have privacy as well. A little cottage where Ty and I could start a life together would be perfect, years from now of course. I had so much schooling still to go before we would be free to settle down and start a life together.

Time flew by as the miles passed. We made our way southeast, and by the time I could see Pilot Mountain on the horizon I was ready for a break from the car. I was anxious to get to the camping site so we could get out, stretch our legs, and spend some time exploring the mountain.

"That's Pilot Mountain, isn't it? We should be there soon, right?" Although Ty had been in the area before with his parents, I had never seen Pilot Mountain before except in pictures. The distinctive peak of the mountain was easy to pick out in the distance.

"It appears closer than it is. We will get there soon enough though. Anxious to get me into a tent are you?" His eyes were twinkling in amusement again, and I knew he was just trying to get a blush from me.

"Perhaps," I replied flippantly, and the twinkle of humor in his eyes turned to a smolder, "or maybe I am ready to get out of this truck and explore."

He smiled that crooked smile that I love and responded. "Don't worry babe. We will get there soon, and after we set up, we can explore until dusk. After dusk, you will be able to spend your evening alone in a tent with the love of your life."

I relaxed back into the seat and watched the miles fly by again. When I had cell service, I tried to call Lucy again, but this time it only rang once and went to voicemail, signifying that she had declined the call. With that I dismissed trying to get in touch with her from my mind, it was no longer a priority. Maybe she would decide to call me this week or she could just wait until next week if I even felt like apologizing then. I would be an adult and out of the house soon while Lucy was still basically a child, and one suffering from a sense of entitlement at that. She had so much more freedom than I did at her age, but instead of being happy that she benefitted from my good behavior she always gave me a hard time because I got to do things that she didn't. I was really tired of trying to play nice with her and having to apologize because I snapped when she pushed too far. Perhaps it was time for her to apologize to me. I closed my eyes and let my mind drift with the smooth movement of the truck.

∞ ∞ ∞

I sat in the comfortable folding chair that Ty had sat out for me watching him pull things out of the back of his truck with the utmost ease. I was always amazed at how confident he was in everything he did. His movements were always smooth and purposeful. It was a pleasure watching Ty do anything.

"Babe, do you need all of these suitcases tonight?" He asked as he peered into the back of the truck.

I stood and walked over to the truck. "No, I'll just need that small one tonight. I really wish you would let me help you."

"You can help me once I get what we need unpacked."

I wandered around the campsite. It was rocky and surrounded by trees just coming into their full green after a winter of being leafless. I loved the newness of spring. The campsite felt alive with spring colors and scents. It was very quiet, and as I looked around, I realized that there were only a few other campsites occupied. I didn't think much of it as I took in the beautiful landscape surrounding us.

Once I saw that Ty had finished unloading all he wanted to from the truck I went to help him get the tent set up. He and I worked well together, and I followed his directions as we worked to make sure the tent was up and secure. We are a good team, I thought as we finished up. Ben and Jules were in the campsite beside ours fighting over every step of putting the tent up.

"Jules, no! Not like that! Listen to what I am trying to explain to you!"

"You aren't explaining, Ben. You are yelling! I can't help you if you just yell at me." Jules started to cry.

Ty kissed my cheek and whispered in my ear that he would be back before heading over to Ben and Jules. I saw him pat Jules on the shoulder and whisper in her ear. She turned to walk back to me while he started helping Ben construct their tent. Ty kept their conversation low and quiet. When Jules reached me, I gave her a quick hug.

"Ty said I should come over here and hang out with you for a while. I'm sorry we were fighting. He's just so stubborn, and he assumes that I can understand what he is telling me to do. I just don't though. Maybe I'm just stupid."

I led Jules over to the chairs and sat her down. "You are not stupid in any way. Ben has never been any good at giving directions. He's like a general who speaks French to American troops and then gets mad when no one follows orders. Ty will get the tent set up with him, and that will take care of the problem for now. I hope that by the time they are finished Ben will have found a better mood. If not you and I can bring out our inner bitch on him."

Jules laughed, and it was a lovely sound. There were times like earlier when they were discussing living on a farm that I could picture she and Ben living a happily ever after life. However, at other times, like now, I had to wonder why she stayed with him. They were either madly in love or just darn mad. Their relationship was based on extreme emotions, and while I would say that my love for Ty was complete and binding, we didn't have those extremes.

Jules and I decided to get the sleeping bags set up in the tent Ty, and I would share. Once we were done, we sat chatting until the other tent was set up. We were looking at the park map and talking about the trails when Ty and Ben walked over to join us. Ty placed his hand on the back of my chair and gently rubbed my neck with his thumb.

Ben was wearing his best I'm sorry face when he kneeled down in front of Jules. He grabbed her hands in his and softly apologized to her. I could feel the sincerity in his words, and it didn't take much talking for him to convince Jules that he was, in fact, genuinely sorry.

"So, Jules and I were looking at the map. I think it would be cool to go hike the Ledge Spring Trail. We can take Grindstone Trail from here to get there. It goes along a spring that follows a cliff. I think it sounds beautiful. What do you guys think?" I could feel the excitement for a new adventure filling me. I hoped everyone agreed with this plan. This trail looked like the best one that the park offered.

Ty took the map and looked it over. "Looks like it could have a challenging spot or two. Everyone up for it?"

Everyone agreed. After changing into hiking gear, I grabbed my phone so that I could take some pictures to send to Mom and Dad once we had cell service again. As we hiked, I took pictures of everything. I must have had twenty of the mountain peak, capturing every angle I could. A new flower blossom in a brilliant blue was a fantastic subject. I giggled out loud as I tried to get a picture of a lizard scurrying along the rocks on the sides of the trail. It was the most uncooperative subject I had ever tried to capture.

The birds were singing all around us, unlike the ones at home that had been strangely silent when I took Sampson out earlier. I had forgotten to ask Mom if he was back to normal yet. I would have to try to remember to ask about him when I next called. When we got back to the campsite, I would ask Ty to drive me to where we had cell service so I could call home and check in. I hadn't called Mom since our lunch stop, and I knew she would be worried if she didn't hear from me again today. Ty had promised her that we would check in tonight, and I was sure that he wouldn't mind taking me back down the mountain so that I could make a call.

The trail was a fantastic choice, I thought as we headed back toward the campsite after the hike. It had meandered along the rock face of Pilot Knob in a circle. I felt like a bird as I looked out over the valley below, imagining an eagle would see the land much as I was. Jules got a bit nervous when we had to go up and down narrow rock stairs, but we all completed the hike without incident. Walking right alongside the rock face of Pilot Knob, I found myself amazed at the sheer size of it. I am not sure that I had ever felt so small before.

Once back at the campsite Ty mentioned that I needed to make a call home, saving me the need to remind him. I quickly changed my shoes and hopped into the truck. Ty drove us down the mountain to where we actually had cell service. After Ty found a spot to pull off the road, I stayed in the truck to make the call home while Ty got out to make his own call home. I was surprised when the phone rang a few times before my mother finally answered, out of breath.

"He... Hello?"

"Mom? Is everything all right?"

"Oh, hi sweetie," the change in the tone of her voice sounded forced. Fake upbeat wasn't her normal tone, and it just sounded odd. "How are you doing? How is the trip going?"

"Everything is going great Mom. We just did an amazing hike around Pilot Knob. You wouldn't believe the views. I'm going to send you some pictures I took on my phone when we hang up. The campsite is set up, and Ty just brought me down the mountain so I could give you a call. You sound upset though, is everything all right?"

"Oh, sure honey. I was just trying to help your dad with Sampson and walked away from my phone. Everything is fine here. Not a thing for you to worry about. Did you get in touch with your sister?"

"Sampson? Is there still something wrong with him? As for Lucy, no she sent my call to voicemail when I tried again. I decided that I have done enough. She can call me when she gets over it."

"I don't know why Lucy is being so difficult this time. I'm sorry sweetie. Don't worry about the dog. Dad talked to the neighbors, and all the dogs are behaving a little strangely today. He thinks that maybe the dogs are all picking up on a high pitched noise or something electrical coming from somewhere nearby. It's possible that they could all be impacted by something that we aren't able to feel or hear. I'm sure it's nothing. You just go enjoy! Call me tomorrow when you get back on the road. I love you!"

"Love you too Mom. Tell Dad I love and miss him."

"Will do sweetie. I'll talk to you soon." I heard my dad yell for my mom as she disconnected the phone. I took the few minutes before Ty got back into the truck to send a few of my mountain pictures to my mom.

"How are things at home?" Ty asked as he climbed back into the truck.

"I don't know," I replied thoughtfully, "things seem weird. Mom was so worried about me leaving with you guys. I figured that she would be sitting by the phone waiting for me to call, but she wasn't. In actuality, it took her a few rings to answer. She said that Sampson is still acting strangely, and the other dogs in the neighborhood are behaving strangely as well, according to the neighbors. She told me not to worry and that everything was fine but it just seems bizarre to me."

"I talked to my dad," Ty said. "He mentioned that some weird things were going on. You know he pays attention to all the crazy conspiracy theory websites and such. He didn't mention any specifics and didn't tell me to come home. He just told me to be vigilant, but that isn't unusual."

I gave a small laugh. "Well, I wasn't really thinking end of the world. I just thought that the dogs are really messed up."

Ty looked at me seriously. "Babe, I know you don't believe in any of the 'end of the world' stuff that my dad worries about but it is possible that something will happen one of these days."

"Possible, but not probable right?"

Ty smiled at me. "Not probable, at least not tonight. If something ever happens, you know that I am prepared to protect you, right?"

"I know that you would always protect me, no matter what the circumstance." I leaned across the seat and placed a gentle kiss on his lips. I had never felt anything but safe with Ty. Even when we had been hiking up the narrow steps earlier, I knew that with Ty right behind me I would never be in any danger. He would never let me fall or injure myself in any way. He was my anchor in a storm.

"Stop trying to distract me," he smiled down at me. "I should probably try to get in touch with Ken before we go back up to the campsite. You and I both know that they won't be here tonight, but we must keep up appearances."

I leaned back in my seat as he placed the call. I glanced down at my phone, expecting to see a return text from my mom but was surprised to see that she hadn't replied. I checked to make sure that the pictures had sent. Each picture said delivered, but not read. I sat pondering what was going on at home while Ty talked to Ken. After just a few moments, Ty's voice got a frustrated tone which was a sure indicator that one of his friends was being particularly annoying.

"Sheesh Ken, you know that this trip was about all of us getting to spend some time together before we all end up going our separate ways. I can't believe that you are just going to blow us off because Mandy wants to..." Ty was apparently cut off because I could hear Ken's voice. Although I didn't catch the words, I could hear the pleading tone.

"Fine, whatever man. Hopefully, we will see you at the house sooner or later, but I won't hold my breath. Enjoy your trip."

I could tell Ty was frustrated when he disconnected the call. He and the twins had been friends since preschool and Ty had been really looking forward to having this time with them before they all took off to different colleges or basic training in the fall. I'm sure he was very disappointed by the choices that Ken was making.

"I'm sorry," I said quietly. "I guess that Ken and Mandy won't be joining us tonight."

"No, I guess not. If I am going to be completely honest though, I wasn't really expecting them. A part of me knew that Mandy wouldn't camp. All Ken said is that Mandy wanted to take an alternative route and that they would be in a hotel tonight. I have to wonder if they will even make it to the beach. I am sorry that I convinced you to invite her. I just didn't think that Ken would come if she weren't invited too."

"Don't apologize to me. I mean, maybe it's my fault. I have wished that she wasn't coming with us. I hate how Mandy talks down to Jules, and she isn't exactly nice to me either. She acts like we should be grateful that she lets us hang out with her. Her comment about seeing how the poor people did the beach was really just, well, obnoxious. I have never been able to understand what Ken sees in her, well, except big boobs." I felt my face redden. "I can't believe I just said that aloud, and to you."

Ty let out a big laugh and gave me a quick hug before he started up the truck. "Thanks, babe. You can always make me laugh, even when you aren't trying. Ken or no Ken, Mandy or no Mandy, it's going to be a great week just because I get to be with you."

Ty turned his attention to the mountain road, and I turned mine to the beautiful shades of the sunset that could be seen on the horizon. I loved when the sky turned to the gorgeous pinks, reds, and oranges that a sunset could bring. The blending of the new colors with the blue of the sky and the white marshmallow clouds was creating an exceptionally artistic display of splendor, I thought. Once again, I grabbed my phone and took a picture. I quickly tried to send it to Mom, not knowing if it would go through or not.

Many cars seemed to be coming back down the mountain, but we were the only ones going back up. Day hikers and tourists, I assumed, off to spend the night in a local hotel in Mt. Airy or some other town nearby. They would sleep in their hotel beds, fall asleep to late night TV, and get up in the morning to rush off to their next stop. I preferred our plan to spend the evening sitting beside a campfire eating hot dogs and s'mores. After that, I would be lying down in my tent tonight beside Ty. My comfort was found in the company I kept and the natural beauty of my surroundings. As much as I enjoy my creature comforts I did not need them to be happy.

As we pulled into our campsite, I saw that Ben had gotten a fire started and Jules was gathering some food from the coolers for dinner. Ty went over to check to see if Ben needed help with anything and I went to offer help to Jules. She and I gathered groceries that we had brought for dinner. There wasn't much to it considering we had brought hot dogs, buns, condiments, and chips. My mom had contributed some homemade cookies, double chocolate chip, my favorite. Once the food had been sat out on the picnic table, the guys grabbed sticks that Ty had brought and began cooking hot dogs over the fire. Soon there was a plate full of hot dogs ready, and we all grabbed some food and sat around the fire eating.

As we were finishing up our meal, I felt Ty tense beside me. I looked up and saw an older man approaching from one of the other campsites. As he got closer, I realized he was not as old as I had initially thought, probably only in his 20's. He was dressed in clothes that appeared to have seen better days. His jeans looked a few sizes too big and were torn from wear and tear. As he approached the fire, Ty stood, positioning himself in front of me. The man stretched out his hand to introduce himself, and I saw that they were caked with dirt. Ty didn't remove his eyes from the man's face as he extended his hand. I noticed that Ben had quietly stood and moved in front of Jules as well.

"Howdy Y'all. I guess we will be neighbors for the evening. I'm Max. Just traveling through the area with my brother, Wayne."

The man made all the right gestures and said all the right things to appear friendly, but there was something in his eyes that I didn't trust. After Ty shook the man's hand, he casually put his hand in his pocket, in the process making sure that the man could see the customized 1911 pistol that he carried in a holster on his right side. Ty and his father were well versed in the gun laws for each state that they planned to visit. Ty had been trained with guns from a young age and was very comfortable handling whatever type of gun that might be available to him. This particular gun had been a gift from his father for his eighteenth birthday. Ty knew that state law in North Carolina gave him the right to legally open carry in the state at the age of eighteen. He had been doing so since we crossed the state line, which was perfect for the current situation. Max looked at the gun warily and visibly tensed.

"I'm Ty, and this is my friend Ben. We will just be staying here one night. Just passing through ourselves, on our way to somewhere else. It's a beautiful area, and we just wanted to stop and explore for a day. My friends and I are planning to enjoy a quiet evening by the fire. We won't be disturbing you with any loud partying." Ty paused and looked around. "I don't see your brother around?"

"Wayne, he likes to explore, and he just hasn't found his way back yet I guess. I'd be worried, but he has a sixth sense about finding his way back from nowhere."

"That's a handy talent to have," Ben stated from his spot in front of Jules. "You can't be too careful out in these mountains though, wild animals and such."

"We've actually been camping here for a few days. He's been out exploring before and never had any problem getting back." Max looked around nervously, perhaps realizing that he had just contradicted himself. "I don't want to keep you folks from enjoying your fire. Y'all have a good evening and if you need anything we are just across the way."

He walked away, and my eyes followed him back to his campsite. The campsite gave the appearance that the occupants had been there for more than a few days. It definitely didn't appear to be inhabited by someone just passing through the area. There was much more thrown around than the few supplies that would be needed for a stay that would last a night or two.

I noticed the look of concern that Ty flashed to Ben once Max was gone. Ty kept eyes on him for a while. I wanted to ask questions, but Ty's demeanor did not seem to welcome an intrusion of his thoughts. I saw Max sit down in a chair that was positioned just outside his truck. He seemed to just be watching what we were doing. I wasn't sure if it was creepy or sad.

After a few minutes, Ty turned to Ben and motioned to him. They stood a bit away from the fire in the shadows talking and watching Max. They were between our campsites and Max's and appeared to be blocking his view of where Jules and I sat. I stood and motioned to Ty that I would like to speak to him. I didn't want to draw attention to myself or Jules because I sensed that Ben and Ty were doing all they could to make sure that Max's focus wasn't drawn to us.

Ty walked over to where I stood in the shadow of our tent and pulled me into his arms. He held me close, but I could sense that his focus remained on Max and his campsite. Ben had left the shadow where he stood and started walking the perimeter of our campsites, seemingly looking for something.

"That guy is creepy," I whispered. "He contradicted himself too. First, he said they were just passing through, and then he said that they had been here a few days. I don't like his eyes either. He just doesn't seem like someone we should trust."

"I agree with you babe, but I won't let him anywhere near you. I find it odd that he says that he is here with a brother, but we've seen nothing of him. There is only one chair set up over there. Why would that be if his brother is there with him? From what I can see in this light, it also looks like his truck is full of stuff. I don't know where two people would sit in there. Ben is walking around and looking though, just to be sure that there isn't someone lurking about around either of our campsites. I don't want any surprises. What I want you to do is to go back and relax with Jules. Do whatever it is you would normally do. Ben and I will both be back over there in a few minutes."

"But..." Ty leaned down and stopped my protest with a quick kiss.

"No buts. I don't want either you or Jules to be alone right now. I promise I will be over there in just a bit."

As I walked back to where Jules sat by the fire, I thought I could hear a conversation coming from the other campground. I glanced over very quickly as I sat down and was a bit confused to see Max sitting in the chair talking. I just wasn't sure who he was talking to. I saw no one else there. He had not started a fire and didn't seem to be preparing himself a dinner or anything. I also noticed a young dog chained to the ground beside him. It seemed to just be lying there whining, kind of like Sampson I thought. Maybe the guy was talking to the dog.

Despite my earlier feelings about how creepy he was, I started to wonder if he wasn't just some guy who was down on his luck. Perhaps we were all just being overly cautious. When Ty returned to the campfire, he took the seat that faced Max. I leaned over to him and told him about my new observations and thoughts. Ty did not look convinced, but he asked me what I wanted to do.

"We have a lot of food left from dinner. Can you take some of these hot dogs, a bag of chips, some sodas and a cookie or two over to him and the dog?" Ty looked at me like he thought perhaps I had lost my mind. "I know that you don't trust him, and that's okay, but what if we're wrong? What if he's just a guy who doesn't have money for food or to move on from this campsite? The least we can do is give him our leftovers instead of throwing them into the fire. After you have given him the food you can go right back to watching him like a hawk with your most evil, I'm watching you eyes."

"The things I let you talk me into," Ty sighed. "Fine, gather up the leftovers on a plate, and I'll take them over after Ben gets back. I want someone over here with you and Jules, and I want someone covering my back. I still don't trust this Max guy. There is something off about him. Not to mention, going against my instincts is not something that I am comfortable with."

I smiled a thank you at him as I got up to gather up some food to send over. Ben walked back into the light of the fire just as I was finishing up. He and Ty stood together talking for a few minutes before Ty walked over to where I had the food waiting for him. He took the bag of food that I had put together from my hands and leaned down to give me a quick kiss.

"You are too kind for your own good sometimes," he muttered before he walked away.

I headed back to sit down by the fire with Ben and Jules, sitting where I could see Ty approach Max. I could tell that Ty was tense but attempting to appear relaxed and friendly as he approached the other campsite. Max stood as he approached, but the dog lying by his feet just remained there, whining. From this distance, it appeared to be looking up into the trees. What, I wondered, could be causing such a widespread weirdness in all of the dogs that I had seen in the past day? I pulled my focus back to Ty and Max. Although I could not hear the words of their conversation, their body language did not appear to be confrontational.

Ty handed Max the bag of food and shook his hand. I could see him relax a bit as he took a casual stance. He stood to talk with Max for a few minutes longer. Once Ty turned to walk back to the campsite I saw Max reach into the bag and take out one of the hot dogs. Rather than keep it for himself, he leaned down and gave the piece of meat to the dog, making sure he took a moment to pet the dog before he stood back up. He then seemed to stand still for a moment, looking up into the trees where the dog had been previously fixated.

Ben visibly relaxed when Ty got back to our campfire. Ty sat down in the seat beside me, taking my hand in his and caressing it with his thumb, as he often unconsciously did. I'm not sure if he did it to soothe himself or me, but it was one of my favorite things.

"Well," Ty said to us, "I'm not sure what is going on with that guy, but he did appreciate the food. His truck is full of things, no room for another person. Maybe he just didn't want us to think he was alone. I am not quite as worried about him as I was, but as my father would say, we should be vigilant."

"You are always vigilant." I smiled up at him.

"Then I guess it's just business as usual," Ty replied as he leaned towards the fire. "In that case, where are the marshmallows? I want s'mores."

I laughed as I got up to retrieve the marshmallows, chocolate bars, and graham crackers. We sat by the fire for hours, long after the brilliant colors of sunset had faded from the sky. By all outward appearances, we would appear to be a group of relaxed teenagers enjoying a camping trip, but I could tell that Ty and Ben were both still guarded. Both had a firearm handy, and they seemed to take turns getting up to walk around the campsites to stretch their legs, or so they would say. There was no sign of the brother that Max had mentioned. In fact, there was minimal movement in the other campsite at all. Max just seemed to sit quietly in his chair with his dog by his side. He had no campfire to warm himself by, and although it was late May in North Carolina, it was a chilly evening on the mountain. When I mentioned this to Ty, he told me that Max would be fine, before distracting me from the odd man across the campground.

As the fire died down, I began to yawn. I was shocked when I looked at my phone and saw that it was already midnight. The day had started early, and I was ready for bed. I looked over and saw that Jules was curled up on Ben's lap, both seemed quite tired themselves. The only one of us who appeared to be fully awake was Ty. He sat in his chair before the fire looking relaxed, but I could see that he was still casually watching Max's campsite. I touched his hand to get his attention, and he turned his eyes to me.

"I'm getting tired. I think I need to go lie down. Are you going to come with me?"

Ty looked longingly at me and then at the tent that we had so happily set up together earlier. "As much as I would like to go in there and curl up beside you right now I feel as if I need to stay out here, just to be sure. I don't trust the guy, and I need to be sure that you are safe. Ben and I talked earlier, he will come out in a few hours and take over for me. So don't be afraid when I sneak in there and lie down with you later."

"I'll stay out here with you then," I stated resolutely.

Tyler stood and pulled me up to him. "No, my love, you won't. Now, don't get that pouty determined look with me. I am going to put a few more logs on this fire to keep it going, and you are going to go to sleep. I want you well rested for all the fun we are going to pack into the next week."

Tyler gave me a hug and a quick kiss before turning me towards the tent. I went without arguing any more. He had enough to worry about without me making it worse, I thought. I looked back and saw Ty grab a few logs and position them on the fire. Ben and Jules had slipped away to their own tent as Ty and I had said our goodnight.

Ty moved a chair so that it was close to the fire, yet had a tree at its back and a view of both Max's campsite and the area surrounding ours. It felt wrong to leave him out there by himself, but I knew he would not welcome my company. I made my way into our tent and settled myself into my sleeping bag. It would be a long night for Ty, and I didn't anticipate that I would get much sleep either. Sleep, in fact, did take a long time coming and when it did, it was uneasy.

Chapter Three

May 23rd

When I opened my eyes, it was still dark and quieter than I had ever experienced. For a moment I wondered if I was still dreaming, but then I heard a crackle from a campfire in the distance and the rustle of the tent flap which I had zipped closed earlier. When the flap was quietly pulled aside, I saw the outline of Ty slipping into the tent.

"Well hi stranger," I whispered in a quiet, sleepy voice. "I guess your shift is over? Anything concerning?"

"Shhh," Ty whispered as he slid into his sleeping bag that was laid next to mine. "You should be asleep. Nothing going on out there for you wake up and worry about. I'm sorry I woke you."

Ty reached over and pulled me, sleeping bag and all, to his side. Even though the sleeping bags were between us, it seemed very intimate. We had never actually spent an entire night together, and we definitely hadn't slept cuddled up together for any significant amount of time. As I let myself relax I realized that it felt right to be curled up to sleep in Ty's arms. It was easier to drift off to sleep this time, and my rest was peaceful.

It was light the next time I opened my eyes. The warmth I had felt in Ty's arms hours before was gone, and so was he. I could still smell his distinct scent, a hint of his cologne and body wash lingered on his sleeping bag and pillow. I could hear Ty and Ben talking in low, quiet voices outside of the tent. I wasn't sure if they were trying to stay quiet so they didn't wake me or because they didn't want anyone in the other campsites to hear them. I took a minute to stretch before I pulled on sweatpants and a hoodie, slipped on some shoes, pulled my hair into a messy ponytail and made my way out of the tent.

Ty looked at me and smiled when I stepped from the tent into the bright sunlight. "Good morning beautiful. How did you sleep?"

"Amazingly well for the last few hours. How about you?"

Ty walked from Ben to my side and slipped his arms around me, whispering down into my ear. "The last few hours were heaven. I believe I would be happy if I could wake up that way every day for the rest of my life."

Jules called out a hello from their campsite and Ty released me so I could go take care of my morning necessities. After I went to the restroom and did a quick brush of my teeth and hair, I went to help Jules make some breakfast for our protectors. As we cooked up some eggs and bacon on the camping stove Ty had brought, I noticed that no one or nothing stirred in Max's campsite. Even the dog seemed to have found somewhere warm to go sleep quietly.

It was a beautiful morning on Pilot Mountain. The sun had risen on what was a crisp, clear spring day. The sky was a beautiful azure blue, and there were fluffy cotton candy clouds sprinkled liberally for as far as the eye could see. I was happy to hear the sounds of the bird's songs echoing in the trees. I sat nibbling on fruit as Ty and Ben feasted on the eggs and bacon that Jules and I had made. I listened to them discuss the plan for the day, routes, and timelines.

I must have zoned out because the next thing I knew Ty was kneeled down in front of me. I blinked and looked into his eyes. They twinkled with humor, and I guessed that he had probably been trying to get my attention for a few minutes at least. I had always had a tendency to get lost in a daydream. I could create great stories in my own mind. When I was younger, my mom would come into the kitchen as I was doing dishes to find me talking to myself. Apparently, the characters in my daydream would be having conversations with each other that I would be speaking aloud. Hopefully, I hadn't randomly started that old habit again.

"Babe, I asked you if you would help me start packing things up. We are all ready to get on the road."

"Oh, sure! I'm sorry. I was daydreaming I guess."

The group made quick work of packing up and making sure that we were leaving the campsite in good condition for the next group of campers. Max had come out while we were packing up and watched us. After a while, he seemed to get involved with his own campsite, and it looked as if he might be packing up to leave as well. Max seemed to be just randomly picking up things that were laying around his campsite and tossing them into his truck with no particular rhyme or reason. I hoped he remembered to leave room for the dog because without a plan there was no way everything he had was going to fit into his old truck.

When both Ty and Ben's trucks were both packed up and ready to go, we made the decision to drive up to the top of the mountain before hitting the road. I was anxious to get one more view from the top of the mountain before heading to the beach. Max seemed to be in an urgent state of packing when we drove past his campsite. I looked back as we turned to go up the road towards the peak of the mountain and saw him pause in his frenzy to watch us go.

The overlook was an easy walk from the top parking lot. The view when we reached the end of the path was spectacular. It was still relatively early on a Monday morning, and there were very few people wandering along the trail. I saw a bald eagle perched on a nearby tree, seemingly watching us. I caught my breath as it took off in flight, appearing to soar and drift on the wind. It was mesmerizing. I jumped when Ty gently touched my shoulder to get my attention.

"I was doing it again, wasn't I?"

"You looked almost hypnotized by the eagle. I hated to pull your attention from it." Ty said gently. "We should really hit the road soon though. I need to get down the mountain and call to check in. You probably should as well."

I smiled as I looked up at Ty's handsome face. "Thank you for bringing me here. This is a beautiful place, and it's so peaceful here. I hate to leave, but my soul longs for the beach. The ocean tides have always carried my worries away. The beach sunshine warms my soul. I am at peace on the beach."

I took a last look at the picturesque view that the overlook provided before turning and heading back down the path where Ben and Jules had already gone. Our progression didn't seem to disturb the natural inhabitants of the area. The birds continued their songs as we walked beneath their resting spots. Occasionally a lizard would scurry here or there, once right in front of Jules who shrieked and jumped. We were all still laughing about it when we walked into the parking lot. I noticed that the few people who were in the parking lot had all stopped and were looking at the sky. I stopped walking and looked up as well. To my surprise, I saw what appeared to be falling stars. I had never seen a falling star in the day and said so out loud. I heard Ben say something about not knowing there was supposed to be a meteor shower.

I was unable to pull my eyes away from the sight. It seemed both beautiful and frightening. I knew that if we were able to see this many rocks entering the earth's atmosphere in the bright morning sunlight, there was probably something very wrong. Ty grabbed my hand and almost tossed me up in the truck. He was yelling back at Ben and Jules the entire time to get in their truck and meet us at the bottom of the mountain because he needed to get to where he could make a phone call now.

He took off down the mountain before I could even get my seat belt fastened. He was driving faster than he should around the twists and turns, and I knew he was solely focused on the road ahead. So as not to distract him I bit my tongue to stop myself from asking him what was going on. He pulled his phone out of his pocket and tossed it to me.

"Watch it and let me know as soon as I have service. I need to call my dad, like now!"

I grew increasingly more nervous as I watched his phone, waiting for the no service banner to disappear. We were already to the bottom of the mountain, and Ty was cussing before it finally left the screen.

"Got it!" I cried out. Ty recklessly pulled off the side of the road and grabbed the phone out of my hand, immediately hitting the speed dial for his father who seemed to pick up the phone before it could even ring.

I could hear Mr. Robins talking in a stern voice. The words seemed to pour through the phone and Ty listened intently, nodding his head and making sounds of acknowledgment occasionally.

"Okay, Dad. I got it, and I will get us there. I'll have Elli call her parents to let them know too. Ken isn't with us, so I'm going to try to get in touch with him when we hang up. As soon as Ben and Jules get down here, we will be on our way. I'll fill up the tank and make sure that the reserves are full before we leave the little town that is near here. Is there anything else I should try to get?" There was a pause while he listened to his dad speak again. "All right, I'll have Elli go into the store while I gas up. She can get any specifics that she might need. We will see you soon. Love you. I'll stay safe, you do the same."

Ty took a deep breath and rubbed his hands over his eyes in a frustrated gesture before turning to face me. I could see him steel himself in preparation for telling me what was going on. It took another deep breath before he was ready.

"Okay Elli, I need you to stay with me and stay calm. You also need to be open-minded and have faith that my father knows what he is talking about. According to Dad, they have just announced that a very large bolide is heading directly for Earth. They aren't releasing many details, but they think it will hit on the west coast, which means we should be safe from impact. Things are going to go bad quickly according to Dad. He wants us to go to our cabin in the mountains. It's about three and a half hours from here, and we should be isolated enough there to be safe. He wants you to call your parents. He has a vehicle for them that will be able to make the trip up the mountain roads, and he is more than happy to let them come as well. We will have all we need there for now."

I started to ask questions, but he stopped me. "Do you trust me?"

"Of course, you know that I do but..."

"I'm sorry there is no time for buts right now. Please, call your parents. They should already have heard the news. Someone will need to go to school to get Lucy. Dad will be getting in touch with them as soon as he takes care of a few other things. Tell them to gather what they will need, any medication or other like things that they have to have. Medicine will become an issue very soon. I am going to try to get in touch with Ken while you call home."

I had so many questions, but I didn't doubt that what Ty had told me was true. I grabbed my phone and saw that I had a few texts that had been delivered while we were sitting there. I ignored them and hit the speed dial for my father's cell, thinking he would be the easiest to talk to about the situation. I was shocked when he picked up the phone sounding happy as if it was just any other day.

"Good morning! I hope you had a wonderful night. Your mom showed me the pictures you sent. You're right it's beautiful there. So..." he was mid-sentence when I interrupted him.

"Dad, Dad! Don't you know what is going on?"

"Wha...what are you talking about?"

"Have you watched any television today? Listened to the radio? Had any contact with the outside world?"

"Well, no we haven't. We have a huge presentation coming up before we can leave for the beach and we have been locked in the office going over the data. What's going on sweetie? Are you okay? Has something happened?"

"Okay Dad, have Mom turn on the TV. Hurry, I don't have much time." I heard him tell my mom to do so and gave them a moment to listen before I continued. "Okay, Dad... Dad!"

"I... I... I don't believe this."

"Dad! Listen to me. Are you listening?"

"Yes, I'm sorry."

"Okay, Ty just talked to his dad. He says it's going to get really bad. I don't have the time or the information to tell you everything. This is what he said though. Is Lucy at school?"

"No, she said she was sick and stayed home today."

"Even better. You and Mom need to get home and gather up everything that you need. Medicine is important so if you have any that you need make sure to bring it. Mr. Robins told us to go to their cabin in the mountains. He said he will be in touch with you and that you can meet us there. Okay?"

Just then the line went completely dead. I looked down at my phone at the same moment that Ty looked down at his. I looked at him questioningly, and he shrugged.

"Dad told me one time that he wondered if they would take cell service down if something big happened. I guess they did. They must need the lines clear for their own use. They may be getting some sort of atmospheric interference or something."

"So, what's going to happen? What do we do? I'm scared Ty," I sobbed. I just wasn't good with stress or sudden change.

He pulled me to him and held me close. For a minute he said nothing, just held me. "I know you are babe. This is scary stuff, but I'm prepared. My dad is prepared. We will get to the cabin, and he will meet us there. I will not let anything happen to you, no matter what. Do you trust me?"

"With my life."

"Good, then just listen when I tell you to do something. I know you always have questions, but I may not always have time to explain. If I tell you to run, you run. If I say duck, you duck and cover. If I tell you to leave me behind, you do it."

"I will not do that."

"You do it, no questions asked."

I didn't argue about it anymore, I knew it wasn't the time, but I also knew that I would never leave him behind. It didn't matter what happened or if he told me to leave him I would never do it.

It seemed like it took forever for Ben and Jules to join us at the bottom of the mountain. They didn't seem to have any clue about what was going on.

"Dude, why did you take off like that? We were watching that spectacular meteor show and heard you yelling something, and when we looked up, you were gone. I want to get Ken on the phone to give him hell before we hit the road. I assume we have service here, give me a minute."

Ty and I just sat there staring at Ben. He wasn't even really paying any attention to us and didn't appear interested in our response to anything he had said. Jules seemed to be looking for something in the back of the truck as Ben grabbed his phone to make the call. I could see him get frustrated when he discovered that he still had no service.

"I assumed you stopped here because you could make a call, but there is no service. I need to go to where there so that I can call Ken. Let's hit it!" We both just sat there, and finally Ben paused to actually look at us. "What the hell is wrong with you two?"

Ty cleared his throat to try to get Ben to listen to him. Ben was the one in our group who made the most fun of Ty and his family's prepping efforts. He didn't believe that anything would ever go wrong that would require a "bug out" situation. As far as he was concerned humans are invincible and nothing would ever cause a catastrophic event of that level in his world, it wouldn't dare. Ben thought the entire idea was ridiculous.

"Okay, I talked to my dad, from this spot, before cell service went down. It appears that there is a large bolide set to collide with Earth. It is projected to hit somewhere on the west coast. That is why you see all of the smaller meteors. Things are going to go bad quickly. Dad says we need to go to the cabin in the mountains. It's about three and a half hours from here."

Jules was listening intently from her place by Ben's truck. Her face went almost colorless, and I could see the fear in her eyes. She knew Ben wouldn't believe Ty, but she also knew that Ty was telling the truth.

"Not funny dude. Don't be an asshole. I need to find out where the hell Ken is and we need to get to the beach."

"I'm not kidding. Look, Ben, I know you don't believe in this shit, but I don't have time to deal with you and your mocking of my family right now. We need to get to the closest town, fill up the gas and reserve tanks. I'm going to drop Elli off to go to the local store to pick up anything that she thinks might be important. After that, we are going to the mountains, and that is it. Now get in your truck and follow me to the gas station."

"I'll follow you to the station because I need fuel, and I should have cell service by then, but I am not going to your cabin in the mountains. We are going to the beach."

Ty didn't argue, he just got into the truck, started the engine, and assumed that Ben would follow. None of us noticed the old truck leaving the park and following us. If we had, I'm sure we would have wondered about Max's timing and why he just happened to be going the same way that we were.

∞ ∞ ∞

Ty drove into the little village that was near the park. The gas station was directly beside a small grocery store. Ty pulled into the parking lot and shifted to look at me.

"Grab large quantities of anything you will need that Dad wouldn't have stocked at the cabin. I don't know what. Perhaps those little caramel candies that you love, or tampons? Any of those secret girl things that you might have to have that I wouldn't know anything about. Definitely get chocolate though. You and I both know that sometimes you just need your chocolate."

I certainly didn't want to discuss tampons with Ty, but it was sweet that he was concerned with my needs considering everything that was going on. Ben pulled in beside us, and Jules jumped out. I grabbed her by the hand to pull her into the store with me. I looked back and saw Ben messing with his phone again. Ty got out of his truck and tapped on the driver's side window where Ben sat. They were still talking when Jules and I walked into the store. It was quiet inside, and only one cashier seemed to be working.

The cashier gave us a bright, welcoming smile when we walked in.

"Howdy girls."

Although from a distance I initially would have guessed her to be in her mid-40s, her face was lined from hard living, and when she spoke to us, her voice was rough, the sound of years of cigarette smoking. Her hair was so blonde that it was obvious that it had been bleached and styled in what I could only think of like a messy 80's throwback. She was wearing a name tag that said Jeana.

"It's very quiet this morning," she continued as we walked in. "I guess all of this excitement about some big rock heading towards California is keeping everyone in their house. Boss told me to go home, but I got no one to go home to. I

42

thought that I'd just stay here and keep the place open. I expect sooner or later everyone is going to realize that they better hightail it down here to get some supplies. You two ain't local. You been staying up there on the mountain?"

"Good morning ma'am. Yes, we spent the night camping up on the mountain. We are just on our way back out of town, but circumstances being what they are my boyfriend wanted me to grab things that I might need or want." The cashier smiled and waved us in to do our shopping.

I headed to the candy aisle first for chocolate and caramel for myself and some of Ty's favorite Bit-O-Honeys. From there I went to the health and beauty aisle to grab tampons and other such girly items. I knew Ty's dad would be stocked with pain relievers and first aid supplies, but I grabbed some anyway, along with some antibiotic creams, band-aids, and other everyday necessities. I looked around for Jules and saw that she had only picked up a thing or two.

"Jules get a cart and get everything that you will need. You aren't going to have many options in the near future according to what Ty's dad said."

"El, I don't have the money to buy things. I'm so confused. I don't know what to do. You know Ben thinks Ty is overreacting, but he isn't is he?"

I stopped grabbing things off the shelf and turned to look at her. "I wish he were, but he's not. We shouldn't have been able to see those meteorites considering how bright the sun is out there today. As far as money, don't worry about that. Fill up the cart with anything you need, not perishable foods though."

Jules nodded and determinedly grabbed a cart. She started heading up and down aisles like she was on a mission. She seemed thoughtful and serious about the items that she chose to put in her cart. Once she was convinced to begin shopping, she wasted no time in finding the items that she felt that she would need. Jules's cart was full, and she was ready to go before I had finished pulling things off the shelves in the first aid section.

Once I had finished gathering items I met her at the front of the store. Jeana starting scanning the stuff from our loaded carts.

"By the looks of everything in your cart," Jeana commented, "it seems that Y'all may have a better idea about what is going to happen than most folk. The government ain't telling us much."

I looked into her eyes, trying to decide what I should, or could tell her. Her eyes were tired, but they were also the most beautiful shade of green that I had ever seen. There was kindness in them, and fear as well. I reached out and stopped her hand from picking up product and scanning it.

"Things are going to get very bad. I really don't have all of the details to give you, but my boyfriend's father has a way of knowing about these kinds of things."

"Is he one of those doomsday preppers? I have a friend who does that. He has a big bunker all prepared for the end of the world. Is it really that bad?"

"End of the world? I don't know. I know that he told us to get to the cabin, and I heard him say that this ... I forget the word he used, but it wasn't meteorite... this rock's impact on the west coast is going to have worldwide effects, and they will be long-term."

Jeana's eyes went wide with fear and concern. "I thought that it would be bad, but not that bad. I... I should go. Where should I go? What should I do?"

"You said your boss told you to go. I can almost guarantee there will be looting and such once people figure out how bad things really are going to be, and you shouldn't be here. Pack up your car with supplies for yourself and get out of here. When we leave, you should lock up the front door and go. I don't know how much time we have. You said you have a friend who has a bunker and if he will take you in go there. I think it's your best hope."

"Okay, that's what I'll do. You two go on out of here. Take your things, I ain't going to take your money. Hell, it won't be worth anything soon anyway. I'm locking the door behind you, filling up my car, and bugging out."

Jeana quickly bagged all of our things and escorted us to the door. She gave us both a quick hug.

"Thank you, girls, for being honest with me. Good luck on your journey and stay safe."

"Good luck Jeana."

I heard the door lock behind us and turned towards the parking lot. If it was possible the little town seemed to be more deserted than it had been when we went into the store. Ty and Ben both had their trucks parked in the spots closest to the door, and we made our way to them quickly. I saw relief flash in Ty's eyes at the sight of me and I wondered what he had been worried about. He quickly walked away from Ben's door and made his way to help me find spots for the bags in the already overfull truck. Ben moved to help Jules do the same.

I could hear the two of them arguing in low voices as Ben tossed the bags into the truck. Jules' voice was adamant, and her tone was one that I had only heard her use once before, with her mother when she tried to demand that Jules return home.

"No! Ben, we are not continuing to the beach, and we are not going back to Columbus. We are going with Ty and El to the cabin like his dad said."

"I'm not driving there Jules! I'm telling you he's just overreacting and it's going to ruin our entire trip."

"Ty," I said quietly, "what's going on with Ben? Why is he being such an ass?"

"He's in denial. He doesn't want to believe. He thinks if we just continue on nothing will happen. He's also worried about Ken. I talked to Ken. I told him where we were going and to get a map. He was there with us once, and he remembers the general idea of where it was. He believes me, but he has to convince Mandy. I am done trying to convince Ben. He can come or not, but I don't have time for his bullshit."

At that precise moment, I heard Jules yell out.

"Fine, be a stubborn ass! I'm going with El and Ty. He's your best friend, and you are being an idiot. El! Make some room for me. I just need a small spot somewhere, but I'm coming with you."

She turned away from Ben, effectively dismissing him, and walked towards our truck. I looked back to Ben and saw him drop his head in defeat.

"Jules," he called out to her, pleading in his voice. "C'mon baby."

When she didn't turn around, he seemed to give up the fight. "Okay, okay. I can't fight you all. You win. Get back in the truck. If all this crazy shit is really going down, we need to get on the road. I have no idea what is going to happen, but we need to get as close to where we need to be as soon as possible."

Jules turned around and ran back to him, jumping back into his arms, and placing kisses all over his face. He carried her to the truck, buckled her into her seat, and quickly tossed the rest of her grocery bags into the truck. Within a few minutes, we were on US 52 headed south towards Interstate 40. Once on I-40, we could travel most of the way to the cabin. The road was deserted, and I wasn't sure how things could get any more bizarre.

I remembered that I had a few unread texts which I had been too busy to look at earlier. I began frantically searching through my things for my cell phone. I finally found it at the bottom of my purse. I quickly went to my texting app and saw that there were two messages from my mom, one from my dad, and one from Lucy. Mom and Dad's texts had both been sent before I talked to them. I was sure that they were just comments on the pictures that I had sent. I clicked on Lucy's text first, which appeared to have been sent while I had been talking to my father. Tears came to my eyes when I read the fear that her words represented. It read:

"Eli! Eli! I just saw something on the news. I don't believe it. I'm home alone, and Mom and Dad won't answer their phone. I'm scared! What's going on? Why did you have to leave now! I'm sorry I was such a jerk yesterday. Call me, okay? I'm scared!"

Ty was focused on the road, but he reached out to rub my leg. "Baby, what is it? What's wrong?"

"I'm worried about my family. What if something happens to them? What if they are wrong about where that rock is going to hit? What if Mom and Dad won't leave with your dad? Lucy was home alone. She sent me a text, and she was so scared. I should have been there for her." The tears were rolling down my cheek. How could everything have gone so wrong so quickly?

Chapter Four

It took Ty a while to calm me. The tears just wouldn't stop flowing no matter what he said to reassure me. I knew what he was telling me was true and as much as my parents had always considered Mr. Robins eccentric, they knew that he would never give them false information. With the news reports to back him up, they would know that they needed to do just as he said. I tried to send a message back to Lucy even though I was sure that she was safe with my parents by now, but the phone just said it was sending and never said sent.

When I had no more tears to shed I quietly looked out the window watching the world fly by and wondered if I was seeing the world as I knew it for the last time. I could see the flicker of televisions through the windows of the homes that we passed. Occasionally a person was working in the yard or playing with a dog. I hoped that these families would be able to continue on with their lives, watch their favorite television shows, run to the market for milk, go to their jobs, and watch their children grow and have families of their own.

I was lost in thought when I felt the truck sharply swerve. I thought we were wrecking or that maybe we had gotten a flat tire.

"Ty, what's going on?" I exclaimed.

"Hold on! I need to get the truck safely stopped. I hope Ben can keep it together back there."

Ty managed to slow the truck down and pull off to the side of the road. I realized that it wasn't the truck or Ty's driving that was the problem, it was the actual road itself. The pavement seemed to be moving. It looked like the road in front of us had turned into waves, and the telephone poles seemed to be dancing to some strange tune.

"Is this a freakin earthquake?" I asked, panicked.

Ty and I jumped out of the truck when it came to a stop. Ben seemed to be struggling to control his truck, and I was afraid he was going to flip it. "Move out of the way, back into the grassy area!" Ty yelled as Ben's truck headed for us. I ran towards the grass and heard tires screeching behind me. I hoped Ty was following me.

When I hit the grass, I realized that I was holding my breath. I exhaled slowly and stopped running, leaning down to put my hands on my knees. For a minute I thought I might hyperventilate. I was gasping for breath when Ty sat down beside me and pulled me into his lap, trying to soothe me. I knew I was having a panic attack. They had happened once or twice before in moments of excessive stress. His low, quiet, calm voice was comforting, and after a few seconds, I began to relax.

The earth was still moving beneath us, but it didn't seem as overwhelming now. I realized that I hadn't heard a crash, so Ben must have gotten the truck under control and stopped. I turned and looked back towards the road. Ben's truck had swerved around Ty's and come to rest about twenty feet further down the road. I saw both Ben and Jules on the opposite side of the road. Both appeared to be unharmed, at least physically. I didn't think I would ever be the same again mentally, and I wondered if any of us would.

It took another deep breath before I was finally able to talk. "So let me get this straight, not only do we have to worry about a giant rock crashing into the earth but we also have to deal with earthquakes?"

"I think the earthquake means that either the bolide that hit the west coast was really much bigger than anyone ever anticipated it would be, they projected the wrong impact area, or we have also had a bolide impact somewhere near here. Either way, all we can do is keep moving forward as soon as this freaking moving stops."

"Is there anything else we should be worrying about? Anything that I should know of beforehand? You know, so I'm not taken quite as off guard as I was this time."

"It would have taken some time for the earthquake to get here. There was the possibility of radiation, but it would have gotten here first. Dad didn't think it would be an issue. According to his sources, it wasn't a concern, but there wasn't a lot that could have been done for us anyway since we didn't have anywhere to shelter nearby. The other imminent issue will be a possible air blast. Dad said we shouldn't have to worry about that if we are close to the mountains because they will deflect it, but if the impact was closer, or there was a second impact closer to here, it could be a problem. If the wind speeds are too high, we will be screwed unless we can find a cave or somewhere to shelter in place. I have earplugs to help with the sound, but we can't withstand excessive hurricane force winds. We just have to hope for a little luck."

"Is there any such thing left in this world? Everything is gone. The world that we know is going to be gone, isn't it? How do we go on? What is left to go on for?"

Ty took my face in his hands and looked deeply into my eyes. "We are what's left. You have me, and I have you. Our families are still out there trying to get to us. There is still life, it will just be different. You may not be able to go to the store and buy your favorite ice cream or to the movie theater, but there is still life."

I relaxed into Ty and thought about what he had said. Life would be different going forward, but I still had the things that were most important to me. My family was trying to get to me, and I still had Ty. We had a place to go where we would be safe, thanks to Mr. Robins. At this point, we were much better off than most of the people in the United States.

"It's enough," I said quietly. "We are very lucky aren't we?"

"Compared to other people and what they will have to deal with in the days, weeks... months to come, yes we are fortunate. If you want to call it luck, Dad would just say we were better prepared. However, I suppose if the bolide had struck anywhere near us things would be very different. Yes, we are very lucky." Ty held me close for a few seconds before I heard Ben and Jules approaching. Ben was cussing, and Jules was crying again.

"What the hell Ty? That wasn't some rock falling from the sky! It was a freaking earthquake!"

Ty sighed and stood, placing me gently on my feet. "It was a freaking earthquake caused by a bolide impact with the earth."

I went to try to calm Jules down, even though, in my opinion, Ben should be trying to do it instead of yelling at Ty. It wasn't Ty's fault that the world was falling apart. He didn't have to let Ben come along to the cabin. I took a moment to take in everything I could about Ben. Yes, he was yelling at Ty, and he was also pacing. There were worry lines on his face and fear in his eyes. That was it, he was afraid. I was afraid. Jules was afraid. The only one of us that didn't have fear in their eyes was Ty. He was, as always, calm and confident. At that moment, I knew that we would be all right. Ty would make sure that we got to where we needed to be. Ty was the leader we needed, and Ben needed to realize that.

"Ben!" I yelled from where I stood with Jules. "Stop yelling at Ty. This isn't his fault. We're all scared, but we need to listen to Ty and do what he needs us to do. So stop yelling and listen."

Ben snapped his mouth shut as if he just realized that he had been standing in the middle of a field yelling at his best friend. Once Ben was quiet Ty shared with him the things that he had shared with me a few moments before. Ty seemed to genuinely think we would be completely safe from the immediate danger if we just made it to the cabin. With everyone calm and more knowledgeable than before we all headed back up to the trucks. Ty walked around both vehicles, making sure there was no damage anywhere.

We were just getting back in the trucks so we could get on our way when we heard the sound of vehicles approaching. Ty and I both looked down the road to see who was coming. Five military vehicles were moving relatively quickly down the road. I heard Ty cuss under his breath. He turned to me and told me to stay in the truck before jumping back out. I saw that Ben was getting out of his truck as well and walking back to where Ty now stood on the side of the road.

The approaching trucks slowed to a stop when they saw Ty and Ben standing beside the truck. I saw a man get out of the passenger side of the first vehicle, followed by one man from each of the vehicles behind the first. The first man stood and looked Ty and Ben top to bottom while the others walked to his location with their hands resting on their weapons. All the soldiers wore camouflage and the first, who appeared to be in charge, was the picture of what I had always thought an American soldier should look like. Even in his camo uniform he was distinguished and had an air of power about him that was almost tangible. He had quite a few bars on his uniform, and the other soldiers looked to him for direction.

The older soldier said something to the others, and they seemed to relax. He then walked over to where Ty and Ben stood. The driver's side window of the truck was open, so I could hear the conversation that followed.

"Good morning. It looks like you guys may have run into a bit of trouble. Everyone all right?"

"Good morning sir," Ty replied with a tone that carried the utmost respect. "The ground shaking just took us by surprise. We are all fine, and there was no damage to our trucks."

"Yes, it was a bit unexpected. Are you kids traveling? Did you not get the news that you should be sheltering in place?"

"Sir? No, sir. We were camping last night in the mountains and are now on our way to my father's cabin. Is something wrong? Are we under attack?" I didn't understand why Ty was not being honest with the officer but was sure that he had a good reason.

"Attack? No, nothing like that. I can't really give many details. Troops are being ordered west to provide civilian assistance. You really shouldn't be out on the road at this point. We can transport you to the nearest shelter."

"Thank you for the offer sir but we aren't going to be going that far, and my father is waiting for us. I wouldn't want him to worry." The officer looked directly into Ty's eyes as if trying to discover something there. He must have been satisfied with what he saw because he made a gesture to his soldiers and they began returning to their trucks.

"I believe you probably will be just fine without our assistance, won't you son? I wouldn't want your father to worry. Don't stay out here long. Things are going to get rough when the true gravity of the situation is figured out on a wide scale. Get to where you are going and plan to bunker down. There won't be military around to help you. Do you understand what I'm telling you?"

"Yes, sir, I do. I will take care of my friends. I have one favor to ask you, sir, please." The officer had turned to head back to his vehicle but paused and turned back to Ty. "I have a brother stationed out of Fort Jackson, Captain Trevor Robins. If you happen to run into him could you let him know that his family is alright? Tell him that Ty was on his way to the cabin to meet our father."

The officer shook Ty's hand and wished us luck before returning to his vehicle. We sat and watched the army vehicles roll past before we got ready to go again. The mood was somber, and things seemed even more severe than they had before if that was even possible. I sat quietly in the passenger seat as Ty focused on the road. Ben had fallen in behind us. I picked up my phone to flip through the pictures that I had taken on the mountain yesterday and saw a text message notification. Maybe it's just a failed send notification, I thought. I clicked on the app and saw a one by Lucy's name.

"Ty, I have a text from Lucy. How did that happen? I thought you said that cell service would stay down."

"It must have slipped through at some point. What does it say?"

I clicked on the message and read it. Immediate relief went through my body, and I felt myself relax. "It says, '*El, I don't know if you will get this, but I'm going to try to send it anyway. Mom and Dad came home, and things got crazy. Ty's dad came and brought us one of his trucks. I guess it will be better to get us where we are going to meet you. We are leaving Columbus now. I hope you are okay. Stay safe!*' That means they are all on their way to meet us. I'm so relieved."

Ty smiled my way. "I didn't think any more messages would go through. I'm glad she got that through to you. It makes me feel better too. Would you check my phone to see if my dad or mom sent us any more instructions?"

"Sure, where's your phone?"

"Right here in my front pocket. You can reach right in there and get it. I wouldn't want to take my eyes off the road or my hands off the wheel." I saw the amusement in his eyes and maybe a little bit of a dare. I unbuckled my seatbelt and slid across the seat, slowly reaching into his front pocket. He lifted his butt off the seat and straightened his hip to give me better access. I carefully reached further into the pocket and slowly pulled his phone free. "You can leave your hand in there if you want," he teased.

I felt myself blushing again. I slid back to my side of the truck and buckled my seatbelt before turning on the screen of his phone. He had two unread messages. I turned to look at him. "You have two."

Ty motioned me to go on, so I clicked on the app and saw that they were both from his mother. "They are both from your mom. The first one must have been sent early before the service went down. It just says that she loves you and to be safe. The second one says that they are all heading south. It says your dad's sources say that the radiation won't be an issue and that as long as you stay on the east side of the mountains, we should be safe from the air blast. She said that when we get close, we should check the two-way radio. They will start calling when they are in range. She ends with they love you and be safe."

Ty took a deep breath, and it struck me that, although on the outside he appeared calm and confident, I should have known that inside he was worried as well. I looked over at him and took one of his hands from the steering wheel. I held it in my own. "I'm sorry. You've been worried, and I should have realized that. You're just always so in control. I'm here for you too."

"It's my job to be here to take care of you, to keep you safe. The messages from my mom help. They are safely on their way. Getting out of the city was going to be a big challenge. According to what Dad told me earlier, they were more than suggesting that people shelter in place, they were insisting."

"We are here to take care of each other, and you are going to have to get that through your thick skull." I knew that he had difficulty with that concept but in this world, he was going to have to learn to accept it. "So, what your dad told you, is that why you lied to the officer?"

"Yes, I didn't want him to think that we were going to be traveling far and force us to go to some shelter somewhere. We need to get to the cabin. The shelters are great for people for now but what's going to happen when supplies don't show up, and there aren't enough resources for everyone? So that is actually slowing down our progress some because I can't drive as fast as I want to or we will catch up to them. If they run into someone else and stop, we might catch up to them though. It's risky to stay on this road, but it's the fastest way."

Just then I noticed the rest area sign. "Do you think we could stop there? I could use a restroom break, and it would give us a little bit more of a buffer between them and us. We could look at the map. Maybe there is a side road that runs parallel to this one."

"That's one of the reasons I love you. You're so smart and such a good problem solver." Ty smiled at me and turned on his signal so Ben would know that we were going to exit soon.

∞　∞　∞

I opened the door of the truck and stepped out into an eerily quiet world. There were no sounds of travelers stopping to take a quick bathroom break. No one walked their furry family member. No families picnicked beneath the pine trees. The silence went beyond the lack of human inhabitants in the area. No sounds were coming from animals, insects or birds. It was so quiet that the sound of Ty closing his truck door made me jump, it seemed so out of place. We suddenly seemed like uninvited visitors, maybe not just in this place but in the world. Perhaps the universe was finally rejecting mankind, and what we have done to the earth, I thought. It could be that we are just out of time like what happened to the dinosaurs.

We all stood on the sidewalk in front of the building seemingly entranced by the lack of all things normal in this place that should be full of everyday human life. There were no other vehicles in the lot and nothing that would indicate that anyone else was anywhere nearby. Ty seemed to be taking in everything, scanning for danger. Finally, he cleared his throat to get us all in motion.

"One second," he whispered to me as he headed back to the truck. He seemed to rummage around for something, and I couldn't see what he had in his hand when he returned. He pulled me to him, in what would appear to others as a hug, but I felt him slip something into the back waistband of my jeans and pull my shirt over it to cover it. A gun. He had made sure that I knew how to shoot, insisting on teaching me one weekend not long ago. I looked up into his eyes questioningly. Once again he leaned down and whispered into my ear, "By all appearances, we are here alone, and hopefully you won't need that, but something just feels off. Maybe I am just overly sensitive or cautious, but I want you to keep that with you ... on you... going forward. You know how to use it and in this world, if there is danger don't hesitate."

I looked into his eyes and gave a slight nod. I wasn't going to spend any time arguing with him or doubting what he said in this world. I didn't know if I would ever be able to shoot someone, but I would try to protect myself if I needed to. Ty pulled away and said, aloud, "Okay, why don't you ladies go in to take care of your necessities and I'll just look at the map here."

Ben had picked up on Ty's discomfort with the situation, and his situational awareness seemed to increase. He walked back to his truck, opened the door, and pulled out his rifle. "I think I'll just take a look around. Walk out some of the kinks from sitting in that truck for so long. If you need me just holler."

Ben wandered to the opposite side of the building from where Jules and I would enter to go to the restroom. He would appear causal to the untrained eye, and I was glad that he was trying to help Ty ensure that the area was safe and secure. I didn't know if the facilities would be working still, with running water and such, but I really hoped that I could use the bathroom and wash my hands and face. I took Jules by the hand, and we walked together to the ladies restroom. I opened the door cautiously and peered inside. I could sense eyes on us, but I was sure that both Ben and Ty were watching to make sure that we safely got into the restroom without incident, so I tried to convince myself that I was simply imagining things. Ty had moved closer to the building and appeared to be studying a road map of the state.

I heard no noise in the bathroom. There was no dripping water, no squeaky door hinge, nothing that indicated someone was in the room. Jules and I quietly slipped inside. I bent down and looked to see if there were any feet visible under the stall walls. I didn't see any, so I slowly walked down the line and pushed each of the doors open, holding my breath the entire time. When I reached the handicap stall, I slowly pushed the door open, half expecting someone to jump out at me. The door banged against the wall, and Jules jumped and let out a small scream.

"Jules, there's no one in here but you screamed, and they'll be freaked out. Yell out that we are all right!"

Before Jules could even get the door pulled open to yell, Ty was there charging through the door with Ben on his heels. Ty had a look of panic on his face, and his eyes immediately swept the room looking for danger and me. His eyes found mine, and I saw him take a deep breath before once again sweeping the room for danger. "What happened? What's wrong?"

"I'm sorry!" Jules looked ready to burst into tears again. "I just... El swung the door open, and it hit the wall. It scared me. I'm so sorry."

"It's okay Jules," Ty tried to reassure her. "I heard the loud bang and was already on my way here when you screamed. Seems like you guys are safe in here so I'll just head back out."

Ty turned and walked out the door. I started to go into the stall when I heard the sound of a shot being fired. I grabbed Jules and covered her mouth to prevent another distracting scream before I quietly made my way to the door. I did not want to rush out and distract Ty from whatever had happened outside that door. I whispered for Jules to not say a word. I tried to tell her to go to the back stall and lock herself in, but, she adamantly shook her head no. She had tears streaming down her face, and I felt guilty, but I needed her safely out of the way. I quietly pulled the gun from the back waistband of my jeans and showed it to her before motioning her back to the stall again.

I could hear Ty's voice through the door, but it wasn't clear enough to understand. I slowly cracked the door, hoping that I could better hear what was going on. I couldn't really see anything or anyone, but I could hear the situation better. Ty was yelling at someone, and I could hear the tension, mixed with authority, in his voice.

"There is no way that we are going to let you leave in that truck. Just back away from it and I'll let you go on your way, no harm no foul. If you move one more step and continue to try to get in that truck or take anything out of it, I will shoot you. I am a damn good shot so don't make me do it."

"Kid, you got more than you need here and it's only right to take care of your fellow man in times like this. Besides, I know that it's just you. Your friend over there is out cold on the ground. I took care of him. Yeah, there are those two little girlies in the bathroom, but they're girls. They ain't going to be of much help to you. You can't stop me, it's just you. So, go on and put that weapon down. Then I'll leave... with the truck. You will still have plenty to tide you over until things get back to normal."

Ben! My heart chilled at the man's words. Was Ben okay? There had to be something that I could do to help, especially since the sexist pig thought that Jules and I were just girls who couldn't do anything. I felt trapped in this restroom. Without seeing where everyone was, I didn't know what I would walk out into if I opened the door. I might end up being a distraction to Ty. I looked around the small room and noticed a window in the very back stall that would come out on the back side of the building. I quietly let the door swing back closed and went to the last stall.

"Jules let me in and help me get out of this window."

"What? No, you can't go out there until they come to get us. Someone just fired a gun. It's not safe out there."

"Someone is trying to steal one of the trucks, and I can't let that happen. It seems like Ben is hurt and Ty is in a standoff with the guy."

"What?? Is Ben hurt? How bad? What happened?"

"I don't know, but I'm not leaving Ty out there by himself with the crazy man who hurt Ben. Is there anything we can stand on to get out that window?" As soon as she heard that Ben was hurt, Jules sprang into action. She climbed up on the toilet and began forcing the widow out. It was one of those old windows that pushed out from the bottom and latched closed. It was old and heavy, but by the time I got into the stall to help her, she had already forced it wide open without making a sound.

"All right," I said. "Ty gave me a gun before we came in here. I'm going to climb out and sneak around. You stay in here, it's safer."

"Ben needs me, I'm not staying in here. I'm coming too."

"You can't defend yourself, and you'll be a distraction to Ty."

"I'm not staying!!"

"Fine!" I didn't want to waste any more time arguing. "Just stay behind the building until it's safe. I'm not sure where Ben is but if you just run out, it will make things worse." Jules nodded her assent, and I lifted myself through and out the window. It was a short drop to the ground, and I tried to land as quietly as I could. Once outside I could hear Ty and the other man clearly again. I looked around to get my bearings and knew that if I followed the building to the left, I would come to the door where the ladies room was, which is where Ty should be standing. I looked in that direction and saw Ben lying face down on the ground.

When Jules landed silently beside me, I whispered to her, "Ben is lying down there. It looks like the man pulled him behind the building. Go as silently as possible down to see if he is all right. If you make noise, you will distract Ty. Can you be silent?" Jules nodded to me, her eyes wide and determined, before silently and cautiously heading towards where Ben was on the ground. I turned to the other side of the building, trying to figure out how to best proceed. I knew that both trucks were parked in the middle of the front of the building and one would think that the man was standing near the trucks with his attention focused on Ty.

"This is the last time I am going to warn you," I heard Ty tell the man. "Walk away from the truck and back into the woods where you came from. That's the only way you are getting out of here unharmed. I can shoot you before you ever get that gun out of your waistband. Just walk away... NOW!"

I took a deep breath, preparing myself to peek around the building when I heard another shot. I hesitated, not knowing what to do now. I didn't want to turn the corner and distract Ty, but I certainly didn't want to leave him out there on his own.

"Hey now," yelled the stranger. "That almost hit me, but you missed. Ain't such a good shot are ya?"

At that, another shot rang out, and the stranger cussed loudly. "You shot my hat you son of a bitch!"

"Told you I was a good shot so you really shouldn't insult my mother again. That's the last warning shot, the next one will strike flesh. Back away from the truck and put the gun on the ground. Obviously, you cannot be trusted."

"I'll step away from the truck but I ain't puttin' my weapon down." I finally peeked around the corner and saw the man take one step away from Ben's truck. "Now, you just lower your gun, and we'll get along just fine. I'm sure we can work this out real friendly like without any more shooting."

From my angle, I could see that the man had another gun in the back waistband of his pants that Ty could not see. He slowly lowered his left hand. The next minute was a blur. The man quickly tried to grab the second gun, a shot rang out, and I stepped from behind the building and pointed my gun at the man who was now laying on the ground, blood pooling around his foot.

"You shot me you son of a bitch," the man yelled.

"Good thing he did because if he hadn't I would have and I'm not nearly as good of a shot as he is. Who knows where I would have hit you. Why didn't you just walk away? Why did you have to reach for your gun?" I was screaming at the man, and my hands were shaking like crazy. Ty yelled at me, concern in his voice.

56

"Babe, lower your gun and make sure the safety is on. Your hands are shaking like crazy, and I don't want an accidental fire. I've got this asshole covered." Ty walked over to the man who was still cussing up a storm and took both weapons from him. He quickly patted him down and also removed a wicked looking hunting knife which was strapped so that his pants and boots made it invisible. "I'll be okay here. Go check on Ben please."

Jules yelled out from behind the building, "I'm with him. He's got a big knot on his head, but he's starting to come around."

"Okay. You're going to get up and walk away from the trucks. Go sit on that bench over by the building." Ty motioned the man toward the building.

"Are you crazy? You shot me in the foot. I can't get up and walk anywhere."

"Well, then I guess you are going to have to crawl or scoot on your ass. I don't care how you get over there just get over there!" I could tell that Ty was getting frustrated with the guy. "Of course if you choose not to I could just shoot you again and leave you where you lie. The choice is yours, my friend, because it doesn't matter either way to me."

The man began scooting towards the bench, cursing the entire way. His progression was slow, but he finally made it. There was a trail of blood from the truck to where he sat, and I looked away so I didn't get sick. The sight of blood and I didn't agree with each other. I really didn't want to look like such a baby in front of Ty, but throwing up would just make it all that much worse.

"Up on the bench," I heard him say. The guy struggled but managed to get up from the ground and onto the bench. I walked over to where Ty stood a bit away from where the guy was sitting.

"What are you going to do with him?" I asked quietly so the man couldn't hear me. Rather than answer me, Ty just glared at the man and walked over to the back of the truck. I saw him pull something from the back and then turn back to the man.

"Mister, you aren't very intelligent. In this world, you just walk away when someone is holding a gun on you. People aren't going to mess around with your stupid thieving ass. You're lucky I love my girl because I'd just as soon leave you here to bleed, get an infection, or whatever but I think she'd be upset by that, so I'm going to patch up your foot and let you hobble back to whatever rock you slithered out from."

Ben and Jules came around from the side of the building as Ty was getting ready to patch up the man's foot. Ben was rubbing the back of his head, and Jules seemed to be helping him stay up and mobile. "Kill the son of a bitch," Ben mumbled as Jules led him over to his truck. "Not only did he hit me he was going to steal my truck."

Ty made quick work of bandaging the man's foot, and then he handed me the first aid supplies. "Can you put these back in the truck and bring me back some of the paracord that's in the glove box please?"

I quickly got him the cord and was surprised to see him tying the man's hands to the bench. "You're going to leave him tied here?"

"Yes."

"But... What ... How will he survive if he can't get free?"

"He better hope he can get free or that someone comes and unties him. I'm going to leave a note here too, explaining why he is tied up. I wouldn't want him fooling some other innocent person so he can steal their stuff."

Once Ty had the guy tied up I felt it was safe enough to turn my attention elsewhere. I went over to Ben's truck and checked on him. He claimed that he was fine, just a headache. Jules seemed to be a bit shaken up, but she was holding up better than I would have expected her too. I really wasn't very good at the nurse thing, so I left Ben's care to Jules and went back to where Ty was standing with a can of spray paint. I wondered if he had everything packed into the back of his truck and realized that he probably did. What was it grandma would have said? Oh yeah, everything but the kitchen sink. Ty made quick work of painting a message on the sidewalk in front of the man. Once his message was complete, he turned back to face me.

"How are your hands? Still shaky?" I held out my hands so that he could see that they were steady now. "Okay, good. I need to go scan the woods to make sure that he doesn't have friends out there nearby. My guess is that he's from that house we passed not that long ago, and he's here alone, but I need to be sure. Can you keep a gun on him? I'm going to have Ben do so as well, but I don't know if he's clear-minded enough yet to shoot straight."

"Sure, I've got this." I still wasn't sure about leaving this guy just tied up out here, but I would never say anything to contradict Ty's decision in front of this random guy who would have shot him if he could have. Ty gave me a quick kiss and walked over to where Ben sat in his truck. I saw him give Ben his rifle, which Ty had picked up from the where it had been left lying in the grass. I also heard him tell Ben, almost too softly for me to catch, that he should learn not to leave his keys in his truck going forward.

"I won't be long," he called out as he headed towards the woods that were in a semi-circle around the sides and back of the rest area. "If you need me yell. I won't go far enough that I can't hear you. Actually, let Jules yell, she's louder than you." Ty winked back at me and disappeared into the woods.

As soon as Ty was gone the man started whimpering. "Girl! Girl! You can't let him leave me here like this. What if nobody ever comes? And my foot hurts something fierce. Even if I get loose, I won't be able to walk anywhere. You have to make him take me with you. You can't leave me here to die!"

"Stop talking." I tried to ignore him, but he just kept rambling on and on about how we couldn't leave him at a rest area to die. "Stop talking! There is no way I would take you with us. You tried to steal our truck and supplies. You were given multiple chances to just walk away and then you tried to pull a gun on Ty. You probably would have shot him if he hadn't shot you first. You didn't care about our wellbeing or survival when you were doing that, did you? Just STOP TALKING!!! I am not going to help you so you can do this to someone else. It's your own fault that you are in this predicament."

The man seemed to give up, hopefully realizing that he was never going to convince me to go against Ty, and he went back to whimpering pitifully. I started to pace and wondered what was taking Ty so long. It seemed like he had been gone for an eternity. "Jules, how long has he been gone? He should have been back by now right?" I wanted to continue pacing, but I knew that I needed to keep my eyes on the stranger. I forced myself to stay still, trying to appear relaxed and confident. I could see that the blood was beginning to seep through the man's bandage. A part of me really wanted to help him, the part that was used to helping anyone in any way that I could. That part that of me still lived in a world where my mom and dad could fix any problem that might arise, and as much as I wanted to live in that world, I knew that the peaceful, safe world of yesterday was gone and it wouldn't be coming back anytime soon. I sighed deeply and steeled myself against the man's pitiful whimpering. I couldn't help him in this world. He had made bad choices that had hurt my friends.

I heard the sounds of someone walking through the woods on the opposite side of where Ty had entered. I positioned myself so I could see both the man and the woods, just in case it wasn't Ty came out. When I saw him walk through the trees, I felt like I could finally relax.

"I don't see any companions, but I do see a cabin on through the trees to the back. He probably came from there. Maybe someone will come looking for him if he's lucky. Hey babe, why don't you take Jules and go use the restroom so we can get out of here."

Jules and I headed to the restroom, again. As we walked away, I saw Ty make his way over to where Ben was sitting. Once in the bathroom, I took care of the necessities quickly, not wanting to leave Ty for too long. I knew that he was more than capable of taking care of himself, but it didn't feel right to leave him out there with the psycho man too long. I was trying to rush when an idea popped into my mind. I quickly checked and was happy to find that the water was still on. I called to Jules that I would be back and I hastily ran out to the truck. I grabbed the Styrofoam soda cup that I had picked up at the gas station yesterday and ran back to the restroom to fill the cup up with water. Jules was ready by the time I was done, so we headed back out.

I cautiously approached the man on the bench. I didn't want to get close to him but to leave the water where he could get to it I knew that I would have to walk up to where he sat. I could sense Ty watching my every move. I placed the cup as close to the man as I could get it on the bench. The straw was relatively long, and I hoped that he could bend down far enough to get a drink.

"This is what I can do for you," I said to him while looking into his eyes. "If you happen to get free, and God gives you another chance, make better choices. I would have helped you if you had just asked."

I turned and walked to Ty without looking back. Ben was sitting in the driver's seat of his truck, and he looked much better. His color was returning, and he looked almost like his usual grumpy self. Ty walked me over to his truck and lifted me up into the passenger seat. He walked around to the driver's side, got in, and turned the ignition to start the truck. As he backed out of the spot and pulled out into the driving lane, I turned and looked back at the man on the bench. Ty reached over and grabbed my hand. "Don't worry baby," he reassured me. "I left the cord loose enough that he'll be able to work his way out of them relatively quickly. I guess we're both too nice for our own good. My father wouldn't be proud."

Chapter Five

"I'm proud of you," I squeezed his hand. "Your dad may have handled that differently, but you did what I think is the right thing. Even if the world is falling apart, we cannot let ourselves lose our humanity. If everyone left after this event, or whatever you want to call it, becomes immune to the needs of others what kind of world will this be?"

"A crappy place, but I think the world is headed there anyway, whether we try to do the right thing or not. I have to put you before anyone else. If your life were at risk, I would have killed the guy, no doubt about it. Once people begin to realize that grocery stores aren't getting restocked, that the sun is not coming back out, and that temperatures are getting colder things are going to go crazy. Things will get even worse when the grid goes down, and there is no military around to keep peace and order. Chaos will ensue, and I don't think it will be long before that happens. I just hope that we can get to the cabin without any further incidents."

"The sun isn't coming back out? Temperature changes? What... what do you mean?"

"If the impact was as large as I think it must have been I believe that it will send a big cloud of earth, rubble, or just crap way up into the atmosphere. Think about it. When you drop a pebble into the water waves emanate out from it. Right? The cloud of crap that is going to go up in the atmosphere will be like if you were to drop a rock onto a pile of loose dirt. Think about how all the dust flies up, or sparks and such when you throw a log onto a fire. It will be much the same as that, just on a much, much grander scale. I'm not sure how far it will spread, but we felt the earthquake, and I'm guessing we will be dealing with a dust cloud too. Hopefully, Dad will have some idea of what we should be expecting and when."

"So what do we do?"

"We keep going forward, babe. That's all we can do at this point. The good news is that we should be far enough behind that military caravan that we shouldn't have to worry too much about catching up with them. I will proceed with caution, as I would have done regardless, but I don't think we will see them again. If everything goes well, we should reach the cabin in about two and a half hours."

"When should your parents and mine get there?"

"They'll be a few hours behind us, about double our time at least. We had already driven a few hours south yesterday, and they still need to get south. Not to mention they have to travel through some large cities, which actually means that they will have to circle them because they won't be able to get through or even use the outer belts. We have to go through two fair sized cities, Winston-Salem and Asheville. I have plans to go around anything we need to and hopefully, we don't run into any issues, but I'm not sure what will happen. The earthquake could have caused issues, or people could cause issues. Hell, even Ben could cause issues if he makes more stupid mistakes like letting that guy get the jump on him and leaving his keys in the truck. He needs some common sense."

"What should I do? How can I help? I feel useless just sitting here."

"There's not a lot that you can do really. Just keep your eyes open for anything that I might miss. Keep the gun on you. If you need to use it, don't hesitate. I was so proud of you back there. You were so brave. Not to mention you looked pretty damn sexy trying to protect me."

I laughed a little. Even during such a serious situation Ty still had to flirt with me. Was it like a natural guy instinct or something? Were they programmed to always think about sex and the continuation of their genetic line and now the entire human race? I just shook my head and looked at him. "Really? Sexy? Even now you want to flirt with me."

"Baby, even if the world is going to end I am going out flirting with you. Well, you could convince me to do more than flirt. I don't think it would even take a lot of convincing on your part. Just say the word, and I'll pull the truck over. We can find ourselves a nice little spot for some quality one-on-one time."

"So you want my first time to... well... to be... what ... in a field?" My face felt hot, and I knew without a doubt that I was blushing a deep red.

"Well, no, but since you brought it up, you would look beautiful lying in a field of wildflowers."

"Okay, okay...let's focus on the task at hand. Staying alive and getting to the cabin. You are going to get both of us distracted, and then we will miss something we should be seeing. You focus on the road, and I'll keep an eye open for anything that looks strange. There should be a town coming up soon. Do you think they will be blocking the roads or anything?"

"I don't think that will be a worry in the small towns, but I'll slow down, and we will approach cautiously. I think we are better off to keep going through and not try to stop. I don't know how much information the government has released yet and even though I really want to know what the updates are my gut says avoid towns, big or small, at all costs."

"Do you think they would be broadcasting on the radio?" I asked. We both looked at the AM/FM button on the trucks updated sound system like it was some sort of alien contraption. No one listened to the radio anymore. We had been listening to a SIRUS station when we got out of the truck last night, but in all the chaos of the morning the volume had been turned down and forgotten.

"Elli, you are brilliant. It is possible that they are broadcasting emergency information. Turn it on and let's see if we can find anything." I pushed the button and was disappointed when all we heard was static. "It's still on SIRUS, turn it to the regular AM/FM and see if you can find anything."

I hit the radio button and once again, heard nothing but static. Of course, it could be that nothing was on that specific radio frequency so I started scanning to see if we could pick anything up. Finally, I heard a man's voice and stopped the scan. The voice sounded automated, robotic.

"...This message will repeat." The loud, ever-annoying emergency broadcast system tone sounded and went on for what seemed like an eternity. Ty and I both held our breath as we sat quietly, listening to the tone, and waiting for the message to come back. At home, if the tone came on while I was watching television, I would immediately get annoyed and mute the sound, but now the tone seemed to represent the only way we had access to current information.

"Attention all Americans," the automated man announced in his monotone voice. "This is not a test. Repeat, this is not a test. This is an actual emergency for all citizens of The United States. A huge asteroid has hit the southwestern coastal area of the United States. The impact was centered in the Los Angeles area. Specific details are unavailable at this time. Loss of life is anticipated to be massive. Currently, military forces are being diverted west to provide what assistance they can to survivors as well as local and state authorities. Communication systems are impacted. Environmental impacts will be experienced throughout the entire country. Citizens are to shelter in place until further instructions are released. Repeat, shelter in place. Additional details and instructions will be released as they become available. This message will repeat."

I wasn't sure what to say at this point. The emergency announcement had made the entire situation seem more real, direr if that was possible. This wasn't a dream that I was going to wake up from. Life was forever changed. I wasn't going to get to go to college. I wasn't going to get to walk down the aisle in a big church wedding with Ty. Where would I fit into this world? Ty had been groomed and prepared by his father for this world, but I had no clue what to do. I had no skills for this world. Once again it was all too much, and I felt the tears begin to roll down my cheeks. I was trying to cry silently. I did not want Ty to once again have to put me together. I kept falling apart while he was calm and collected. I needed to be strong in this new world, not be someone who would hold Ty back.

Concerned by my silence after hearing such news, Ty glanced over and saw the tears. Immediately, he was once again trying to comfort me and keep me together. "Babe, it will be okay."

I tried to think of something calm and confident to say, but the words wouldn't come. "How will it be okay?" I sniffled as I tried to wipe the tears from my cheeks. "I'm really trying to hold it together here, but nothing will ever be the same. The life that just yesterday I thought we would live isn't possible anymore. I won't go to OSU in the fall. We won't buy a house on the beach or have kids. It's all gone because of a rock!"

"It's not all gone. Things will be different, and our focus will change, but we will have a life. Things are going to be tough for a while, but when the dust settles, you and I will still be here. We will have an amazing life, I promise you that. The things that are truly important in life are still here. I have you, and you have me. We have our families, who are racing to meet us. We will have food, shelter, and believe it or not power. We may not be able to search the web for whatever bit of information we need, but we have many of the creature comforts of home. Our dreams just have to change, but we can still dream. We can still live long lives and have a family together. All is not lost. Can't you see that?"

"I'm afraid," I whispered, looking down and away from Ty's beautiful eyes. "I'm afraid of this world, and I don't think I have a place here."

"Look at me!" I reluctantly turned back to look at Ty. "Your place is right beside me, now and always. If you aren't strong enough, I will carry you, physically or emotionally. You are mine, and I am yours, still, as it always was meant to be. Life is scary right now, but it won't always be that way. This is the unknown to you, and the unknown has always frightened you. Remember when I made you climb that tree in your Easter dress? You were afraid, but you did it anyway. How many times has something similar happened? I will lead you through this change, and you will be awesome, as you always are. I know you though, and you need your moment to be afraid, so, for now, I will just hold you. Once you are ready, you'll come into this new world fighting."

I unbuckled my seatbelt and scooted over to nestle beside Ty. This was my spot, beside him. He was right, this was where I belonged, in any world.

∞ ∞ ∞

Ty approached the small towns we passed with caution, but we never came across anyone trying to stop our progress. Well, to be honest, we didn't see anyone at all. Everyone must have been following the announcements direction and sheltering in place. People should be preparing, I thought. Stores and warehouses should be giving away their supplies so that people will be able to survive as long as possible. Perishable foods could be prepared to last longer while people had power, but, by keeping people in the dark about how bad things were going to get, the government was actually doing them a disservice. My heart broke for all the families, tucked away in their homes waiting for information about what they needed to do. They weren't prepared. Their children would suffer, and they most likely wouldn't make it. That was the real tragedy of the entire situation. Good people would die. Children would die. There was nothing that I could do to help them, but I could help myself and my family. The strong people, the ones who could adapt, would find ways to survive if at all possible. At least I hoped that they would. I took a minute to say a prayer to God, who was hopefully still listening to me. It was all I could do for all the people tucked away in their houses. If I spent too much time dwelling on their fate, it would become incapacitating. I needed to let it go. I couldn't save them. That thought alone was heartbreaking, but I knew that the only thing that I could do at this point was help Ty save us.

I pulled my mind away from the people in the towns and tried to focus on looking beyond what I would typically see. In this new world, I would need to see different things. I needed to look for danger and threats, which could be hidden anywhere. "Do you think that people will already be turning to desperate tactics? I mean, I know the guy at the rest area did, but will most people be to that point already? Are there really going to be dangers everywhere?" I asked Ty.

"Well, no not yet most likely. Most normal people will be sitting in their homes watching or listening to the emergency announcements. They think that the government will take care of them. I don't know that the government won't try to help, once they figure it out but they won't be able to help everyone. Right now they are pulling all military west, but I'm guessing that most of the west coast is now unlivable if not gone. The earthquake that we felt was caused by the impact, but I have been wondering if an impact that large where there are so many tectonic plates wouldn't cause other area fault lines to have quakes too. You know how they used to joke about the big California quake that would finally send that part of the country into the ocean? What if that happens too? Not to mention, radiation from the initial impact and the dust cloud... oh and the air blast that will destroy most everything in its path. The devastation to the west coast, and beyond, will be complete. I think survivability is about zero percent in that part of the country. Once they call the military back to help the people that they can, it might be too late. Time will tell." Ty paused, seeming to re-center his thoughts. "We won't have to worry about the people who are waiting for the government to take care of them yet. It's the people who know, like my dad, that we have to worry about. There are the doomsday people out there who didn't prep like my family did, and they are the ones who are going to be a problem right now. They will be devious, and they could be anywhere or anyone. While we may not have to worry about everyone we do have to worry that anyone could be the guy that we have to worry about."

I thought about his logic for a minute, and it made perfect sense to me. It didn't mean that we could be any less vigilant. Even though most people would not try to harm or stop us, anybody could be the person who would try. I looked out the window, watching the road ahead, scanning the hills and any exit or entrance ramps to the freeway that we passed. Danger could be lurking anywhere. It was maddening to think that danger could lurk anywhere and my stress level was unbearable, but I knew I just had to deal with it. The radio continued to quietly repeat the same message but other than that the truck was noiseless as we progressed down the freeway.

We were quickly approaching Winston-Salem, and I knew that we would have to circle around the city in some way. I was sure that Ty had a plan, but I didn't know if he had shared it with Ben. I had stopped seeing signs of life in the houses that we passed, and I had to wonder if somehow the families had been gathered up and forced to some unknown place. As I was pondering, Ty started the slow the truck. I looked out the windows and all around but did not see any reason for concern. As if he was reading my mind Ty explained.

"I think I should explain to Ben my plan and the reasoning for circling around the bigger cities. He needs to be on board so that he doesn't do something stupid and mess up. It also would be a good idea to see how he's doing. That was a hard hit to the head and, even though he's hard-headed, it could have done more damage than he is willing to admit. He refused to let Jules drive. Lastly, I want to let them know about the emergency broadcast if they haven't heard it yet."

"Good plan. Sometimes he doesn't think things through as well as he should. It'll be nice to get out and stretch my legs for a minute too."

"Really, you need to stretch those tiny little legs?" Ty teased me. "You have plenty of room in here to maneuver. I'm the one without any space over here."

I was laughing as Ty brought the truck to a stop on the side of the road. He asked me to stay inside for a moment as he got out to make sure that he didn't see any danger lurking in the area. Once he had looked around, he opened my door and lifted me out of the truck. The world seemed very peaceful here. There were no houses in our line of sight and as far as I could see everything was green and new. Some of the fields looked as if they had been planted recently and little green plants were pushing their way through the newly turned and loose dirt. I hoped they would survive the upcoming dust storms, or whatever Ty was talking about, and be around to feed those who needed it when autumn arrived.

Once Ben and Jules got out of their truck, and it was determined that Ben did not seem to be suffering any lingering effects from his head injury, Ty got right to the point. "All right, I want to waste as little time as possible here because we need to keep moving forward as quickly as we can. First, if you two have not had your radio on you need to turn on the AM/FM and listen to the emergency broadcast. It's just the same message repeating but it might change and give us more information as we progress or if they learn something new." Ben tried to interrupt, but Ty stopped him. "Just listen to it, and you will know the same things we do. Now, as we proceed, we need to do so cautiously. People will start to figure things out and when they do they will become increasingly more desperate. We don't want to deal with anyone else like the rest area guy. Just make sure you are keeping your eyes open for danger. If you see anything flash your lights. I'll see them in my rearview and know you need to speak with me. As we go through the larger cities, I will be changing our routes. We do not want to attempt to go through on the main roads. I'm guessing they will be barricaded and/or manned with military or police force to enforce the shelter in place request. We do not want to be stopped by anyone or forced into a shelter at this point. A shelter would be the worst place for us. We need to come out of Winston-Salem on the western side, heading west on I-40 so just keep up and follow me. Got it?"

I was feeling tense when we got back into the truck and headed back onto the road. We were getting close to the city and, although I had the utmost faith in Ty's ability to maneuver us around the city itself, I couldn't shake the thought that something was going to go wrong and someone was going to try to force us somewhere that we didn't want or need to go. 'For our own protection,' of course, they would tell us. I couldn't help but think that everything would be better once we got to the cabin. I knew that it was going to take us longer than the three and a half hours it would have on a typical day, but it felt like we had already been on this journey for a lifetime.

A few miles up the road Ty eased the truck onto an exit ramp and exited the freeway. I sat on the edge of the seat, waiting for something to go wrong. Would the police be waiting at the top, I wondered. The ramp curved and the spot where it intersected with the road was hidden by a thick grove of trees. Finally, the empty intersection came into view, and I released the breath that I hadn't realized I had been holding. No one was waiting there to try to force us somewhere. No one was monitoring the roads, at least not this one.

Ty turned left onto the two-lane road, and we began making our way towards Interstate 40. Unlike the freeway, the road we now traveled on had houses sprinkled alongside it and, occasionally, I could see someone peek out from behind a curtain. I mentioned this observation to Ty, but he had no clue why the people from the freeway houses were gone while these ones were still sheltering in place.

"Maybe someone came and picked up the other people for some reason, and whoever it is just hasn't made it here yet. It just adds another reason for us to look very carefully and move as quickly as we can. We need to get out of these populated areas. It's a good observation on your part. Things like that are what we need to be looking for."

I continued to watch the landscape as we drove. Every once in a while I saw a house or building that appeared to have been damaged in the earthquake. There was a collapsed barn with flames licking the wood and a few houses with damaged walls or chimneys. As we made our way away from the well-traveled and well-maintained roadways there also appeared to have been damage to parts of the road. In some spots, it looked as if the road had cracked and been pushed up from underneath, while in other places the entire berm had collapsed and rolled down a hillside.

Ty made multiple turns onto different roads which kept us moving in the right direction. He seemed to know exactly where he was going without the aid of GPS or a map. Soon the houses thinned out, and the landscape was sprinkled with farms here and there. Fields had crops growing or animals grazing as if nothing unusual had occurred. Of course, nothing probably seemed uncommon at this point to the animals. Once the earth was done shaking they had most likely gone right back to their grass eating activities, unaware that the world they knew would soon come to an abrupt end.

Ty slowed as we approached the top of a big hill. There was no way to see what was on the other side and forests had been closing in the space around us. He slowed the truck to a stop.

"Something just doesn't feel right about this. I'm going to get out and look. Stay here and lock the doors when I leave. The tinted windows will prevent anyone from being able to see you from outside. Have your gun out, and ready. I need you to back me up if there is something set up on the other side of this hill and they catch sight of me. Can you do that?" I nodded and gently kissed him as he got out of the truck. He whispered back over his shoulder, "Lock it," as he closed the door quietly.

I locked the door and turned to watch Ty as he walked to Ben's truck. Ben had remained inside, I assumed because he didn't want to get out and do anything that Ty would consider wrong. I saw Ty talk to him for a moment or two before Ben slipped out of his truck with his shotgun in hand. Ty motioned for Ben to circle to the other side of the trucks. Once Ben was in position the two moved forward simultaneously. They slowly made their way forward and, from where I sat in the truck, I couldn't hear a sound.

I watched them make their way up the hill, both trying to blend into the trees which lined each side of the road. I realized that, yet again, I was holding my breath. I forced myself to release it in a long, slow exhale. The breath holding is becoming an annoying habit, I thought to myself. One of these days I would probably pass out because I was holding my breath without being aware of it. When Ty and Ben got to where they could see over the hill, I saw Ty pause and slowly look around. He seemed to take his time and scan everywhere, the road ahead, the trees on both sides of the road, the area behind us, the horizon and even the sky. Finally, he motioned to Ben, and both walked out into the middle of the road at the top of the hill. They appeared to talk for a moment before turning and walking back to where the trucks were parked.

Ty approached my side of the truck, I unlocked the door and climbed down. He pulled me to him and gave me a big hug. I could feel how tense his body was and knew that the stress he was feeling was probably a hundred times more intense than mine. He would feel responsible for all of our safety. It was an enormous burden for him to carry.

"Does everything look okay," I asked as I leaned into his arms and gazed up into his eyes. They were serious when he looked back down to meet my gaze.

"I can't see anything of concern. It looks like we are going into a section of the road that is hilly and lined with trees. That's not to be unexpected really, but it makes me a little nervous. We will have a series of these types of hills to go through, but I really want to stay on this road because it will take us to I-77, which we can then take to I-40. The hills are going to slow us down most likely because I intend to be cautious on each one. If I were trying to set a trap for someone, I would pick someplace like this. It's an easy trap."

"I trust your instincts completely. I will follow you wherever you say we need to go."

We all got back into the trucks. Ty led the way slowly up and over the crest of the hill. His entire body was tense as we progressed. "Keep an eye out for anything that doesn't look right. Even if you just feel like something isn't right, you tell me. Okay?"

"Yes, I will be vigilant." I didn't take my eyes off the countryside that we were rolling through. The forest seemed to be quiet and nowhere did I see anything moving. It was like the world around us had been paused like a favorite television show when you are desperate for a snack in the middle of the most critical scene of the season. There were no birds to be seen soaring in the sky, no squirrels jumping from tree limb to tree limb. There didn't even appear to be any movement of leaves on the trees.

Before we reached the top of the next hill, Ty stopped the truck again to repeat his safety check before we continued up the next incline. The process was repeated at each hill as we progressed. When we reached the top of the third hill, Ty did his usual scan of the area ahead but stood staring down at the road ahead longer than he had on the other hilltops. He just stood and stared down. I knew he wouldn't stand there exposed like he was if it wasn't safe. After what seemed like an inordinate amount of time, I decided that I would go to him to find out what he was seeing that was halting our progression. I carefully looked around before unlocking the truck and getting out. I quickly made my way up to the top of the hill as quietly as I could.

"Ty," I whispered softly as I approached, not wanting to startle him. "What's wrong?"

I walked to his side and slipped my hand into his. Looking over the hill, I tried to find what had caught his attention. As I gazed down the hill, I saw what appeared to be something large in the middle of the road blocking the way. "What is that?"

"I think that the earthquake caused a landslide which is blocking the road ahead. Damn it! We can't go this way. We're going to have to go back. What a waste of time!"

"It's okay. We'll turn around and go back. We'll just find another way."

"That's the only option." Ty sighed, and I knew that he was frustrated. "I knew we would run into delays, but I really was hoping we wouldn't have to deal with them yet. There is nothing that we can do but turn around I guess. Standing here bitching about it isn't going to help."

We turned together and headed back to where the trucks were parked. Ben and Jules were out of their truck, waiting to see what was going on. When Ty explained the issue, Ben immediately began cursing and complaining.

"Shut it and get in your freaking truck. Turn it around and follow me. I do not want to hear any more complaining from you, or you can find your own way to someplace. I've got enough to deal with without adding your attitude to the list. Your choices are either help or shut up and follow. If you can't do those, then go where ever you want as long as it isn't with me. Got it?"

Ben put on his pissed off face and stomped off to get back into his truck. Once the trucks were turned around, we were ready to get back on the road.

Chapter Six

We backtracked down the road we had been traveling on, trying to make our way to the last exit ramp. Ty was hoping to find a way around the blockage that the landslide had created. We had crested the hill which we had last gone over and started back down the other side when I felt the shaking begin again. It felt worse to me this time around. Fortunately, we weren't traveling that fast, and Ty was quickly able to bring the truck to a stop. Rather than telling me to get out, this time he insisted that I stay inside. We stopped not far from the top of the hill. If we went further down into the ravine, which the road followed between the two hills, rocks that were being knocked loose by the quake would put us in danger, Ty explained to me.

The shaking seemed to go on and on, increasing in intensity. I started to wonder if the world was going to shake itself apart. A noise, similar to the sound of thunder, caught my attention. Ty began maneuvering to get a better view of what was going on outside of the truck.

"Ty, what is that? Thunder?"

"No, it's not thunder. Look."

I looked out the window to where he was pointing and saw parts of the rocky hillside starting to fall. The rocks were tumbling down the hill. They were picking up speed and gathering in mass as they progressed. I couldn't look away as the jumble of rocks and dirt made its way down the hillside. At some point, the earth stopped shaking, but I was too mesmerized by the chaos unfolding in front of us to notice. The entire mass eventually collided with the road at the bottom of the ravine, and a large cloud of dust flew into the air. When the dust settled, I could see that the road was completely blocked. We were trapped. I felt panic rising inside me. I looked at Ty and saw that he was simply sitting in the driver's seat staring at the road below.

I tried to calm myself, but I couldn't think of any way that we were going to be able to get around this new problem. We couldn't turn around and go back, that way was blocked. We couldn't go this way now because it was impassable as well. I could feel myself begin to hyperventilate, but there was no way I could stop it from happening. I was incapable of calming myself. The only thing I could think was that we were now trapped. We were stuck between these two hills. I couldn't even force myself to look away from the enormous pile of rubble blocking our way, and I couldn't breathe.

"Babe? Babe! Breathe!" A part of my brain heard Ty calling to me, but I couldn't focus on him. I couldn't think of anything except being trapped. I felt Ty gently turn me away from the window towards him. He filled my vision, and I wasn't able to see the road below any longer. I could hear him talking to me in a calm and quiet voice. "Elli, focus on me. We have to get you calmed down. You have to breathe. Just focus on me and listen to my voice."

He took my hand and placed it on his chest. I could feel the rise and fall of his breath under my hand. "Okay, try to match your breathing to mine. Listen to what I am telling you. I will get us out of here. This is a problem, yes, but it is not insurmountable. Do you trust me?"

I nodded slowly. I tried to focus my mind on Ty's words and match my breathing to his. He continued to reassure me and slowly I was able to calm myself enough that I could draw an almost normal breath. After I was able to get a few normal breaths, Ty pulled me into his arms and held me close.

"Damn Elli, you scared the crap out of me!"

"I'm sorry," I whispered to him. "I scared me too."

We sat together for a moment in silence. It felt good to feel his arms holding me. With my eyes closed and cradled in his arms, I could almost pretend that we were at home enjoying a normal afternoon before the world fell apart. Ty would have picked me up in his truck, and we would have driven to one of the state parks or lakes that were relatively close. Once there we would have enjoyed a day spent hiking or swimming. That kind of day always included some quiet cuddle time; this was undeniably my favorite part. A knock on the window startled me, bringing me back to the here and now. I looked up to see Ben, looking even grumpier than before, glaring in the window at us. Ty slowly opened his door and got out to confront him.

"Well, what the hell are we going to do now Ty," Ben exclaimed as soon as Ty opened the truck door. "You're the expert. You know everything, right? So, what exactly are we going to do?"

"Back off Ben! I am not going to deal with shit from you right now. I'll figure this out, but you need to back up. Just go back to your freaking truck and comfort your girlfriend. She is crying and probably scared, and you are up here being an ass. When I figure it out, which I will, I will let you know. So just go sit on your ass and wait for me to take care of it."

Ty turned around, got back in the truck, and slammed the door. Ty usually didn't lose his temper with Ben, even though he was almost always an ass. He generally just ignored him and went about what he had to do.

Ty took a deep breath. "All right, are you okay for now?"

I nodded at him. I certainly wanted to be okay. I didn't want him to have to expend energy worrying about me, especially when he had so many other things to worry about.

"I'm going to walk down the hill to see if I can see any way for us to get over, around, or through that landslide. I don't want to drive down because, if there is another landslide, we could get trapped in an even smaller area or even worse."

"What? No! You can't walk down there. What if there is another landslide and you get trapped or... or..."

"Elli, I will be fine. I'm fast, smart, and in relatively good shape. I will be fine. I'm going to go look. I'll be right back."

I wanted to cry. He couldn't go down there and leave me here. What if something happened to him? I didn't want to cause him any additional stress, so I went with humor as a distraction. "Yes, you are all those things. Modest too, right?"

Ty leaned in and kissed me, then looked into my eyes. "I will be back. It's going to be fine. Can you find that faith and optimism that you have always had? It's one of the things that I love so much about you. To be honest, it would really help me out right now."

Ty got out of the truck and gently shut the door. He took a second to look around, taking stock of the area before beginning a brisk jog down the hill. My eyes did not falter from their task of following his progress. He got smaller and smaller as he made his way down to the pile of rocks and rubble. He seemed so small and fragile compared to the walls of rocks that lined the road. If just one of the large boulders came loose at the wrong time, it could be fatal. I had never noticed how all these rocky hills seemed to be dotted with precariously perched boulders, resting like large, hard hats waiting to tumble down on unsuspecting victims. I wanted to hold my breath again as I watched him, but I consciously forced myself to breathe in and out slowly. Occasionally I would take a deep breath, hold it and then slowly exhale. Ty finally reached the spot where the landslide had come to rest. He seemed to study it from the middle of the road before walking to either side and examining it from each angle. Finally, he climbed to the top and stood. He took a long time to look around before I saw him raise his hand in a wave. He made his way back down the pile and started the jog back up to the truck.

I allowed myself to relax slightly when Ty finally got back to a spot where I could distinguish his features. I jumped out of the truck and ran to meet him. He was only slightly out of breath when I jumped into his arms. He held me close, whispering in my ear. "I'm okay and, more importantly, I see a way out. It'll be okay."

"You really see a way out? I mean, I had faith that you could get us out but is there really a way around those rocks?"

"Around them? No, but over them, yes."

∞ ∞ ∞

"You think we can do what?" Ben exclaimed.

"I don't think, I know," Ty replied calmly. "My truck has been customized to be able to go places and do things that other vehicles cannot. My truck is a converted military H1 pickup. Dad has this thing customized with anything and everything that I could possibly need in this type of situation. It wasn't the truck that I wanted, but it is the vehicle that he insisted that I have. It has airless tires that will be able to make it up and over the landslide."

"I will not leave my truck here. Are you crazy?"

"No, I'm very sane and trying to get us all to someplace where we will be safe in the coming months. A little cooperation from you would be greatly appreciated. We can all fit in my truck." Ty turned to look at Jules. "Jules, get your clothes and Elli can help you fit them into my truck."

"I am not leaving my truck," Ben screamed at Ty.

Ty walked to where Ben stood and began to talk to him quietly. I went to Jules and helped her grab her things. I could hear small snippets of their conversation.

"... Think about Jules' safety... It's just a truck..."

"... Let me try... Can't hurt..."

When we had gathered all of her things, Jules and I took them to Ty's truck. It was a bit of a challenge to find room for them, but we were able to shove them into the bed. I felt slightly guilty for packing so much. My suitcases were taking up an inordinate amount of space leaving little room for the additional things we were trying to add. When Ty walked over, I asked him if I should take out some of my things to make room for some of the other things from Ben's truck.

"Babe, you leave your things right where they are. Other than their clothes, there is nothing that we will need to bring from his truck. He brought boogie boards, kites, and Frisbees. We won't need any of that for this journey or once we get to the cabin. You keep your things. I'll make sure his clothes and the things that he really needs will fit. He wants to try to drive his truck over. I think its wasted effort even to try, but I suppose that I don't have the right to tell him no. I'll do everything I can to help him, but I won't let him risk your life, or Jules's life either. You know how he is.

He's not going to just get into my truck and come peacefully. Go ahead and get Jules settled into the back seat of the truck. I'm not letting her get in there with him while he's behaving like an idiot. The only life he gets to risk is his own."

I walked over to make sure we didn't have a bunch of crap piled in the backseat. I heard Ty tell Jules to get in our truck. She gave Ben a quick hug and called back to him to be careful as she walked away. I could see the worry in her eyes. Ben tended to let his stubbornness get him into situations that he was incapable of handling appropriately. He had a problem with authority, didn't like to be told what to do and always had to be right. Even though they had been friends for years, it seemed to irritate him the most when Ty seemed to know more about something than he did. It was often a point of contention between them and had been the cause for more than one fight over the years.

Ty spent a few more minutes talking to Ben, and when he walked back to join Jules and me, he was shaking his head. "All right ladies," Ty said with fake brightness when he settled into his seat, "buckle up and hold on tight. It might get a little bit rough, but we will get over. Once we are up and over, I am going to climb up to the top and motion for Ben to try to make his way over."

Ty started the truck, and we made our way slowly down the hill. When we reached the landslide, Ty slowly eased the truck forward. We barely seemed to be rolling but inch by inch we made our way up the rocks and rubble that were blocking the road. The process felt like it took forever. Once or twice the truck tires seemed to lose grip and slip, but they caught again almost instantly. Finally, we reached the top. Ty slowed the truck down even more, which I wouldn't have thought was even possible. We crested the hill and started the trip down the other side. The journey down proceeded much as the trip up had, slowly and carefully. Ty maneuvered the truck with precision, seeming to know exactly where to go, when to speed up, and when to slow down. Once we were on the actual road again, we all seemed to take a deep breath and slowly release it.

Ty pulled the truck forward a bit, presumably to leave room for Ben behind us. We all climbed out and looked up at the enormous pile of rocks that we had just conquered. It looked even more daunting from this side of the road. Jules and I found a comfortable spot on the side of the road where we could sit in the shade. Ty started his climb up the pile. Occasionally I would see the rocks slip from under his feet, yet it looked like he was seamlessly making his way up to the top. When he eventually reached the top, I could see him standing to one side of the peak. He seemed to be yelling directions to Ben, but the wind was blowing away from where Jules and I sat, and his voice was being carried in the opposite direction. I could hear Ben's truck engine revving. It didn't sound as if he was approaching the mountain of debris with the same caution that Ty had.

I stood and walked to the bottom of the rock pile. It sounded as if Ben was causing rocks to come loose from the mass and crash down to the ground below. His truck engine appeared to be growling. Ty was yelling at him to stop. The engine noise ceased abruptly, and I heard Ben's truck door slam.

"Damn it, Ben! You aren't going to make it up the pile that way. Just wait. I'll hook you up to the winch; then I can pull you up."

"I can do this myself, Ty. I've got this. I definitely don't need you to save me."

"Stop being a stubborn ass and let me help."

I didn't hear Ben answer, but I caught the sound of the truck door slamming again. The truck roared to life once more, and almost immediately the growling started. Ty was looking down at him shaking his head but seemed to have given up trying to convince Ben to approach the situation differently. The sound of falling rocks increased. I heard Ty yell out, panicked, for Ben to stop. The noise that followed was horrific. Nothing good could have happened after a sound like that. It was the sound of a loud crash intermingled with crunching metal.

I saw Jules look in horror towards the pile of rocks. I felt my feet begin to move of their own accord towards the pile of debris. Before I could even think to do so, I was climbing up the loose rock pile. I could feel some of the rocks slipping out from under my feet as I tried to make my way quickly to the top. When I looked up, I saw that Ty was no longer standing at the peak. I quickly scrambled my way to where he had been standing just seconds ago. When I looked down the other side, I saw Ben's truck upside down at the bottom. The truck was a mess. The cab was so crushed down that it appeared almost flat.

Ty slid to a stop at the bottom of the rubble pile and stood by what remained of the truck. He was yelling for Ben, but there was no answer. He bent down and looked into the cab. I saw him reach into what remained of the cab and try to pull what appeared to be Ben's arm out. Just then the world began to shake again. The shaking was even more severe than the other two quakes that we had felt.

"Ty!" I screamed. When he looked up at me, there was a look on his face that I had never seen before. Was it fear? Panic?

"Elli! Get back down and get to the truck. Get Jules and drive it to the top of the hill. NOW!!!!"

I hesitated, he didn't. I saw him try to pull Ben out of the truck one more time. When the thunderous sound of rocks began again, he turned away from the truck and the rock pile. He ran away from them, up the opposite side of the hill. Seeing Ty run away from Ben's truck kicked me into motion. I turned back towards Ty's truck and started back down the rock pile. There was no way to get down the pile of rocks and rubble quickly and safely. I ended up sliding, and at one point rolling, down the rocks. I felt cuts and scrapes as the jagged rocks cut through skin, but didn't let it stop my progress.

When my feet hit the pavement, I started running and screaming. I could hear the rocks behind me picking up speed and mass. The sound was deafening. Making everything worse, the ground was still shaking violently. It was so hard to keep running, but I knew that I couldn't stop until I got to the truck.

"Jules! Get in the truck! Get in the truck now!" Jules was still sitting on the side of the road and seemed to be in shock. "Jules!"

Finally, the sound of my voice penetrated her fog. She turned to look at me, appearing confused. "Get in the freaking truck, now!"

Jules started moving and, by the time I was able to throw myself into the driver's seat, she was in the passenger seat with her seatbelt buckled. I started the truck and threw it into gear. Tires squealed as I took off to the top of the hill. I could hear the rocks crashing behind us but, by some miracle, nothing hit the truck. When we reached the peak, I slammed on the breaks and put the truck in park. I quickly jumped out. Jules remained sitting in the passenger seat, seemingly back in her trance. I knew that Ty would have told me to stay in the truck because the ground was still shaking, but I needed to see what was going on.

First, I started scanning the hill for Ty. Panic set in when I didn't see him. I expected him to be at the top of the other hill, but he wasn't there. Had he been hurt? Had he been hit by one of those boulders that were currently rolling down the hill and crashing into the rubble left by the last landslide? What was I going to do if he was hurt or worse? I knew screaming for him wouldn't help. He wouldn't be able to hear me over the crashing rocks. All I could do is continue to look. I knew that he had to be somewhere, didn't he? I refused to acknowledge the evil, little voice in my mind that whispered that Ty could be trapped near Ben's truck, under the new rubble that was starting to cover up the entire area. If the rocks kept falling we wouldn't even be able to see where the truck was laying. I couldn't think of Ben. I knew that I couldn't help him right now. Ty would know what to do. He would know how to help Ben. We wouldn't survive without Ty. We would never make it to the cabin. I was overwhelmed with panic and anxiety. I finally gave up, sat down on the ground, and cried.

When the shaking stopped, I tried to pull myself together enough to come up with a plan. Tears were still streaming down my face, but I stood up again and started scanning the other hill. Ty had to be there. I refused to think that he was somewhere in the massive pile of rock and rubble. He wasn't standing at the top of the hill, so I slowly scanned from the right side of the road to the left down the entire hill. Finally, about halfway down, I saw movement in the trees on the right side. It was Ty's arm waving in the air. I screamed his name but doubted that he could hear me. I turned and ran back to the truck. I told Jules that I needed to check on Ty, but I didn't think she even heard me, so deep was she in her stupor. I hesitated for just a moment before turning to run back down the hill. I started to make my way over the rubble.

I am not a runner by any stretch of the imagination, and I am definitely not an athlete, but I think I made world record time getting back down the hill. Of course, gravity was on my side since I was running downhill. I got to the rock pile and started working my way over. The new rocks made the climb even more precarious, but it didn't matter. There was nothing that was going to stop me from getting to the other side where Ty was. I picked my way up the pile carefully, but quickly. There were a few times during the journey when I was sure that I was going to go crashing back down onto the pavement and rubble below. Luck must have been on my side because I made it to the top of the pile.

I paused and looked back to where I had seen Ty's arm. It was no longer waving in the air, and I couldn't see him at all in the tall grass. I yelled his name as loud as I could but didn't see an arm or any other indication of a response from Ty. I tried to not look at the spot where I knew Ben's truck was buried and specifically made my way down the pile of rock and rubble away from where small bits of red paint were barely visible through the newly fallen rock. I made my way quickly, yet cautiously, down the rocks. Even with the cautious approach, I slipped and slid about halfway down the pile, scraping knees and hands once again. As soon as I hit the ground, I turned and ran up the hill. Pain from a fall and scrapes did not stop me from sprinting as fast as I could up the hill to where I thought Ty was.

I tripped and fell over rocks and other debris in the road as I tried to get up the hill. Finally, it was just one fall too many, and I just couldn't physically or emotionally get back up. I lay on my back on the road as tears streamed down my face. Staring up at the sky, I whispered a prayer. How could the sky still be so blue and the clouds still be fluffy white cotton balls? This cannot be the way the world ends, I thought, and the world cannot go on unless Ty is in it. He promised me he would keep me safe, but where was he now?

I'm not sure how long I lay there, praying and staring at the sky. It could have been thirty seconds or hours. I was lost to the world and my surroundings. Maybe I'll just lie here forever, I thought. The pavement was warm and smooth under me, which was nice since the area around me was littered with rocks or clumps of dirt. I wondered if anyone would ever find me here, trapped between two landslides.

The logical part of my brain kept telling me to get up. For every self-defeating thought that popped into my brain, the little, rational voice in my mind came up with a reason that I needed to get up and keep going. The pavement was warm, but Ty was out there somewhere, and he needed me. The world was ending so why bother, but I told Jules that I would be back. What was the point because we weren't going to make it, but Ty needed me. My woe is me brain was arguing with the logical voice. Through the haze of all the internal noise in my head, I head a faint shuffling sound.

"Great," I muttered to the world at large, "more rocks are going to fall and crush me. Well, I'm tired, and I'm just going to lie here and let them!" In a childish outburst, I stuck my fingers in my ears, because if the rocks were going to fall and crush me, I didn't want to hear their approach. The world went silent. I closed my eyes, waiting for whatever was next.

∞ ∞ ∞

After a bit, it felt ridiculous to be lying on the ground with my fingers stuck in my ears, especially since the rocks hadn't come tumbling down the hills to crush me. I slowly took my fingers out of my ears and didn't hear any landslide sounds, so it felt safe to open my eyes slowly. Pure joy shot through my body when the first thing I saw was Ty sitting beside me, gazing at me curiously with his beautiful eyes. He looked worse for the wear. He was dirty, and there was blood on his face. My concern increased when he didn't move to touch me or say anything.

I tried to sit up and realized that my entire body was sore. With all the climbing in the dirt and rocks, as well as the scrapes and bruises, I probably looked horrible. I eased to my knees and scooted over to where Ty sat, knees pulled up to chest with arms locked around them. He looked distraught. I had never seen him with such a look before, and seeing him this way was more frightening for me than anything that had occurred since we left home.

"Ty?" At the sound of my voice, his eyes met mine. They seemed empty, so different from the usual warmth that could be found there. "Ty, are you all right? Are you hurt? What can I do for you?"

I reached up to touch his face but saw that my hands were covered in my own blood from all the cuts and scrapes that I had gotten during my foray over the rocks. I didn't want to smear blood on his face, so I pulled my hand back looking for something to wipe it on. My clothes were covered in dust, and I didn't have any clean surface on which I could wipe away the blood and dirt. As I was scanning for something, I saw Ty's hand reach out. I looked back up into his eyes and saw fear, guilt and something I couldn't define. It broke my heart. Ty took my hand in his, caressing it with his thumb. We sat there in silence, tears streaming down both of our faces. I couldn't look into his eyes, they were just sad, and I couldn't stand to see him that way.

Finally, Ty said very quietly, "I'm sorry. This is entirely my fault. Then I saw you lying there. You weren't moving. I thought I'd lost you and it was just too much to bear. I'm not sure how I will ever live with what has happened here as it is. Just because my dad knows how to be prepared, and tried to make sure that I was as well, doesn't mean that I am. I'm struggling to get us all to the cabin safely, and I've failed. Ben is gone, and that is my fault."

I hadn't let myself focus on Ben and what his ultimate fate had been, but now that Ty had mentioned it, my mind wouldn't stop thinking about Ben. Was he really gone? Couldn't he have survived and just be stuck in the truck?

"We don't know that he's gone! Maybe he's just stuck in the truck. We should go try to get to him!" I started to stand, and Ty tugged me back down.

"He's gone, Elli. I know he's gone."

"How do you know?" I knew that Ty wouldn't lie to me. If there were any possibility, he would already be down there trying to get to Ben. I didn't want to believe it though. I desperately repeated, "How do you know?"

"He didn't have a pulse. When I got down to the truck after he flipped it, he didn't have a pulse. I checked, more than once. I was going to pull him out and do CPR, but he was pinched in. He was... he was really messed up from the crash. I wouldn't have been able to bring him back, even if I could have pulled him out. Even if the world hadn't gone to shit and we could have gotten him to a doctor or hospital, I don't think he would have survived that crash. I would have tried everything though, you know that, but then the earthquake started again. I was afraid that if I didn't move, I would be crushed in the next landslide."

I sat quietly for a moment not knowing what to say. Ben had been my friend for as long as I could remember. I couldn't imagine him being gone. As much as it hurt me to think that Ben was truly gone, I knew that it hurt Ty more. Ty, Ben, and Ken were like triplets. Their mothers had been best friends since high school, and the boys had been born less than a month apart. They had gone through everything together including learning to walk, starting school, learning to drive, high school graduation and everything in between. They'd done it all together, as a group. Ben was a good and lifelong friend to me, but to Ty, Ben was a brother.

I linked my fingers through his, tugging on his hand until he looked at me. The hurt and loss in his eyes was almost tangible. "Tyler." I never used Ty's full name. His mother was the only one who called him Tyler, but I wanted to reach him in the darkness and ensure that he was truly listening to me. "This is not your fault. You loved Ben, even when he was pushing your buttons and trying to annoy you. I loved Ben. We both know that Ben was stubborn, hard-headed. He was just difficult and contrary sometimes. That didn't make us love him any less. It's just who he was, and ultimately that is why he is gone. He didn't understand what was really going on and he wasn't mentally prepared. That is why he's gone. You tried to convince him to come over with us, but he insisted on taking his truck. When the truck wouldn't make it you told him to wait, and you would pull him, but he wouldn't even do that."

"I should have made him stop. I knew he wasn't going to make it and I let him try anyway. I should have just made him get in my truck." Ty shifted his gaze back away from mine. "I am supposed to be the one who is prepared, the one who can protect everyone, and I've failed miserably."

"You did not fail! No matter what you think, you are not responsible for all of us and our safety. You have done nothing but try to keep us all safe. We all know that you have been preparing for a situation just like this one and that you would best know what to do. He should have listened to you. He made his choices, and they were the wrong choices. Am I sad? Yes, I am, but I'm also damn mad at him because this is his fault. I trust you completely. If anyone can get me to my parents safely through this mess, it is you."

"What if I can't?" I had never heard him lack confidence.

"Look at me. How many times have you asked me to have faith in you?"

"Many."

"So now you have to have faith in me. Can you do that? I know that you are hurting right now, but you cannot let this stop you or destroy your confidence. I need you to have your confidence because your knowledge and abilities are what will get us through this safely. We NEED you! Jules and I need you to keep us safe. You tell us what to do, and we will listen and do it. Can you do that?"

Ty must have heard the pleading in my voice because I could see some of the old Ty return to his eyes. He slowly stood, faltering slightly. He held his left side stiffly as if he were in pain and my eyes were drawn back to the blood on that side of his face.

"You're hurt!"

"I'm fine," Ty replied trying to brush off my concern. "I'm certainly not hurt. Compared to Ben, it's a scratch."

"What happened?" I closed the distance that he had put between us and gently examined his face. He had a gash on his left cheek that seemed to still be seeping blood. His arm had a large scrape that went from shoulder to elbow.

"Rocks. I wasn't fast enough."

"Where else?"

"My back and my side, but I'm fine." I grabbed his shirt and tugged it up so I could see for myself. His back and side were both covered scrapes, and bruises were already beginning to pop up as well. Ty gently pulled his shirt back down. He must have seen something in my eyes because he said, "I am fine. We need to go."

When I started to protest, he continued. "We have to get out of these hills as soon as possible. I don't know why we are still getting earthquakes, but if there is another that causes more landslides we could get trapped in here. I don't want to waste any more time. We need to go."

His confidence was back, and I knew I needed to listen to what he was telling me. "Okay," I replied quietly.

Ty must have heard the worry in my voice because he leaned down and gave me a quick kiss before reiterating that he would be fine until we got somewhere safer. That was enough motivation to get me moving. I followed him to the rock pile, well aware of the fact that he wasn't moving with his normal strong, confident strides. He gingerly began making his way over the pile, often stopping to take a breath. After we made it up the first few feet, he motioned for me to move ahead of him. That way, he explained, if he followed right behind me on the way up, he would be able to catch me if I slipped and I also wouldn't be hit by any rocks that he might knock loose as he climbed. Of course, I thought, the flip side of that was that anything that I knocked loose would fall down and hit Ty. I took each step upward very carefully, trying not to dislodge anything from the pile. I didn't want to cause him one more second of pain.

The trip over and back down the pile was slow and methodical. Ty kept pushing me to move faster. I knew that he wanted to get out of the area quickly, but I was just too afraid to move too fast. I completely understood his urgency, but I couldn't seem to make my hands and feet climb any quicker. I was afraid to fall and send us both tumbling down the pile. It seemed like it took forever, but finally, our feet were back on the ground, and on the same side of the heap as Ty's truck. I could see that Jules was still just sitting in the passenger seat.

Ty's face was somewhat ashen, and I tried to convince him to sit and take a break before walking up the hill to the truck. He refused, insisting that if another earthquake hit every second would count. We made good time up the hill, and when we got to the top, I immediately went to the passenger side of the truck to check on Jules. She was still in a daze sitting where I had left her. Tears were streaming down her cheeks, and her hair was chaotically coming out of what would normally be a very neat ponytail. It looked as if she had grabbed handfuls of it and pulled at some point.

"Jules," I said to her quietly as I touched hands that were clenched in her lap. "Jules, we have to get out of here in case there is another earthquake."

No response. "Jules! Can you hear me?"

Still no response. "Ty, there's something wrong with Jules. She won't respond to me. I think she must be in shock or something. I don't know what to do."

Ty made his way over to where I stood and began to quietly talk to Jules. She wouldn't make eye contact with him and didn't respond verbally in any way to his questions. He spent a few minutes trying to get her to acknowledge him before he turned to me shaking his head. "You're right. I think she's probably in shock. I don't know what we can do for her right this second. If there is room, we should get her to lie down in the back seat. Just keep reassuring her that she will be okay. Keep her comfortable and warm. Make sure she doesn't start to freak out or anything. I'll drive us out of here if you can keep her comfortable and watch for a change. I wish we could stay here until she is better, or we could get her somewhere that could provide her professional help, but we just don't have that luxury right now."

"Okay. I will do whatever you think we need to do. Let me get her in the backseat, and then we can get going."

I went back to Jules and told her that we needed to go and that she needed to get into the backseat so that we could get back on the road. When I took her hand, she let me help her out of the truck and then help her into the back. I was able to get her to lie down, and I tried to fasten a seat belt around her as well. Once I had her settled in, I got myself settled into the front seat. Once again we were off.

Chapter Seven

From the top of this hill looking down, I could see no landslides. Ty started the truck, and we began to move forward, more quickly than we had progressed over the hills earlier. One more, I thought to myself. We had traveled over three to get to where the landslide occurred, we'd made it back over two, and the cost was high. I said a quick prayer that we would be able to get over the last hill without any further incidents. Even though we were traveling faster and less cautiously than before, it seemed like it took forever to get back to the top of the last hill. I couldn't stop myself from holding my breath until we hit the peak and I could see that there were no big piles of rubble waiting for us at the bottom of the hill. Ty must have pushed down on the gas pedal because the truck picked up speed and we seemed to be flying down this hill.

The truck made quick work of plowing through or over the small piles of rocks, which were scattered here and there in the road. After reaching the other side and seeing the relatively flat road ahead of us, I was able to breathe a little easier. I asked Ty to pull over so I could get a better look at and clean his wounds, but he insisted on waiting until he had gotten us away from the rocky hills that still lined the roads. We flew down the road, making our way back to safer ground.

The earth seemed to have gone silent again. I saw no birds flying, no animals scurrying away at the sound of our approach, and definitely no sign of people out and moving about. I wasn't sure if that was a good sign or a bad one. We passed a few roads which would take us off of the route we were on, but Ty passed them by and continued to backtrack to where we had been. When I looked at the radio clock, I saw that only a few minutes had passed since we had made it over those last few hills. Finally, when they had diminished to smaller, grass-covered mounds, Ty pulled over to the side of the road and audibly exhaled. He put the truck in park and turned off the ignition. We sat quietly for a minute, and I realized that Jules had begun making a whimpering type of sound in the backseat.

"I need to check your wounds and get some antiseptic on them if nothing else. I would like to take a few minutes to try to get Jules to snap out of the daze that she is in as well. That is if you think we can take the few minutes."

"Yes, of course, we can take a few minutes for Jules. Go take care of her first."

"No, after your scrapes and cut are cleaned up to my satisfaction I will try to talk to her again. I know she is upset and probably in shock, but you are hurt. That takes priority."

I got out of the truck. After Ty got the back cover opened, I climbed onto the back bumper so that I could rummage through the piles of necessities to find the bag of first aid supplies that I grabbed at the little store outside of Pilot Mountain. The bag was quickly located, and I snatched it before heading to where Ty stood, leaning against the truck. I started by trying to clean up the gash on his cheek. Some of the blood had dried, and I knew the alcohol that I was using to clean it had to sting, but Ty didn't flinch. When I finally got the blood all cleaned off, I liberally applied an antiseptic ointment. I grabbed some of the butterfly bandages that I had taken from the store out of the bag. The cut was about two inches long, and a couple of the butterfly bandages pulled the sides together nicely.

After the gash was taken care of, I moved on to the scrapes. The one on his arm had gravel and dirt embedded in it. I tried to clean it as gently as I could. Ty said that he didn't want a bandage on his scrapes. Once they were cleaned up, I sprayed them with a liberal coat of antiseptic spray. I knew that he had to be hurting from all of the scrapes and bruises, so I got him four pain relievers and a bottle of water before I turned my attention to Jules.

I had forgotten my own small cuts and scrapes, however. Ty stopped me before I could go back to the truck. He gently cleaned up all of my cuts and scrapes, applied antiseptic and put a bandage on anything he deemed too serious to be left open to the air. He took the job of cleaning each injury, no matter how slight, seriously and apologized over and over for the fact that I had been hurt. When he was finished, he gently kissed me on the forehead. He put his hands on my cheeks and looked directly into my eyes. "Don't worry me like that again. You were just lying there, not moving and I thought that I had lost you too. I was so afraid, and I am so sorry that I left you alone back there."

Ty pulled me into his arms and hugged me tightly. It felt like the contact was to comfort himself as much as me. I held him tight and whispered what I hoped were reassurances for him. We drew our strength from each other, and as we stood there securely enveloped in each other, I could feel strength and confidence returning. When Ty pulled back, he seemed to be his old confident self. "Go check on Jules. I'm going to study the atlas for a few minutes."

I stretched up, giving him a quick kiss, before walking back to the passenger side of the truck. I was actually a bit relieved to find that Jules's animal-like whimpers had turned to tears and sobs. She was no longer lying down. She was sitting up, gazing out the rear window, with tears streaming down her face. I opened the door and eased into the front seat, turning to face her. Quietly I spoke, "Jules, are you okay?" As soon as I asked I knew that of course, she wasn't. She was still looking out the window, so I tried again. "Jules, it will be okay. I promise you that Ty will get us to the cabin safely."

I knew that she wasn't worried about that, but I didn't know what else to tell her. I couldn't mention Ben, and I knew that is what she needed me to reassure her about. She wanted to hear that he would be popping up behind us in his truck. That he was fine, but I couldn't give her that reassurance. I reached out and gently took her hand. I wish that I was better prepared to help her, but I didn't have words that could help her and I wouldn't lie.

"Ben?" Just the one word, said so quietly that I almost didn't hear it.

"I'm sorry." I didn't know what else I could say. I was sorry. Ben was her everything, and he was gone. I realized that I felt guilty because we had left him behind, but I understood why it was necessary. I didn't think Jules would understand, and to be honest, if it had been Ty in a truck under a pile of rocks and rubble back there I wouldn't understand leaving him behind either.

"Is he... Is he... Where is he?"

"I'm sorry Jules. He's gone." Jules seemed to retreat into herself again at my words. Her eyes had a faraway appearance, and she curled into a fetal position, lying back down. I really wished that I knew what to do to help her, but I hadn't been trained in this yet. I had wanted to go into psychology. I had wanted to be a therapist and help people cope, but I couldn't figure out what to do for Jules.

Ty slid into the driver's seat and looked at me questioningly. I shook my head no, to indicate that Jules was not really doing okay. Ty sighed and started the truck. "So I studied the map, and I think I have a good route around the city that will get us back to where we need to be. Let's buckle up and hit the road again. I'm anxious to get there as soon as we can. Babe, why don't you see if you can find another station with the emergency broadcast system playing? I would love to know what is going on with all of these earthquakes. They probably won't tell us anything new, but it's worth a try."

We had turned the radio off again when it became too annoying to hear the emergency tones over and over. At Ty's request, I reached over and turned it back on. The station we had been receiving before just played static now. Whether that was due to us leaving its range or the station going off the air, I wasn't sure. I scanned through the stations, but nothing seemed to be broadcasting. I think Ty could tell I was getting frustrated because he patted my hand and then turned the radio off. Except for the sounds of Jules sobbing in the backseat and the tires on the road the world was silent. It was frightening.

Ty followed the road we were on for a few more miles and then turned on to what looked like a well-traveled country road. We seemed to be circling the hills that we had been trapped in. Farms dotted the landscape here and there, but they were all down very long drives. I could see what appeared to be damage from the earthquakes here and there on the properties. There was a barn collapsed here, damage to a house there, and fallen trees all over the place. When we got close enough to the hills, there were piles of rocks lying everywhere. I still didn't see any people out and about, but there were cows and horses, as well as other farm type animals, wandering around fields.

Ty made a few more turns before coming out on what seemed to be a state route. Once on the road, he started traveling a little faster. "This will take us to I-40. I know I said we should stay off the main roads to avoid the military, but after the rock slides, I think maybe it is more important to stay on roads that are generally more well-traveled. Wider roads are less likely to be completely impassable, not to mention the wide berms on the sides of the main roads give either the rocks room to pile up there or us room to go around other types of blockages."

"Sounds logical to me," I replied. There were entirely too many rocky hills and eventually mountains on the route we would need to take to expect that we would be able to make it to the cabin without any other road issues. Two-lane roads through the mountains were likely to be difficult to follow at this point, so it was best to avoid them until they were a necessity. Ty focused on the road ahead of him, and I tried to vigilantly watch out the window for anything that looked even slightly suspicious.

Jules was still quietly sobbing in the backseat, but she seemed to have calmed some. It broke my heart to hear her, but there was nothing that I could say that would diminish the pain that she was feeling right now. Ben was the one person that she had felt safe with, and now he was gone. Her father had left her, and her mother didn't care where she was or who she was with. Jules had always known that in her mother's eyes drugs were a higher priority than her daughter and that knowledge had left her damaged. After learning about her home life and family, I was shocked when she allowed Ben into her heart, but she explained to me once that, while Ben might seem cocky and narcissistic, he was really insecure and wanted to be loved for being himself, not as half of Ben and Ken. She also told me that, even though he put on a show in front of everyone, he worried about what everyone thought of him. She explained that when they were alone, he was kind and gentle with her. He made sure that she was taken care of, which was something no one had ever done for her before. The world had fallen apart, and she had lost the one thing that represented safety to her. She wouldn't even have that security going into this new, scary, and unknown world. I was sure that she felt beyond devastated.

I watched Ty as he drove and tried to imagine how I would feel if he was the one that we had left behind under that rock pile. I wasn't sure that I would have been able to go on if it had been him. I don't think I could have left him there. I would have refused to leave unless we were able to get him out and bring him too. Would Jules have done the same thing if she weren't in shock? How would I continue on? I didn't even know where we were going really, so how would I have ever gotten there? If something happened to Ty now, I thought, how would I find my way to my parents? The thought flitted into my mind and took root. I tried to not think about it and focus on other things, but the thought kept coming back to me until finally, I couldn't take it anymore.

"Ty, what if something happens and you can't get me to the cabin?" I asked timidly. I didn't want him to think that I didn't have faith in him, but I needed an answer.

"I will get you safely to the cabin if it's the last thing I do."

"I know, but what if something were to happen to you? What if the falling rocks had hurt you more seriously, or worse, and I needed to get both of us to the cabin? I can drive the truck, but I don't know where we are going."

Ty was quiet for a moment while he processed what I was trying to tell him. "You're right. You should absolutely know exactly where you should go. I'll mark the map when we stop next time to show where we are going and my planned route. I'm sorry babe. I wasn't trying to keep you in the dark it just didn't occur to me. God forbid something were to happen to me, but if it did and I was unable to get you to the cabin, I want you to leave me and go. I will do everything in my power to make sure that I am here to protect you every step of the way, but I guess, considering what has happened so far, I can't really make a promise that I will be here to get you to the cabin. I will write down all the details for you."

"I hope it won't be necessary for me to ever even look at the map, but it will make me feel better if I know the information is there in case I need to take over and get you to help. We're in this together, you and me. If I got hurt, you would make sure you got me to where I needed to be to get help. If you get hurt, I want to be able to do the same thing for you. Me and you, we still have that, and that is all that I need to keep moving forward. I will do whatever I have to to keep you safe as well. It isn't a one-way thing here. Our relationship has never been that way, and it's not going to be that way now. Yes, I understand that you are much better equipped to protect me than I am to protect you, but I will still do so to the best of my ability. Do you understand?"

"I understand completely, my love. You and me, me and you. Together we will get to the cabin, and we will get through this. I think there is a small town up here and I might risk stopping. Maybe someone will come out and talk to us, and we can find out if they have made any more announcements on television or anywhere about what is going on. It wouldn't hurt to fill the truck tank up if we can, but I don't know that we will find anyone who will sell us fuel."

"Sounds like a plan."

"Do you still have that gun on you?" I put my hand on the gun to reassure myself that I hadn't lost it during my forays over the landslide. I nodded affirmation

88

to Ty, and he continued. "Good, keep it on you and loaded at all times. If we stop, you need to be my second set of eyes. Got it?"

"Yes, sir. I will be your eyes and ears and whatever else you need me to be." It was going to be a long trip, I thought. We hadn't even made it halfway yet and look at what the cost had been. Could we really make it the rest of the way?

$$\infty \;\; \infty \;\; \infty$$

As we traveled down this road, I noticed that we saw increasingly more houses. I watched warily out the window hoping to see signs of anyone normal and also to make sure that nothing suspicious was lurking. I was shocked when I saw a few kids playing in a yard as if nothing was going wrong in the world. I mentioned it to Ty, and he seemed surprised as well. They were the first people we'd seen since the crazy rest area guy. Maybe there had been some good news released, and things weren't as bad as we thought.

About another mile up the road we saw a woman out working in her garden. She glanced up and waved as we passed. I couldn't help but wave back. It was good to see some of the routine daily human tasks still taking place. The closer we got to the small town the more people we saw out and about. I felt tiny blossoms of optimism working their way into my mind. I couldn't imagine this entire town of people would be out and about if the emergency broadcasts hadn't given some good news. When we approached the small village, it seemed as if the residents were just going about their everyday life. Cars were traveling on the roads. The post office, grocery store, and gas station all seemed to be open and practicing business as usual.

Ty was cautiously looking around and seemed to be as confused as I was about the normal activities going on around us.

"Do you think this is a sign that they have had some good news," I asked. I could hear the hope in my voice.

"I don't know," Ty replied. "We still need to be cautious. I want to use the same story that we used with the military. We have been camping. We haven't heard any announcements. We don't understand these crazy earthquakes, but they can explain my injuries. We are just heading a short distance to my father's house. Okay?"

"Got it. I'll just keep quiet if I can. What about Jules?"

"I haven't heard her for a while. Did she fall asleep?" I looked into the back seat and saw that she was no longer sobbing. Ty was right, I thought. Jules's eyes were closed, and her breathing was even. She appeared to be asleep.

"It seems that she did, which is probably for the best. I don't know how to make this better or easier for her. I don't even have the right words. A part of me feels guilty because I still have you when she lost Ben. I can't even imagine how devastated she must feel."

"I feel horrible too, but the best thing that I can do for her right now is to get her to safety. There will be time for comfort and healing after that." Ty eased the truck into the gas station and pulled up to one of the pumps. "Stay in the truck unless I call you. Okay? I need you to watch for anyone approaching or anything that seems off."

Ty looked around the area and discreetly checked that his gun was hidden but present. Once he was sure that all was in order, he opened the door and eased out into the parking lot. Locking the truck door behind him, he left the keys inside with me. I watched him turn towards the building, and as he started to walk in front of the truck, an employee walked out. I couldn't hear their conversation, but Ty listened intently to the man. They talked for a while, Ty making a statement to which the man would reply animatedly. I kept scanning our surrounding for anything or anyone that looked suspicious but it really just seemed to be a charming little town where the people were going about their normal lives. Ty tried to give the man some money, but he waved it away. They both moved to the side of the truck where they appeared to be adding fuel. I could hear the rumblings of their conversation and assumed Ty was still probing for information.

After a few more minutes of talking, I saw the young man turn and walk back into the building. He flipped the sign in the window to closed and turned off the lights in the building. As he was coming back out of the building and locking the door, Ty knocked on the driver's side window. I hit the unlock button so he could get in. Once in he started the truck and just waited.

"So," he said. "This gentleman is Trent. He's an engineer, and his wife is a physician's assistant. Dad always told me that we would need to look for someone with medical training if something bad went down because that is the one field where none of us have any experience. An engineer is always valuable as well. We are going to follow him to his place, and they are going to come with us."

"Umm, okay."

"Trent said that the government hasn't released any other information. The emergency broadcasts have stopped, and both television and radio stations have gone silent. That's actually a bad sign. I didn't think we would lose government communication yet. There is no information on why there were so many earthquakes, so I'm still not sure what has happened, but I think this is bigger than what I thought it was. I don't know how that will change anything but the more we know, the better we are able to deal with the situation. If the bolide impact is what started this all we will still see atmospheric changes as well." Trent had gotten into his car and motioned that he was ready to go. Ty pulled out after him and began following him through the town before continuing. "I wonder if there was more than one large bolide impact and that is why we have felt more than one earthquake."

"Is it really possible," I pondered aloud, "that something happened with all those fault lines in California like you mentioned earlier?"

"Yes, I'd say that is very possible. The bolide could have caused an earthquake on the west coast unlike any that mankind has ever experienced. It would cause issues with other tectonic plates and fault lines, not to mention the havoc that such a level of earthquake would cause, aftershocks for example. The quake would be of such a level that people would feel it thousands of miles away."

I quietly pondered this for a while as Ty followed Trent out of town. It was incomprehensible to me that half, or even more, of our country might be gone. Why would the government go quiet, I wondered. Were they just trying to keep citizens in the dark or were they gone somehow? "So why would the government go quiet? What does that mean?"

"Well, I'm not sure. Could be a flaw in the EBS system or it could be some sort of interference preventing broadcast. It could also be that whatever is left of the government wants the broadcasts stopped because they are worried about riots, looting, and such. It could be that everything is in chaos and no one is thinking about creating broadcasts right now. Maybe the staff who handle the EBS has been redirected. I would guess that the president, vice, and other integral government officials are safely tucked away in a bunker somewhere trying to figure out what the heck they can actually do. They may bring it back up when they have new information."

Ty followed Trent down a long dirt drive which led back to a beautiful white farmhouse. As we approached, I saw someone walk onto the porch. Must be Trent's wife, I thought to myself. She was a short woman with very long, poker-straight, black hair. She had the kindest eyes that I had ever seen, and the smile she flashed to Trent when he got out of his car spoke volumes about how much love she had for him. Ty and I sat in the truck and watched them embrace. Ty told me that Trent wanted to explain things to his wife before he introduced us to her. They were still talking intently on the porch when the front door opened. A young girl ran out and threw herself into Trent's arms. Trent picked her up and held her close but did not look back to our truck.

"Ty, did you know that they have a child?" I asked curiously.

"No, he failed to mention that. We can't bring too many people with us. I hope he isn't hiding an entire extended family in there and thinking that we will take them all with us."

"You aren't going to make them stay now, are you? Just because of the little girl?" My heart broke at the thought of her suffering when the sky went dark, or the world got extra cold.

"What?" Ty seemed shocked by my question. "Do you really think I wouldn't let them come just because of the baby? You know me better than that."

"I'm sorry. It's a different world now, and I know that things have to change. I'm guessing that we will have to change too."

Ty turned to face me, taking my hands in his. "You're right they do, and unfortunately, we won't be able to save every child. Look at that beautiful little girl though. We can save her."

At that moment, Trent handed the little girl to his wife, motioning for us to join them. I was wondering if I should get out too, but Ty answered the question for me when he indicated that I should come with him. I climbed down from my side of the truck as Ty exited the driver's side. I looked back to Jules and saw that she still appeared to be sleeping, so I quietly closed the door behind me.

As we walked to the porch, I could not take my eyes from the little girl standing beside her mother. She had her mother's black-as-night hair, but rather than being poker straight her hair had ringlet curls that cascaded down her back. She looked back at me with bright, inquisitive eyes and an infectious smile. She had a teddy bear in one hand, and the other was wrapped around her mother's leg. Her eyes stayed on me as introductions were made. Trent introduced Ty and, in turn, Ty introduced me to the family.

"This is my wife, Bonita," Trent stated, "and this little beauty is Sarah."

Bonita came forward and gave both Ty and me a quick hug. "It is so wonderful to meet both of you. Sorry, I'm a hugger and a talker." She smiled widely. "I am so glad that you chose our little town to stop in. I've been so worried since the emergency broadcast started. I've been praying and then God brought us you."

"I'm pleased to meet you all," I replied, "and we are so glad that you can join us." I bent down to Sarah's level to speak directly to her. "I am so thrilled to meet you, Sarah. What a lovely bear friend you have. I had a bear friend when I was little. His name was Ted, and he went everywhere with me."

Sarah's smile was luminescent. She didn't speak to me, just smiled, popped her thumb into her mouth, and hid behind her mother's legs again. I half listened as Ty spoke with Trent and Bonita, explaining what he had surmised about what had happened so far, and what we could expect to happen in the future. Bonita's smile faded, and her face became paler underneath her deep tan color.

"This is so much worse than we anticipated," she whispered. "Are you sure that things are really that bad?"

"I can't guarantee anything," Ty replied. "I can tell you that my father has made a business out of his "prepping" tendencies. He's been studying possible apocalyptic type events for years, and he has insiders in the government from whom he gets information. The first communication I had from him was a phone call, so I don't have proof of that, but I can show you a text from my mom about what dad's sources said if you want. You probably think that I'm just some crazy kid, but I'm not. This is real, and it will be the end of the world as we know it. You both have skills that will be very valuable, and I have a place I can take you where we will all be safe. If you stay here, you won't be. I'm sorry. You have to trust me. I can't offer much more proof than that, other than the emergency broadcast and the earthquakes which both back up what I am telling you."

"All right," her reply was firm and confident. "How long do I have to pack?

"We should be on our way as quickly as possible. You will just need to bring the essentials. We have everything necessary waiting for us."

"Okay, Trent, you go get the truck and pull it to the cellar door. I know that we are four more people than you are expecting so we will be eating the food and such that you have stockpiled. I have canned and preserved food that we can bring with us. I'll need my medical supplies, which I can get, and I'll need a little bit of time to pack some clothes. I would also like to bring a few personal belongings as long as there is room."

My eyes darted to her when I heard four, and I noticed that Ty's did as well. "Four?" he asked.

"Brandon, step out."

A tall, dark-haired young man stepped onto the porch from behind the front door. A rifle rested causally in his hand, and there was a small smirk on his face. His voice was deep and confident when he said, "Howdy folks."

"I'm sorry," Bonita said. "This is my brother. He was visiting with us when the emergency broadcast started. When I saw your truck coming up the drive after Trent, I asked him to stay just inside the door with the gun just in case something was wrong. He was supposed to keep Sarah inside as well."

Brandon had the grace to look chagrinned at his sister's words, and Sarah ran over and ducked behind his legs. Ty took a moment to consider the situation before speaking. "Okay, there's just the four of you though right? You aren't going to produce Great Aunt Mary or another brother or two before we leave are you?"

"Just the four of us," Trent laughed before turning serious. "I should have told you from the beginning, but let's face it, the situation being what it is, I could not risk that you wouldn't want to bring us with you. I had to either withhold the information or risk safety for my family. You would have done the same, wouldn't you?"

Ty nodded and patted Trent on the back. Trent smiled and then continued. "I'm glad that part is done. Let's get to loading so we can get out of here. Brandon why don't you and Ty get the stuff from the cellar and I will help gather the things needed in from the house."

When everyone started to head off to complete their tasks, I called out to Bonita. "Can I speak with you for just a quick minute?" Ty looked at me questioningly, and I mouthed Jules to him. He nodded and took off after Brandon. "I think our friend Jules is in shock. I was hoping that you could give me some advice about what I can do for her?"

"What happened, or is it just everything?" Bonita asked.

"Well," I started tearing up as I spoke. Talking to Ty about it was one thing but explaining to a stranger what had happened to Ben made it feel even more real. "We were traveling with our friends, Ben and Jules. We were on our way to the beach, going to celebrate graduation and life. We camped at Pilot Mountain last night. We were trying to get through some hilly areas when those last two earthquakes hit. We had decided it might be better to stay off the main roads because of the military. They are all traveling west, and we had already been stopped once. There was a landslide and Ben... well, Ben got hurt and we couldn't help him. Ty said he was gone."

Bonita nodded her head. "You poor things. Let me talk to her real quick, and if she is alright, I'll go get my packing done." Bonita made her way to the truck and pounced up on the passenger seat. She leaned into the back seat and appeared to be talking to Jules. She spent a few moments in the truck, then hopped back out and made her way to me.

"I think she will be fine, given time. This entire situation is very shocking and then, on top of everything else, to lose her boyfriend would be overwhelming. I have a pill that I want you to give her. After taking it she will probably rest more, but hopefully, when she wakes up, she will be more lucid. Come in, and I'll grab the pill and some water for you.

I followed Bonita into her home. It was lovely and had obviously been restored with painstaking effort. The handrails, moldings, and fireplace mantle all appeared to be hand carved and were polished to a glimmering shine.

"You have a beautiful home," I told Bonita.

She paused and looked around before responding. "This morning I would have told you how proud I am of all the work we have put into this old house. Can you believe it was falling down when we bought it? I'll miss it, but there are more important things than this house. Maybe someday we can come back?"

She handed me a pill and a bottle of water. "I hope so," I replied. "Thanks for this and for checking on Jules. I'll let you get to packing now."

I made my way back out to the truck. Everyone but Jules and I were scurrying around collecting things and putting them into Trent's truck. Jules looked at me when I climbed in and, although she seemed calm, tears were streaming down her cheeks again.

"Here you go sweetie," I said as I handed her the pill and water. "Bonita wants you to take this, okay?"

Jules took the pill and the water from me. She didn't hesitate to take the pill before handing me back the water. She curled back up on the seat while I waited, alone. The others were all inside, taking care of gathering things. The world is ending, I thought. I hope it doesn't happen while I'm sitting out here alone.

Chapter Eight

It didn't take long before we were back on the road again. The fact that we once again had another truck following us made me nervous. I couldn't help but think about Ben following us in his truck, and I hoped we didn't lose them too. Ty had made sure to indicate on the map where we were going and as we traveled he let me know where we were and how he planned to proceed. Trent had offered up some suggestions about better routes, and Ty had indicated those on the map as well. Jules had gone back to sleep almost immediately after taking the pill and with Ty focused on the road in front of him the truck was relatively quiet.

We traveled down country roads that had very few homes visible from roads, but I had the feeling that the gravel drives we cruised past led to hidden homes where families sat waiting for someone to tell them what to do. They didn't realize that they most likely were being abandoned by their government and in the days to come they would be at the mercy of the environment that this catastrophe would create. Power would go out, and the sun would be blocked. People would get ill or hurt, and there would be no medical services or ambulances to come help them. Those who didn't have a way to burn wood, a generator to run an electric heater, or propane and a way to heat with it would get very cold very quickly. People would run out of food and water, all the necessities of life, and most would have no idea how or where to go to gather or hunt more.

"So," I broke the silence, "I've never been to this cabin. Aren't we going to be crowded with my family, yours, Jules and now Trent and his family?"

"Well, it's really so much more than just a cabin, although, if someone accidentally came across it they wouldn't really see more than cabins in the area. There is more than one as well as an extensive underground bunker system that links them all together. It's ingenious really. Dad wanted to be prepared for anything."

"I'm sorry that I ever laughed when people made fun of his prepping. I am so grateful to him for allowing me and my family to take shelter in the place that he prepared for your family's survival. He's saving our lives, and none of us will ever forget that. I bet my parents are really feeling bad about how they judged your dad's prepping tendencies."

"As far as my parents are concerned, you are family. You are their daughter, and I think if you and I had stayed broken up they would have picked you over me.

They also know that if you weren't going to be in the shelter with me, I wouldn't be there." Ty glanced at me and took my hand in his. After placing a quick kiss gently on the palm, he continued. "I love you, Elli. My life is both as simple and as complicated as that. No matter what happens in this world, you are what matters most to me. I will do whatever I need to keep you safe and us together. You are my one and only and, if I have any say in anything, we will get married, have babies, and live happily ever after."

"I love you too." I paused, thinking about all he had said. "You really want to bring babies into what you think this world will become?"

"Well, yeah. Someone will need to repopulate the earth, and I think we should do more than our fair share."

"I'm not sure about this more than our fair share thing." I smiled at him. "So tell me more about this...what? I guess I would say compound, that your dad has built."

"Well, it's entirely self-sufficient with redundant systems for all the necessities. Without knowing what exactly we needed to prepare for, we had to prepare for everything. We'll have heat, water, food, weapons, and just about anything you can think of that we might need. Spread out over the property are ten different cabins which are all linked together through the underground passageways. Every security measure feasible has been taken, and there are warning systems in place in case someone comes onto the property. We have vehicles and ways to power them. There are also ATVs that can be used when going from one place to another inside the underground tunnels. We have a communication system set up so the cabins can contact each other."

"Your dad has thought of everything, although I can't say I'm surprised. He's always been so much more aware than anyone else I know. Well, maybe aware isn't the right word. He's a realist, and the rest of us just didn't want to believe that anything this bad could really ever happen. Remember that kid's movie where all the ants prepared for winter, then the grasshoppers came and took their food? You and your family are the ants, and I guess I'm one of the grasshoppers." Ty laughed at my analogy and Jules moved restlessly in the backseat. "Seriously, I don't have anything of value to bring to this situation. I'm just me. I don't have any mad skills or talents that will be valuable in this post-catastrophe world."

"You do. You just aren't confident in your skills and talents yet. Give it all some time. I think we are all still in a bit of shock, you probably more so than me, because I always knew this was a possibility. You, however, still believed in the fairy tales."

"You're right, I did. I understand now, or I'm trying to. There aren't any fairy tale endings in this world. People get hurt, they die. There are some family members who I will probably never see again. Gram... Gran... This is a cruel world, and I don't think I like it so much." I hadn't thought of Gram or Gran since this started. I had aunts, uncles, cousins spread out around the country. They would most likely all be lost. Friends had already been lost, and others would be as well. Ken and Mandy weren't even home with their families. They were somewhere out there on their own trying to navigate this catastrophe. Entire states of men, women, and children were probably already gone. I wondered if the devastation was worldwide. Would other countries be able to come to help us? Could they save some of the families hiding away in these houses that we were passing?

Ty broke my silent introspection. "It is truly going to be a different world. This world will not be as welcoming to life as the old one was, at least for a while. It will have desperate people, but it will have good people as well. We just have to be cautious about determining what kind each person is before we trust them. We will all lose someone, but in the end, hopefully, we can all have our own personal fairytale ending. Find your optimism, try to focus on what is good, because if you can only focus on what you have lost, you are going to go down a very dark path. If that happens, I will walk beside you the entire way to make sure that you are always reminded of the light and hope."

With tears in my eyes, I nodded at Ty and looked back to the road ahead of us. There were so many blessing that I could count and there were so many tragedies. Mom had always told me to make a pro and con list when I was trying to make a decision, but I was afraid to do so in this situation because I was afraid that the cons would outweigh the pros. I knew that I needed to stay strong and I knew that my optimism was one of the things that Ty appreciated about me the most. I needed to try harder to focus on the positives. I tried to think of an internal mantra that I could repeat to myself. *My family is safe. Ty is safe. We have a safe place to go. We will have everything we need. We are luckier than most.* That was the best I could do for now, but it was a start. I just started repeating it over and over again in my mind.

The miles seemed to be passing quickly now, and for some reason, Ty didn't seem to be as cautious as he had been before, so I decided to ask him about it.

"Well, I'm starting to get concerned about how slowly we were progressing. I was hoping that we would get to the cabin before all of the dirt and flying debris starts to block the sunlight. It would just be better if we were in the shelter by then."

His reply caused me some concern, and I found myself watching the sky. Something I'd read once made its way into my mind. I wondered if the words, written so long ago by T.S. Elliott, were prophetic.

This is the way the world ends.
This is the way the world ends.
This is the way the world ends.
Not with a bang but a whimper.

98

For those poor people on the west coast there had most likely been a bang but would the end of the human race come with a whimper rather than a bang? Would the sun be blocked so effectively that it could cause the earth to go into another ice age? They said that was what had killed the dinosaurs. Would it kill us too? I voiced the thought to Ty.

"Well," he said thoughtfully, "I guess in the extreme it could, and if the bolide was big enough, maybe. However, we are smarter and more evolved than dinosaurs. We know how to shelter ourselves. We have prepared for this, and we have a way to create heat, replenish food, and water sources. I truly do not believe that we will become extinct. Unfortunately, I do think that humans, as a species, will become greatly reduced in numbers. Those who didn't prepare and do not know how to adapt will not survive. The earth will need time to recover, and we will have to be adaptive until it does. Most normal people in this world do not know how to adapt."

"I feel like I should be more upset, or devastated, or something. How many people have lost their lives today and how many more will over the next week or month? It's just like this can't be real, it has to be a dream. I'm going to wake up, and it's going to be yesterday morning. Mom will make pancakes and bacon. Then you will come to pick me up, and we can start our grand adventure. It wasn't supposed to be like this."

"I'm sorry babe. It wasn't supposed to be like this, but it isn't a dream. The world has changed, and the change is just too massive for your brain to deal with this quickly. You can't imagine it's real because your brain doesn't want to have to think about the changes and the loss."

I nodded to Ty and went back to staring at the sky. *My family is safe. Ty is safe. We have a safe place to go. We will have everything we need. We are luckier than most.* Repeat.

It was a keening sound from the backseat that interrupted our somewhat tense silence. Jules had woken and was wailing in what could only be described as a howling of grief. The sound was both disturbing and heartbreaking. Ty had been so focused on the road ahead that her wail made him jump slightly. I quickly turned to the backseat and reached out to try to soothe her. I called out to her softly, but she didn't respond to my voice. She continued to wail pitifully.

"Ty, I don't know what's wrong with her. I can't calm her down. What do I do? We can't just let her wail. You need to focus on the road, and I don't know how you could with that sound in your ear. Do you think that she needs medical attention?"

"Okay, okay... I don't know what to do. Keep trying to talk to her while I get pulled over."

"Jules? Jules! Focus on me, sweetie. Come on, listen to my voice." I kept talking to her gently as I patted her hand. The wailing continued.

Ty found a wide spot in the road ahead and signaled to let Trent know that he would be stopping. Once he got the truck stopped, he jumped out to go get Bonita. I unbuckled my seatbelt and climbed into the backseat with Jules. I hugged her, rocking her back and forth trying to both calm and comfort her. I felt tears streaming down my cheeks. That's how Ty and Bonita found us when they got back to the truck. Bonita had an old-fashioned doctor's bag in her hand. She was calm and confident as she asked me to step out of the truck.

Ty helped me down, and Bonita climbed up in my place as I walked away. Ty led me to a large boulder that rested along the side of the road. I scaled up, perched on the rock, and put my head in my hands. Tears continued to stream down my cheeks as I listened to Jules wail. Ty finally pulled me into his arms and rocked me back and forth as I cried for Jules and Ben. After what seemed like an eternity, the wailing died down, and finally, Bonita emerged from the truck, followed by Jules. Jules's eyes were red, and she seemed more aware than she had been in the time since we had lost Ben. Bonita motioned to Ty. He rubbed my back and whispered that he would be right back.

After Ty left, I walked over to Jules. She was standing outside the truck and appeared to be just looking around. She wasn't looking at anyone in the group, simply staring off into the distance as if lost in thought. "Jules," I said softly, "I just want you to know that I'm here for you. Whatever you need, Ty and I are here for you."

Jules turned and focused on me, not speaking. She turned and looked at Ty, and her eyes turned hard and angry. Her words came out in an angry hiss. "I believe that you are my friend and that you might be here for me without his," she motioned towards Ty, "influence, but HE is not here for me. This is his fault, all his fault!"

I tried to calm her. "Jules, you know that isn't true. Ty loves you like a sister."

Her voice just got louder and louder until she was shouting. "It's his fault! He killed Ben! He fucking left Ben there to die all alone. All he is worried about is himself. He knew Ben's truck wouldn't make it over that rockslide, and he let him try anyway. He probably did it on purpose. He was always jealous of Ben. He egged him on, pushing and pushing until Ben had to prove that he was capable."

"Jules, you know that isn't true. None of that is true. You're upset, and you just aren't thinking clearly."

"It is true! If it had been Ty under those rocks, we wouldn't have left, but we left Ben there. You were okay with it! It's your fault too!"

I stood looking at Jules feeling dumbfounded. I had no idea what to say to her. Ben could be annoying, but I had known him forever. I would never have left him there if Ty hadn't said he was gone. Ben had been like a brother to Ty so I know he wouldn't have egged him on or left him there if he thought there was any hope. Then again, we had left him. The world had been falling apart around us. What if Ty was wrong? Had we really left him to suffer and die alone under a pile of rocks?

I hadn't noticed Ty and Bonita approaching until Ty touched my shoulder and moved me behind him. He tried to talk to Jules. "Jules, you know that isn't true. Ben was my brother, by choice. I would never have left him if he wasn't already gone. I..."

I saw Jules raise her hand, and although in reality, the action was lightning fast it seemed as if I watched the exchange in slow motion. The slap was so loud that I thought it might resound for miles in this newly quiet world. Ty's cheek immediately began turning red. He raised his hand and put it on the spot. Jules continued to glare at him, her eyes projecting nothing but hatred. I knew I should step in and say something, but my feet and voice seemed to be frozen. Luckily, Bonita chose that moment to step in.

"Okay, Jules, why don't you come back here with me?" Bonita took Jules by the hand and led her back to their truck. She sat Jules in the passenger seat and then spoke briefly with Trent and Brandon, who had been entertaining Sarah. After a few moments, Brandon and Trent made their way to where we stood, while Bonita seemed to be searching through her medical bag.

"So," Trent stated, "It seems that it might be better if Jules came and road with us for a while. Bonita is going to sedate her, and hopefully, that will help her calm down. She's just not thinking logically right now. She is deep in grief, and she wants to blame someone. You two are the only ones who she can blame right now. She is more than welcome in our truck, but that creates a bit of a tight spacing issue. So we were thinking that Brandon could just trade places with her for now."

Ty was about to answer when we heard Jules screaming again. "I'm not getting in your truck. I don't know you! Why would you help me? I'm not getting back in their truck either!"

The tone of Jules's voice, and the sound of disgust in the word their when she said it, was enough to make my tears start again. I could hear Bonita talking to her in a low, soothing voice, but it didn't seem that Jules had any desire to listen to anything that Bonita had to say. I could see a syringe in Bonita's hand, hidden behind her back. Jules continued to yell and began to scream obscenities as well. She was calling Ty every name I could think of as well as yelling something about Bonita and Trent being human traffickers. She had obviously had a bit of a mental break, and I couldn't necessarily blame her. I could not even imagine what I would feel like if I were dealing with everything going on, and the loss of Ty.

While she was distracted, Brandon quietly made his way behind her. He firmly, but gently it appeared, wrapped his arms around her, effectively trapping her arms with his. Bonita quickly sprang forward and injected whatever was in the syringe into Jules's arm. Jules let out an inhuman wailing sound.

Brandon continued to hold her firmly, but I noticed that he was speaking quietly in her ear. Jules stopped screaming and began to look around widely, her eyes darting between Ty and me. Slowly she seemed to relax, and finally, Brandon was able to loosen his hold. Eventually, he was able to scoop her up into his arms and lay her gently in the backseat of their truck. Once she was settled in Bonita and Brandon walked over to where we still stood with Trent.

"That didn't go quite like I planned," Bonita said with a sigh. "The first pill that I gave her should have calmed her down, and when she woke up, she should have still felt relaxed. Obviously, that didn't happen. The shot I gave her will keep her out for a while."

It seemed as if we all collectively took a deep breath. I looked around at the faces of these people who were really absolute strangers and found the one face that I would know in any crowd. Ty looked back at me, eyes filled with concern. He wrapped an arm around me and pulled me to his side. We all stood for a moment in silence until Ty finally decided someone was going to have to speak.

"There is a sense of urgency for us to move on. What can we do for her, anything? You have a child in your truck. If Jules is going to wake up and start acting like that again, I wouldn't want Sarah to have to go witness it. It would be far better for Jules to go back into our truck, so that doesn't happen."

"She shouldn't wake up again for quite a while, but if she did, I worry about what she would do if she were in your car. She is not thinking logically right now, and I don't think Elli could stop her if she tried something physical."

"Hey!" I replied to Bonita with just the right degree of outrage. "I'm not a baby or a weakling. I can take care of myself, and I could stop Jules if I had to. She doesn't know you two, and she thinks you are human traffickers. If she woke up with you, it might make things worse."

Bonita patted my arm kindly and then answered thoughtfully. "I don't doubt you can take care of yourself, sweetie. However, Jules is angry and irrational right now. I don't think you would want to hurt her if she tried something. I can see how you are hurting. Even though I truly don't believe that there is anything that you or Ty could have done to save your friend I can also tell that you are both carrying guilt. I get it, but there is no time to deal with that right now. You made a good point about her being in our truck too. We have to figure out how to keep Jules calm, or sedated, and get to the compound as quickly and as safely as possible. My family's lives depend on it, and we have put our faith in Ty. So I cannot with an easy conscious put her back in your truck without anticipating the possibility of it causing a problem. However, if there is room in your truck, I suppose that Brandon could ride with you in the back as well just in case."

Ty didn't take more than a second or two to consider before agreeing that Bonita's idea was the best solution available to us. I climbed into the backseat of the truck to make sure that there would be enough room for both Jules and Brandon, while Ty went to get Jules from the other truck. When I climbed back out, I saw that Trent had gone to collect Sarah from where she was picking wildflowers. Sarah tugged on her father's hand, and he leaned down so she could whisper in his ear.

After sharing her secret, Sarah took her father's hand and skipped beside him as he walked back to where I stood. I expected her to take the flowers and give them to her mother so I was surprised when she stopped directly in front of me and held the flowers out. I saw Trent nudge her, but she looked at him, shook her head, and pointed at him before popping her thumb into her mouth.

"Sarah would like you to have these flowers." He explained to me. I reached out, took them, and smiled down at her. "She said that you look sad, and such a pretty girl shouldn't be sad. Pretty flowers always make her and mommy feel better so she wants you to have them so you won't be sad anymore."

I kneeled down in front of her, thinking it would be better to talk to her at her level. "Thank you for the flowers, Sarah. You were so right. They do make me feel better." I smiled at her and was pleased to see that she smiled in return. The flowers that she handed me were white with a distinct pink circle in the center. They were beautiful and represented everything that we would soon be losing in the world. How long would it be before flowers bloomed here again, I wondered. How long before crops could grow?

Sarah darted away and ran to her mother, who was waiting by their truck. Bonita helped Sarah up into her car seat. Sara looked back to me and gave a little wave before she was deposited back in the truck. Ty had settled Jules into the backseat, and Brandon walked to the truck to join her, bag in hand. His eyes were serious and measuring, but he had a half smile that made me want to like him.

"Hope there's room for my bag, just the necessities of course. You know the things I wouldn't want to be without in case we run into trouble. My friends Smith and Wesson, and a few of their friends as well. I also have a walkie-talkie, so we communicate with Trent easier."

"We'll find the room. Climb on in, and we'll hit the road."

Once Brandon was in and settled, Ty turned to me and pulled me into his arms for a quick hug. I climbed up into the truck and buckled my seatbelt. The ride we were on just seemed to get bumpier and bumpier.

Chapter Nine

Once we were all back in the trucks, we blazed a trail down the roads as quickly as we could. I saw the rolling hills stretching before us, and my mind protested at the thought of having to travel through them. Thoughts of landslides and blocked roads causing us to be trapped filled my mind. I did not want to get entombed in those mountains.

"Ty, is there a way for us to go around the mountains? I mean, I know that we have to get to through them but can we go around these ones to get where we are going?"

"I'm sorry babe we really can't go around them. I would rather avoid them too, but the timeline that we need to stay on just doesn't allow for it. It would add hours to the trip to have to try to go around and, eventually, we would still have to go into the hills. This truck will be able to get through most any blockage without issue. I could have pulled Ben over the last time if he had cooperated, but he wouldn't listen. Trent will know the importance of caution. He isn't going to put anyone at risk. I think we will be fine. It's been a while since the last quake so, hopefully, we have nothing new falling. With any luck, which has to be on our side at some point during this journey, we won't come across anything too bad that we can't get over."

"Oh... okay." I couldn't shake the thought that going back into the hills was a mistake, but I knew I needed to have faith in Ty. I also understood that time was of the essence and that we couldn't waste hours going around the hills, especially when we were going to have to go into them eventually. I started to chew on my lower lip, another new stress habit I thought to myself.

"I have to say," Brandon said thoughtfully, "that I agree with your boyfriend. This truck is decked out for off-roading and if you are worried about Trent and the other truck, I wouldn't. Trent may not look like it but he's been running off roads and in and out of these mountains for half of his life or longer. I know, I know, he looks like a nerdy computer guy or something but take my word for it."

Actually, Trent didn't look at all like a nerdy computer guy. His eyes were intelligent, but he was also very muscular, my mother would describe him as stocky. He reminded me of a football player. "The point is," Brandon continued, "that we will get through these hills, all of us. We will make it to your compound, and we will all be safe. Trust me and trust Ty here."

"I trust Ty implicitly, but, to be honest, I don't know you well enough to trust you yet. If Ty thinks we will get through I believe him but after... after what happened with Ben the hills make me nervous."

"I think those hills make us all a little nervous, but in the long run, it's worth the risk," Ty told me. He reached over and took my hand, running his thumb along the palm like he always did to soothe me. The sound of the walkie broke the temporary silence that had settled in the car. Brandon grabbed it and depressed the button.

"Go."

Bonita's voice sounded back. "Trent says that we are going to want to turn left onto the access road. He'll jump out and take care of the gate."

"Affirmative."

When the road appeared to the left Brandon pointed it out, and Ty turned. It headed directly towards one of the hills. The way didn't look as if it was well traveled, and a metal gate blocked access. Ty brought the truck to a stop, and, within a minute, Trent went jogging past. A moment later the gate swung open. After giving Trent a minute to get back into his truck, we started down the new road.

Within a few minutes, the road began to head up. Rather than being between two hills, this road traveled along the outside of the hill. It followed the natural incline, curving along the hillside. There were some piles of rocks and rubble lying along the side of the road, but for the most part, it seemed that if pieces had been knocked loose by quakes and fallen they had continued to roll down the hillside. The road, Brandon explained to us, was a county road that was used most often by emergency vehicles. Trent, in addition to his many other jobs and talents, was on the local volunteer fire department and, as such, had a key to open the access road gates. This road would be the quickest way through this part of the county. Anything quicker was better, I thought. I had been keeping my eyes on the sky and had been noticing for the past few minutes that the sun was starting to look as if it were behind a haze.

Ty kept the truck at a quick pace as we made our way down the road. The path we traveled provided beautiful views of fields in the distance. I could see the colors of the wildflowers dotting the landscape here and there. Pinks, purples, reds, yellows, and whites blended together making intricate designs as they intermingled with the greens of the grass and crops. I had always loved the newness that came with spring. The trees blooming and then getting their leaves, not to mention, all the new animal babies that ran about exploring their whole new world. Now spring wouldn't get to progress to summer. The trees wouldn't produce fruit. The crops wouldn't grow and prosper. The landscape that I was able to see now would be the last of its kind for many years to come. If the earth ever recovers, I thought to myself.

I was trying to imprint the memory of the color of wildflowers in my mind when a white streak in the sky caught my attention. It wasn't as bright as it would have appeared in a clear blue sky. The haze that had settled in made it difficult to track. It looked kind of like a shooting star would appear, but closer.

"Ty, do you see that white streak in the sky? What is it?"

Ty slowed the truck so he could look out the window to where I pointed. He continued to slow, watching the streak come closer and closer to the ground. Eventually, he brought us to a complete stop, opened his door, and stared up at the sky. I followed him out, and Brandon quickly followed. I heard Trent's truck come to a stop as well and soon they were standing with us, staring at the white streak that was getting closer and more prominent. I think we all knew what it was, except for Sarah, but no one was willing to acknowledge what we were watching.

"How big is it, do you think?" Brandon asked.

"I wish I knew," Ty replied, eyes still glued to the incoming mass. "Maybe a meteorite storm following the impact on the west coast? It's possible that whatever struck there was part of a large meteor belt, a debris field, or something. If that is the case, we may see the impact of some of the smaller meteorites that make it through the atmosphere."

We all continued to watch the white streak as it got closer and closer to impact with the ground. Its trajectory didn't seem to put us in any danger, but I still felt dread watching the space rock plummet to the earth's surface. My group wasn't under any imminent threat, but someone out there might be. It seemed to be increasing in speed the longer we watched it. Suddenly, we heard a loud crash and saw a bright flash of light. Flames appeared in the distance, and we all gasped in shock as we watched the world go up in flames.

"There's the bang," I whispered.

Ty looked down at me questioningly. "Hmm?"

"It was so quiet earlier. The quiet brought to mind that T.S. Elliot quote we talked about in English last year. You know the quote about the world ending with a whimper and not a bang. It was so quiet I thought that in this part of the world it might be that way, while on the west coast it probably ended with a bang. Now we've heard the bang here though, and the world is burning. No rescue workers will come, and it will just keep burning."

"Parts of the world will burn, this is true, but the world is not going to end. Not with a whimper or a bang. This is not going to affect us getting to the shelter. Do you understand and believe me?"

I looked up into Ty's eyes and knew that he believed what he was telling me. I nodded and stood beside him as he quietly turned his attention back to the scene below. While everyone else was looking down at the fire, I was looking to the sky. What I saw there was frightening. There was not just one but three more white lines streaking through the hazy sky. Were we now going to have to go forward trying to avoid falling space debris and the fires that their impact ignited?

"Umm, Ty?" He was still staring at the fire, and I really thought he should see the additional three meteorites plummeting towards us. I could feel his eyes on me, and I heard his gasp when he caught sight of what I saw.

"That's not good," Ty said softly, as if to himself, and then louder to everyone else. "That's not good! We need to move! Now! They don't look like they are going to hit us, but we need to make faster progress. I don't know how big this meteorite storm is going to be, but just in case it is more than what we see we need to move faster and get to the shelter. It could be localized to this area. We need to get out of here now."

We all turned and ran back to the trucks. I was climbing in when I heard Bonita yelling for Sarah, her voice panicked. "Sarah? Sarah! Where are you?"

I quickly hopped back out of the truck at the same time that Ty did. Brandon was close behind us. Bonita was standing by the truck yelling, and Trent seemed to be scanning the landscape looking for Sarah. "What happened?" I asked.

"I don't know. I don't know. She was standing with us while we watched the meteorite falling, and she must have wandered away. I can't believe this. She's not a wanderer. She's never done this before. Sarah!"

"We'll look for her," Ty said. "Bonita, we will find her. We will not leave here until we find her."

We all headed in different directions calling for Sarah. I headed up the road, towards the hillside. I looked for her black curls bobbing in the tall, green grass and listened for her childish singsong voice, but nothing caught my attention. What if she wandered into those fields and one of the meteorites hit in the area before we could find her? She could be hurt or even killed. With all of us wandering off in different directions we were more likely to be caught by one of the falling rocks as well. We really needed to find her!

I could hear the others continuing to call for Sarah as we all spread out. Ty was walking on the other side of the gravel road, looking down over the hillside. I continued to call for her and scan the area, but she didn't answer me. I didn't see any signs of Sarah. She couldn't have just disappeared. She had to be here somewhere, I thought. I took a moment to look back up at the white streaks in the sky. They were still distant but approaching none the less.

The road curved ahead and I couldn't see beyond the curve. Something just didn't feel right about the location and the entire situation. I paused again, scanning for Sarah or any sign of danger other than the approaching meteorites. Nothing appeared out of the ordinary, well for a world that was falling apart I thought, but something was off. I didn't want to go around the curve by myself. However, something told me that we would find Sarah somewhere on the other side. I called out quietly to Ty, and he turned to look at me before making his way to where I stood.

Before I could say anything, Ty said, "Something isn't right. Sarah wouldn't have run this far from her parents."

"I thought the same. I didn't want to go any further without you."

"Good instincts babe. Get your gun out and ready." I pulled the gun from where it was tucked in my back waistband and made sure the safety was off before Ty continued. "Okay, I want you to stay a little behind me and close to the side of the hill. Blend into it as much as you can. You need to have my back."

I nodded and headed to walk along the side of the hill while Ty walked right down the middle of the road. He didn't have his weapons out and ready, but I knew that if he needed one he could have it in his hand almost immediately. I was uncomfortable with the fact that he was making a target of himself, but in doing so he was also creating a distraction for whoever might be around the curve. There was someone there, I was sure of it now, and I was confident that whoever they were they had Sarah.

I watched Ty walk down the middle of the road. He exuded confidence as he called out for Sarah. I followed discretely behind him, off to the side, sliding along the hill and trying to stay hidden in the foliage. I glanced quickly behind us and noticed that Brandon seemed to be following as well. He kept an inconspicuous distance and was also careful to stay hidden. I really hadn't gotten a chance to get to know Brandon yet, but his presence provided me some measure of comfort. I could hear Trent and Bonita still calling for Sarah from the other direction, but their voices grew increasingly more distant as we made our way around the curve of the road.

It seemed to take forever but finally, Ty rounded the curve ahead of me. His last call for Sarah ended in a tone that conveyed worry. "Sarah, are you okay?" There was no reply that I could hear.

Ty started walking more quickly down the road, and I tried to follow him as rapidly as I could without drawing attention to myself. I was glad for the heaviness of the gun in my hand as it provided me with a sense of security. Ty's footsteps were beginning to sound distant, and I was worried that he would get in trouble. If that happened, I would be too far away to help him. I couldn't keep up with his pace without losing my cover. Ty's footsteps came to an abrupt halt, and I picked up my pace as much as I could. Finally, I got to where I could see around the curve. I couldn't believe what I saw. My eyes had to be playing tricks on me. It just wasn't possible that what I was seeing was real.

I cautiously peeked around the curve again to where Ty stood with his hands held out to his side in a conciliatory manner and saw Sarah sitting in a truck. The vehicle was familiar. It was an old piece of junk and was packed with even more junk. Not only was the truck familiar, so was the man walking around from behind it. I had seen that exact truck earlier in the morning parked at the campsite. It couldn't be possible though, I thought to myself. How could it be possible?

Chapter Ten

How could Max be here? How was that possible? And why did he have Sarah in his car? It just didn't make any sense, none of this made any sense. I sensed Brandon hiding in the foliage beside me. When I looked at him, he lifted his finger to his lips to indicate that we shouldn't talk before turning his complete focus to the situation in front of us. I could hear Ty trying to communicate with Max.

"Max, how did you get here? We've met, remember? We shared some of our dinner with you last night at the Pilot Mountain campsite, remember?"

"I'm not Max. I don't know you."

"Last night, at the campsite..." Max cut Ty off before he could continue.

"I don't know you. I'm not Max. I do have a brother named Max though. Y'all just need to go. We don't need you or your help. Something is wrong with the world. I can sense it, and Y'all just need to move on. I won't stop you or hurt you if you just leave."

"You must be Wayne then. Max said he had a brother. We will leave you alone, but I need to take Sarah back to her mom and dad. Then we will happily get out of your way."

"I don't know no Sarah," Wayne replied, "so Y'all just go ahead and get on out of here."

"Sarah is the little girl in your truck. Her mom and dad are looking all over for her. I'm sorry if she wandered over here and bothered you, so I'll just go get her. Then we will be on our way." Ty took a step towards the truck where Sarah sat, and I saw Wayne lift a shotgun. He kept his grip loose and held the gun to his side. The threat was obvious, however.

"That there is my little girl, not the Sarah that your people lost. Don't you be going over there and bothering her. Just turn around, go back to your people, and leave. Don't make me do something to make sure that you can't bother my girl. What kind of parents would lose their kid anyway? Bad parents, that's who. This Sarah you are looking for is probably better where ever she is now."

Ty put his hands up again and stopped moving towards the truck. "Woah there, it's all right. There's no reason for the gun. Let's just lay that down and relax. We'll figure this all out without having to resort to any of that."

"We ain't gonna be peacefully figuring this out if you take one more step towards my truck."

I watched this exchange in horror. This man was crazy! He was Max. He was wearing the same oversized, dirty clothes that he'd been in yesterday. I had no idea why he was claiming to be the brother named Wayne or why he was claiming Sarah was his child. I looked questioningly to Brandon, who once again raised his finger to his lips. He whispered to me, almost silently, "I'm going to make my way around. Be ready to back us up, if needed. Stay hidden unless it looks like we need back up though." I nodded in acknowledgment, and he silently slipped away from me and made his way further down the hill. I watched Brandon's progression as Ty continued to try to negotiate with Max/Wayne.

Brandon seemed to be an expert in becoming invisible, blending in with his surroundings perfectly, like a chameleon. If I hadn't been watching him from the beginning of his journey, there was no way that I would have been able to see him make his way along the hill to circle around behind Max. In the time it took Brandon to make his way stealthily behind where Max stood still holding the gun pointed at Ty the situation had escalated. Ty was trying to calmly talk to Max, who was still not making any sense. He didn't falter in his statements. It was like he truly didn't know who Ty was and thought that Sarah was his daughter.

I finally saw Brandon step out from the foliage near where Max stood. Max was so focused on Ty that he didn't seem to hear or even sense him. Ty noticed him immediately. I saw the subtle change in his posture, and he slowly dropped his hands back to his sides as Max ranted. Ty glanced to where he seemed to know I was crouched before appearing to focus solely on Max.

Max seemed to be progressing to a state of advanced agitation. He was starting to pace and wave his gun around erratically. Brandon was silently creeping up behind him, but I didn't think he was going to make it in time. Max looked like he was ready to lose it, even more so than he already had if that was possible. He was screaming about people trying to take his kid away from him, mothers who are unfit, and government systems who punish good men and reward lying, evil women. I was just about to stand up and take aim when I saw Ty casually make a downward motion with his hand. How did he know I was about to show myself?

I settled back down into the tall grass in which I had hidden, watched, and waited. Ty had stopped talking and just seemed to be letting Max rant and rave. When Brandon was close enough to make a move, Ty finally started speaking to Max again, trying to hold his attention.

"Listen, Max, err Wayne. You sure do look like your brother. I'm certainly not going to take your child away from you. Obviously, we've just had a misunderstanding here. You are right though, something bad is going on, and maybe we can help you out."

Max once again focused on Ty and seemed to be listening to him intently. The gun was focused solely on Ty as well. As Ty talked, Max seemed to relax, and eventually, the gun began to lower into a more relaxed position. As soon as it had been completely lowered, Brandon stepped up behind him and placed the barrel of his gun against the back of Max's head.

"All right mister," Brandon said in a low and dangerous voice, "don't do anything stupid. I'll just take that gun from you, then we can figure this out all civil like."

Max tensed at Brandon's voice and the feel of the gun now pressed against his head. His mouth formed a hard, angry line and his fingers clenched around the weapon, knuckles white. Other than the clenching of his hand he didn't seem to move a muscle. He didn't respond to Brandon in any way, just stood as still as a statue keeping a firm grip on his gun.

"I won't say it again mister, hand me the gun. It's a crazy world out there. If I have to shoot you to make sure my niece is safe and back with her mother I will do so without a second thought. You ask yourself if it's worth it. You won't get that gun up to shoot anyone before I pull the trigger on mine."

My eyes were glued to Max. He seemed to take a moment to think through his options. Then the strangest thing happened, Max's entire demeanor changed. His posture, eyes, and facial expression were all different. Everything about him seemed to transform into something else. When he spoke, his voice was even different.

"Hey now, whatca all doin' here? What's goin' on?" He started to raise the gun and tried to turn, but Brandon put his more firmly against Max's head.

"Don't try something stupid. Just hand me your weapon, and we'll figure this out. Then we will be on our way." Brandon stated firmly.

Ty followed Brandon's statement with one of his own. "Max, just hand your gun to Brandon there, and like he said, we will figure this all out peacefully."

"Hey," Max sounded confused, "I know you. Y'all were nice. Y'all brought some food to me and my mutt last night. How did you get here? How did I get here?" Max slowly handed his gun to Brandon. "I'm just gonna sit down against the truck here. I ain't gonna try nothing."

Brandon moved the gun away from the back of Max's head but kept it pointed at him. Max slumped down against the tire of the trunk, staring at his feet. Ty immediately went to the truck and grabbed Sarah from where she was sitting with Max's dog. Brandon continued to keep his gun on Max, but I could tell he was waiting for an all okay from Ty. I could hear Ty's low voice soothingly talking to Sarah and, finally, I heard her small but strong voice answer.

"She's okay!" Ty called to us. Relief filled me as I stepped out of my hiding place and made my way to where Ty was with Sarah. She looked no worse for the wear and, in fact, seemed to be happily playing with the dog and eating marshmallows from the bag of food I had sent over to Max last night.

"I'll stay here with her," I told Ty. "Why don't you go try to figure out what's going on so we can get out of here."

Ty walked back to the other side of the truck and looked down at Max, who was still sitting slouched against the tire staring at his feet. Ty lifted his gun and then turned to Brandon. "Can you take Sarah and Elli and go back to our trucks? I'll be there in just a minute, and then we need to get on the road."

Brandon started to protest, but Ty quickly explained. "Bonita and Trent are still worried sick about where Sarah is. You need to take her back to them. I would just send Elli with her, but it's not safe in this world anymore to just walk alone. Who would have thought this guy was on the road. We weren't cautious, and look what happened. Think about what could have happened. I just want to talk to Max here to make sure that we won't be seeing him again."

Brandon nodded and came over to where Ty was standing. Sarah was playing with the dog. "Hey pumpkin," he said to Sarah in a soft voice. "Mommy is very worried about you. Let's go find Mommy, okay?"

Sarah looked up at Brandon, and her eyes lit with joy. It was obvious that she adored her Uncle Brandon. She lifted her hands to him, and he picked her up, holding her close. "I made Mommy sad? Can we stop and pick her a flower, Unc Bran?"

"Maybe just one flower pumpkin." Brandon turned and started walking back down the road towards our trucks. He turned back, looking at me questioningly.

"I'm going to stay here with Ty," I said loudly enough that they could both hear me.

"Elli, go. Now. Please?"

"I don't want to leave you here alone. It doesn't feel like the right thing to do."

"Please go. I'll be okay. You have to trust me."

I didn't want to leave him there, but he really wanted me to go, and I didn't want him to think that I didn't trust his judgment. I nodded to him and followed Brandon and Sarah back down the road. I could hear Ty murmuring to Max as we walked away, and when I looked back, I saw that he still had his gun in his hand but seemed to have relaxed somewhat. Brandon stopped and let Sarah down so she could quickly pick some flowers for Bonita. I caught up with them, and he picked her back up so we could be on our way. We were walking quickly, and soon we were around the curve. I could no longer see Ty and Max.

When we rounded the curve, Bonita and Trent came back into view. Bonita must have sensed that Sarah was near because she immediately looked up and began running to us. Trent, hearing his wife's scream, turned and ran to us as well. Bonita grabbed Sarah from Brandon and quickly looked her over for injuries.

"Where have you been? You never leave Mommy and Daddy! You know that! Where have you been? I was so worried!"

I opened my mouth to explain where we had found her, but my words were interrupted by a blood-curdling scream followed by gunshots. What came next was even more chilling to me, absolute silence. I didn't hesitate a second longer. I turned and ran back towards where we had left Ty. I felt helpless and angry. I knew better than to leave him by himself but he had insisted, so I had left him there with a man who was obviously crazy. Why did I do that, I thought as I ran full speed back towards Ty. Why wasn't he yelling to let me know that he was okay?

Brandon and Trent both sprinted past me. I can't do this; the thought took up residence in my mind and wouldn't go away. I can't go and see Ty hurt or dead. My feet stopped of their own accord, and I found that I couldn't take one more step around the curve in the road. I couldn't see Brandon or Trent, and no one had made a sound. There had not been one reassuring sound. My knees buckled, and I fell to the rocky ground, tears streaming down my face. I was frozen in fear, unable to go forward but knowing that I could not go back. My hands began to tremble, and it felt like the world was closing in on me.

Someone was talking to me, but I couldn't hear what they were saying. I couldn't seem to focus on their words or face. I knew the world was going on around me, but for me, it had stopped. I was unable to interact with those who were going forward. I heard the voice talking at some basic level because I knew that it wasn't Ty. The tone was off, and it didn't have his confidence. I tried to pull myself together enough to listen, but I just didn't seem capable of doing so. The voice finally stopped trying to get my attention, at least I couldn't hear it anymore. A minute later, or maybe an hour I can't be sure, I vaguely heard the sound of feet hitting the gravel as someone ran away, followed by yelling in the distance.

At some point even sitting seemed to require too much effort, so I curled up on the ground, waiting for I have no idea what. Maybe I was waiting for one of the big outer space rocks to land on me and take me out of my misery. The world was ending anyway, I thought, and for the second time in a few hours, I was sure that Ty was gone. I didn't like this world. I wasn't equipped for living in this world and without Ty what was the point.

Then, quietly at first, I could hear Ty's voice in my head. Get up! The voice became louder and more insistent. 'Elli, you need to get up and go. You are stronger than this, and I need you to get up and go. Come on, don't give up!' His voice was strong, confident and bossy, I thought. He wasn't this bossy in real life, just in my head. Finally, he pushed me enough that I was able to pull myself back to the here and now. I could hear Trent yelling for Bonita to come and bring her medical bag. Medical bag? Maybe Ty was just hurt.

I jumped up and began running towards Max's truck where we had left Ty. I didn't know what I would find when I got there, but I knew that I couldn't just sit here and give up. This habit of checking out when things looked bad was becoming unpleasant, and I really needed to get over it. I needed to be stronger in this world, and I needed to remember that it was essential to be strong when things look like they were going badly. I finally got around the curve and could see where Max's truck was parked. I searched frantically for Ty, but I didn't see him or any sign of him anywhere. I got to the clearing and brought myself to an abrupt halt as I desperately scanned the area for Ty. He was nowhere to be found, but then again I didn't see Trent or Brandon either.

I felt my mind start to disconnect and give up again, but I forced myself to stay focused on the here and now. They had to be here somewhere. Everyone couldn't have just disappeared. I tried to calm my breathing. I stood as still as I could, listening to see if I could pick up on any human sounds. I could hear what I assumed was the sound of Bonita's coming with her medical bag. Listening intently, I could also hear an almost indistinguishable whispering that seemed to be coming from the other side of Max's truck. I turned and walked slowly along the truck, afraid of what I might find on the other side.

When I turned around the front end of the truck, I saw Trent kneeling down beside ... who was it laying there? I couldn't see anything but feet because the person was lying on the ground positioned, for the most part, behind and under the bed of the truck. The shoes? Were they Ty's shoes? I had no clue what shoes he was wearing. Why wasn't I more observant? The feet looked about the right size for Ty, but Brandon wasn't that much smaller than Ty. There was only one way to find out, keep moving forward. I forced myself to take one step after another. Finally, there he was lying there in front of me.

∞ ∞ ∞

Brandon's face was still and pale. Trent was kneeled down beside him, holding his hand and whispering to him quietly. There was blood on the ground around him, and I couldn't immediately see where it was coming from. I was worried that he was gone already, but then I saw his chest rising and falling with regular breaths. Bonita dashed past me, jostling me out of her way as she tried to get to her brother. Trent immediately moved to the side to give her room to work and tried to explain what had happened as she did.

115

"We came around the corner and didn't see Ty, so we ran over to the truck to look for him. When Brandon got to this side, a shot rang out from over that way." Trent paused and looked up at me, "I didn't see Ty. I... I'm sure he isn't the one who fired the shot though. I'm sorry. I don't know where Ty is or what has become of him."

Bonita was checking Brandon over thoroughly, asking him questions. I could not hear him answering, but answering he was. The bullet seemed to have gone through his bicep, Bonita explained, so she needed to get the bleeding stopped and get the area bandaged. I offered to help, but she told me that I should go look for Ty.

"Trent, you go with Elli to find Ty. Both of you be cautious. You both have weapons. Have them ready and use them if necessary!"

"What about Sarah?" I asked. I knew I needed to find Ty, but there was no indication that he was hurt. I didn't see any blood or signs of a struggle, other than the blood that was around Brandon. "Yes I want to find Ty, but I will go stay with Sarah if you need me to do that."

"Sarah is locked in our truck and believe me she will not get out. She is occupied and safe. I'm going to get Brandon bandaged, then I will either drive him and this truck back over there, or we will walk. Don't let Brandon fool you, he can get up and walk if he needs to. You two go find and help Ty. We need to find him and get out of here." Bonita looked to the sky when she finished talking, and I looked up at the reminder of the current state of events. I had somehow forgotten the meteorites, but there seemed to be even more of them in the sky now than there were before.

Bonita only spent a moment looking at the sky, and then focused her sole attention on Brandon. Trent leaned down and gave her a kiss on the head before standing and pulling his gun from his waistband. I made sure my weapon was in my hand and ready before we took off in the direction from which the shot had come. We walked quietly and cautiously, not sure what we would find. There was a visible trail where gravel and foliage had been recently disturbed.

Trent led the way down the trail. He was familiar with the area and seemed to know the landscape well. The trail led to the rock face of the hill we had been driving around and then appeared to go up a very narrow rocky path that also wound up and around. We made our way up the trail as quietly as possible. It was frightening to me. We were much too vulnerable in this position. We were exposed as we walked along the path and anyone could be looking down from above. It would be simple for them to take advantage of us in this weak position. I was on edge, waiting for a shot to ring out.

Trent must have been reading my mind because he paused and turned to whisper to me quietly, "We need to tuck in as close as we can to the rock and work our way up. We are too exposed just walking up on this path, especially since we don't know what we are walking in to."

I nodded and tucked myself in as tightly against the rocky surface as I could. I briefly wondered if hills had rocky surfaces, or if this was this really a mountain. Back home the only rocky surfaces I'd seen on hills were where they had cut through hilly terrain to build interstate 70. Driving east from Columbus on I-70 the landscape quickly transitioned from flat farmlands to the beginnings of the foothills of the Appalachian Mountains. These hills were foothills of a mountain range too, I thought. Perhaps that is why they were so rocky.

Trent pressed his back against the rock and slowly started to move forward. We seemed to be progressing so slowly, and, as much as I wanted to run ahead in case Ty was lying hurt somewhere, I knew that caution was better than just rushing in. We didn't know what the situation would be when we found Ty and Max. Just running full speed ahead could cost someone their life. I understood the necessity of caution, but it was physically painful to stop myself from rushing forward to find Ty. I could stay against the rocks and move quickly, I thought to myself. Could I move quietly and quickly though, I asked myself as I crept along after Trent. I knew I couldn't. I was not trained in this sort of stealthy maneuver. I tried to calm my mind, keep faith in Ty's ability to take care of himself, and focus on the task ahead.

We wound our way around the hillside, silent and cautious. Our progress was slow but steady, and finally, we were rewarded by the sound of a lone voice ranting. We weren't close enough that I could distinguish the owner of the voice, but the tone and cadence didn't sound right to be Ty's. I wasn't sure if that should make me happy or concern me, but I tried to logic my way through it. Unless Ty was there and conscious who would Max be talking to? Could he be talking to himself? Was he that crazy?

Trent paused for a moment to listen and then started moving more quickly along the rock face up the path towards the voice. The feel of the gun in my hand gave me a sense of comfort and security that I desperately needed. The voice grew louder and louder as we approached. Looking up the path, it appeared as if we were approaching a clearing of some sort. The trail seemed to be widening. Max's voice was clear enough now that I could definitively identify it and understand what he was saying. His voice sounded deranged.

"... just stupid! Max is an idiot, and you must be someone he brought here to trick me. Well, it's just not going to work! I know what you are after and you aren't going to get it, and neither is he, the little bastard. He's just a sniveling coward, always just waiting around for someone else to take care of him and the problems that he creates. I have always had to clean up after him, even when we were kids. Dad would yell and then all he would want to do was hide under a bed somewhere while dad took his anger out on me. Well, that didn't work out for dad too well, did it? DID IT?! He's in a shallow grave down in the holler, now isn't he?"

My blood ran cold.

"I think you will join him there right quick. Sticking your nose in where it didn't belong. Trying to steal from me. You're just like his whore wife. I scared her away for good, along with his screaming brat kids. Her constant bitching and them kids screaming and crying all the time. They gave me a headache, and I'm glad they are gone. He whines about it all the time, boohooing himself to sleep. Won't keep a job. What a loser!"

There was no audible response from Ty, but Max paused as if he was listening to an answer. After about a minute of silence, Max continued on his rant. "That's what I thought. You deserve to be in the ground, and I have the perfect spot in mind."

I knew we couldn't wait for even another second, and apparently, Trent did too. He motioned for me to stay down before jumping into the clearing, gun out and ready for whatever he might find. Amazingly he had remained silent as he pounced into the clearing. Max must have been looking the other way because there was no ruckus at Trent's appearance. I inched my way up the path as far as I could. What I could see in the clearing was beyond frightening. Ty was propped up against a tree, his hands tied behind his back. There was blood running down his forehead, and he appeared to be unconscious. Max was kneeling down in front of him and raising a gun, which was pointed at Ty.

Before I could scream Trent yelled to direct Max's attention away from Ty. "Hey! You don't want to do that!"

Max turned immediately at the sound of Trent's voice, the gun now aimed in Trent's direction. I kept my eyes on Ty, hoping that he would show some sign that he was faking unconsciousness, but he didn't move so much as an eyelid that I could see. The situation had transformed, and now it seemed to be a standoff between Trent and Max. They stood, facing each other, guns leveled and ready to fire.

Finally, Max spoke, "Listen, mister, this doesn't involve you at all. Just turn around and walk away. No harm, no foul. Don't make me kill you too. I'm gonna kill this kid though. Can't let him live after he conspired with that no account brother of mine to steal from me. Just can't do it, so you just walk away."

"I won't do that sir. Just put the gun down, and we will figure this all out. I came here with Ty. He wasn't trying to steal from you, and I have never seen your brother. We are just trying to get out of here. Now lower your gun."

I could see a look of determination in Max's eyes. He leveled the gun more securely, preparing to shoot I thought. I couldn't let any of this happen. I had promised Ty I would have his back. Bonita was already dealing with a brother being shot because I hadn't followed my instincts, she shouldn't have to deal with her husband being shot as well. I would do what I had to do! From my hiding spot, I raised my gun and carefully took aim. I tried to remember what Ty had told me about shooting with accuracy. I needed to aim at the center of... well... Max. I needed to keep both eyes open, and I needed to try to stop my hands from shaking. I took a deep breath. On exhale, I pulled the trigger.

Chapter Eleven

The sound of the gunshot was louder than I remembered it being when Ty had taken me for target practice. Of course, I had been wearing protective earwear then. The shot was loud enough to hurt my ears. My instincts told me to drop the gun and jump back, but I forced myself to keep the gun aimed and focus on Max. I could feel myself starting to panic as I saw Max grab his side in shock. I was going to have another anxiety attack. I was sure of it. I knew I couldn't let that happen so I focused my mind on taking care of Ty like he would me.

Blood appeared on his shirt, spreading under the hand he had placed over the wound. I couldn't shake the feeling of horror that came with the knowledge that I had just shot a man. When Ty wanted to teach me to shoot I had been hesitant. I hadn't thought that it was a skill that I would ever need, but now I had been forced to shoot a man to save Ty. I wasn't going to let myself get trapped in guilt. I knew I needed to keep my focus on Max and Ty. I wanted to see what Trent was doing, but I didn't dare take my eyes from Max.

"Drop the gun. Drop the gun. Please drop the gun," I whispered. The gun was still firmly grasped in the hand that wasn't holding the wound. He scanned the area where I was hidden, but e didn't seem to see me in the brush. He started ranting again.

"A coward hiding in the bushes shot me? You son of a bitch! Now I'm going to have to shoot you too. Since you want to hide like a baby, I guess I'll just start with this one!"

Max started to turn the gun back to Ty, but he had obviously forgotten Trent. By the time I could re-aim and pull the trigger a shot rang out from where Trent stood. Trent was a better shot under pressure than I because Max collapsed to the ground immediately upon impact. Blood started to pool around his head, and I knew that the shot had been a fatal one.

I dropped my gun and ran to where Ty was propped up against the tree. He was unconscious, but the only visible new injury that I could see was the gash in his scalp. There was, what seemed to be, a large amount of blood dripping down Ty's forehead from the wound. I started talking to him, hoping for a response, as I was trying to get his hands untied. Trent kneeled down beside me and put his hand on mine to still them. He took a knife and cut through the ropes holding Ty's hands. We slowly lowered Ty to the ground and I began examining the wound on his head.

His poor body was already covered with scrapes, bruises, and cuts from his run-in with the landslide, I thought, and now he had a massive gash in his head. "Is he okay? Do you think he's okay? Why isn't he waking up?"

"Well, his breathing seems to be good, and his pulse is strong. I don't have the medical experience that Bonita has, but I did see some injuries when I was deployed. I think if we give him a few minutes he'll be back with us. Keep talking to him."

"Do you think that it would be okay to lift his head?"

"I think so."

I lifted Ty's head and sat it on my lap. I continued to talk to him, increasing my volume, hoping that he could hear me on some level. I spoke to him about how sorry I was to have left him. I begged him to wake up. I could look right into his eyes but still saw no movement from him at all. I looked up to Trent questioningly, and he told me to just keep talking. I looked up at the sky trying to find strength but what I saw there caused more panic. My voice reflected my increasing anxiety when I started speaking to Ty again.

"Ty, you have to wake up, and you have to do it now! There are more and more rocks falling around us. You have to get us to the shelter. I can't get there without you. I need you to wake up. Do you hear me? I NEED you NOW!!"

I don't know if it was the panic in my voice or something else, but Ty's eyes began to flutter. He moaned in pain and lifted his hand to his head before he opened his eyes. After another low moaning sound, he opened his eyes. I could tell he was confused even before he spoke.

"Wha...What happened?"

He looked questioningly up at me and then shifted his gaze to Trent. I saw a glimmer of concern cross Trent's face before he responded.

"We were kind of hoping that you could tell us."

Ty struggled to sit up, groaning and holding his head. He looked around the clearing, saw Max's body, looked at me and said. "I don't remember. Did I kill him?"

"No, when we got here he was ranting and raving. It was just a bunch of crazy talk. He and I were in a standoff and then Elli shot him. When he moved again, I shot him again. He must have hit you or something because you were out cold and have a big gash in your head. I don't mean to rush you, but we do need to move, quickly. Conditions seem to be rapidly deteriorating. I really don't want to push you but you know the urgency we are facing, and I have a family to think of."

I started to protest. I wanted to say that Ty needed a minute or two at least so we could make sure he was alright, but I knew that Trent was right. We needed to get out of there. Ty got a determined look on his face then held a hand out to Trent to be helped up. I knew that he must be really in pain and struggling because, under normal circumstances, he would not ask for help.

Trent took Ty's hand and helped him to his feet. Ty was wobbly on his feet for just a moment before squaring his shoulders. It only took that moment for him to be ready to go. I didn't look back as we walked away from the clearing. I didn't want to see the body that was lying there again. I couldn't believe that I had shot a man. Had I really shot a man?

∞ ∞ ∞

We made our way back down the trail as quickly as we could considering Ty's condition. He insisted he was fine, but his face was pale and pain reflected in his eyes. A few times I asked him if he needed to stop for a moment, but he was very insistent that we push forward. He continually looked to the sky which inevitably forced him to try to increase his pace. I saw him tense with each step, but still, he kept on going.

The trip down the path seemed to take much less time than the trip up had. We weren't nearly as cautious as we trampled our way noisily down the hillside. When we arrived at the spot where we had left Bonita and Brandon, I immediately noticed that Max's truck was gone. I also saw that more fires had popped up on the horizon. There was even a small fire burning in the field just beyond the road. The impacts were getting dangerously close to where we were.

As we turned to head down the road and back to our trucks I asked, "Are these falling rocks getting closer or is it just me? Is there some way to avoid them or is it literally just hit or miss?"

Ty chuckled at my question, and I knew he was going to be okay. "Sorry babe, it's hit or miss. I think it's unlikely that one will hit us directly, but if they don't lighten up, they are definitely going to affect our travel."

Ty picked up his pace, yet again, and soon he was jogging down the road, with Trent and I following closely behind him. Even being hit over the head and almost killed by a lunatic couldn't seem to slow him down.

We quickly made our way back around the curve in the road, and I could finally see our trucks. Sarah was running around one of the trucks playing with Max's dog. I guessed we would probably have another companion to bring with us now, as she didn't look like she would be willingly parting with him anytime soon. Bonita and Brandon seemed to be going through the things that had been stuffed into Max's truck, most seemed to be piled outside of the truck now. They had a small pile of items sitting on the ground near them, and when Bonita saw us, she began picking up things and tossing them in their truck.

Bonita had everything, including Sarah and the dog, in their truck by the time we got there, and she was quickly at our side with her ever-present medical bag. While she looked at Ty's head Trent explained to her what had happened and Ty's condition when we found him. She looked into Ty's eyes and ears and then continued by asking him a few generic questions about how he was feeling or any specific discomfort he might be experiencing. Bonita quickly declared that it was highly likely that Ty was suffering from a concussion and stated that she would quickly stitch up the wound before we got on our way. Ty tried to argue, but she quickly shut him down and grabbed the necessary supplies from her bag.

I really couldn't stomach the thought of watching her put a needle in Ty's head, so I turned to speak with Brandon. He seemed to be fine now, but I asked him to be sure.

"Brandon, are you alright? Is your arm okay?"

"Oh yeah, it's nothing but a little scratch. No worries." I knew it was more than a scratch as he had a relatively large bandage wrapped around his arm. "Bonita took good care of me. I'm good as new. How's your boyfriend?"

"I think he'll be okay. He got hit on the head, and he was unconscious when we found him. Max was going to, well, he was going to shoot him. He was talking crazy again. We had to shoot him. He's dead. Ty has a big gash on his head. Bonita said he probably has a concussion. She's going to stitch him up and then we need to get out of her. It's starting to look like the sky is falling, and no I'm not Chicken Little."

Brandon laughed, patted me on the arm and told me Ty would be alright with Bonita looking after him. After talking to Brandon, I walked over to the truck to check on Jules. I felt guilty because I hadn't thought of her since we took off to find Sarah. I couldn't seem to focus on the many different things that I needed to while the world falling apart. I peeked in the window and saw that Jules was lying in exactly the same place and position that Brandon had put her in. Usually, I would worry, but I could see the rise and fall of her chest indicating smooth, even breaths.

I silently leaned my forehead forward and rested it against the truck. The metal was refreshing and felt cold against my skin. I knew that everything that just happened was going to catch up with me sooner or later. Sarah had almost been stolen, Ty had nearly been killed, and I had shot a man, a man who just yesterday I had felt sorry for. I had even made Ty take him food. Yes, he was batshit crazy, but he was still a living, breathing human. Even if I hadn't fired the shot that killed him in a way I was still responsible for his death. Did he have a wife and kids, like his alter ego was ranting about? Was he trying to get back to them or was he really just a lunatic?

I was trying to hold back the inevitable tears when I heard someone approaching. Before I could pull myself together and turn around to see who it was, I felt Ty's arms close around me. He pulled my back against his chest and held me tight. He knew I needed him to comfort me and here he was. I took a deep breath and let myself shed a few tears before I turned in his arms to face him. He tipped my chin up, and in a very Ty manner, leaned down and gently kissed me.

"Thank you for saving me," he whispered.

"But I... it was Trent. I didn't... I didn't aim accurately enough. He was still going to shoot you."

"You saved me. I don't care what you say or who fired which shot. You were brave enough to shoot when I needed you to. You saved me." He kissed me again, more deeply this time.

"Well," I whispered, "I said I would have your back. You need to stop sending me away so I can keep that promise. Do you understand now that you aren't invincible? We need each other. Got it?"

Ty looked into my eyes deeply and nodded. "I've got it. I promise."

Chapter Twelve

It took a few minutes to convince Ty that he couldn't be the driver, and once we got him set up in the navigator's seat we were able to be on our way. Brandon took over the task of driving our truck, while I sat in the backseat to keep an eye on Jules. She wasn't much of a risk in her current condition and Bonita was sure that she wouldn't be an issue anytime soon.

Brandon's arm was fine, according to Bonita. It wasn't his dominant arm and, other than some mild pain, he was good to drive and do whatever else he needed to do. I think we were all still in a bit of shock over someone trying to take Sarah and as a result, we were all on edge. For me, at least, it seemed that now that I had faced things that would typically be completely impossible I had developed a new awareness of just how very real and serious the situation was. Yes, Ty had been telling me that it was severe and that people would begin to behave in ways that would otherwise seem unbelievable. When he had made the comment, I thought I understood, but in reality, there was no way that I could have. Once people figured out just how bad things had become and how much worse things were going to get, they would do anything to survive. Anything. It wouldn't matter if it hurt or even killed someone else. If the action had benefit to them and their survival they would do it.

I had heard it said once that when things went wrong, the worst people were always right there, ready and waiting to take advantage of everyone else. Without anyone to deter them the criminals, pedophiles, murderers, and other evil people would start to take over. Areas with a high population would probably become very dangerous for regular, law-abiding citizens. I suddenly became very thankful that we were not at home in Columbus. I was grateful that my family had been convinced to leave as well. If we survived this journey to the shelter, they would be there too. If we could get away from all of these crazy people, I would have my family with me through this journey.

Brandon knew all the area streets and was able to travel along them more quickly than Ty could have done. He drove fast, but safely, and was proactive in watching the roads ahead to make sure that we weren't driving into a big hole or fire left by one of the rocks that were hurtling to the earth. I looked at the sky and was a bit relieved to see that the number of meteorites there was remarkably less than it had been just a few moments ago.

"So," I commented aloud, "it looks like the meteorites seem to be decreasing in number. Can I hope that this is finally something good?"

Ty took a moment to look at the sky before answering. "It does appear as if there are significantly fewer meteorites entering the atmosphere. Hopefully, that means that we have made our way through the debris field, or whatever it was. That, in and of itself, would be a good thing but the more time that passes before we get to the cabin the harder it's going to be. It looks to me as if the sky is becoming even more overcast. Soon the sunlight won't be able to get through all of the crap in the air at all. The smoke from all of these new fires will not help that. We need to move and hope that we make it before that happens."

Brandon seemed to push the accelerator further down at Ty's words, and we picked up some speed. Soon we were off the access road and driving down smooth, paved, county roads. We were still driving through the hills, but they were growing bigger and bigger with each passing mile. I was still nervous about driving through the mountains, but I knew it was necessary. I tried to stay as calm as I possibly could. I noticed that the number of fires that I could see in the distance also seemed to be fewer than what we had initially been able to see. I wondered if perhaps we had just been in a high impact area at the time.

Brandon and Ty were talking quietly in the front seat about what had happened and what we might expect as we got closer to our destination. Brandon started asking questions about what might have happened and what the future might bring. Ty answered his questions honestly and frankly. I loved to listen to his voice, even if the subject matter was distressing, but this time my mind began to wander. I must have drifted off because the sound of squealing tires and cussing from the front seat took me entirely by surprise.

In shock by the sudden stop and yelling, I jumped up to try to see what was going on. We were on a country road with no structures of any kind in sight. Mountains surrounded us, but it didn't feel as closed in as it had before. The road was wider than the one we had been traveling on before, and there was a good berm on the side opposite the mountain. I scanned the way ahead, and that's when I saw what had caused our abrupt stop.

Ahead of us, blocking the road, were a group of military vehicles. There appeared to be a variety of types. The troop transport trucks had multiple soldiers milling around beside them, and other vehicles had visible weapons which seemed to be positioned to deter traffic progression. I was sure that they had seen us. There was no way that they hadn't. Why were they here? Why weren't they heading west like the other military group that we had seen? We all sat in silence, simply staring ahead of us at the military blockade. Apparently, neither Brandon or Ty knew what to say any more than I did. The sound of the walkie seemed to pull us all out of our trance. It was Trent's voice that we heard this time.

"So, this is not the best thing for us to run in to. Any ideas?"

Ty picked up the walkie to respond. "Well, they've obviously seen us, so turning around probably isn't the best option. Not to mention, how much time we would lose backtracking? I think the only option we have is to go forward and try to talk our way through. Elli and I have already done this once today. Bonita, don't share your medical experience. I don't know if they are looking for involuntary volunteers or what."

"Alright, proceed slowly and with caution," Trent replied.

Brandon put the truck back into drive, and we slowly approached the military caravan. Two soldiers in camo stepped in front of a makeshift barricade at our approach. They were armed and appeared ready to use their weapons if it became necessary. Brandon let the truck roll to a stop at a non-threatening distance from the barricade. No one made a move to get out of the truck, delaying the inevitable. Finally, Trent's voice sounded over the walkie again.

"Why don't ya'all let me get out and talk to these good men. Me being a veteran might help us out, you never know."

After Ty responded, I saw Trent's truck door open. He stepped out confidently and made his way to where the soldiers stood. His hands were visible and hung loosely at his sides. Ty and Brandon both opened their windows, hoping to hear Trent's conversation, I'm sure. We weren't parked close enough to the barricade to catch the actual words, but we could try to interpret from the tone of the voices and the body language of those talking. Trent remained relaxed, and the two soldiers speaking with him appeared to relax slightly but remained guarded. Trent looked back to the trucks and then turned back to focus on the soldiers once again.

The conversation lasted for a few minutes before Trent turned and walked back to the trucks. When he was gone, one of the soldiers turned and walked to a Humvee parked on the other side of the vehicles which were blocking the road. Trent walked up to the driver's side window and leaned in.

"Friendly young men, but very serious about their orders. They are supposed to enforce the shelter in place. People who are attempting to travel west are being taken to government established shelters. I think that, for the most part, they are trying to stop people who are attempting to get west to family members. I'm trying to convince them that we are on our way to somewhere safe to shelter in place and that we are not trying to travel much further west. I explained our situation, without sharing specifics, and they went to talk to their Captain."

I looked back to the Humvee and saw the door open. I saw a tan combat boot emerge from the interior of the vehicle. The boot was followed by a camo covered leg and, finally, an entire army officer stepped out from the vehicle. He was tall, and I saw short dark hair before he secured his hat into its proper place. The guys were still talking in the front seat, so no one but me noticed the officer step out and start our way. When he got to the barricade, he paused for a moment and seemed to look quizzically at Ty's truck. He spoke briefly to the soldiers standing there, and the three that followed him, and then headed, alone, towards us. His walk was familiar, and there was something about the way he carried himself that gave me a reason to pause.

"Umm, guys..." I figured that I should alert them to his approach.

They paused in their conversation, and all turned to look at me. I nodded my head towards the barricade, and they all directed their attention out the front window. I watched Ty study the officer approaching. His eyes widened, and he jumped out of the truck, taking off in a sprint towards the officer. It only took a moment for me to figure out why. Walking toward us was not just an army officer, it was Trevor.

I hadn't seen Ty's older brother in a few years. Trevor was eight years older than Ty. Cousins by birth, Trevor was the biological son of Edward, Mr. Robins's older brother. Edward had worked for the CIA, and when he died, he had been assigned to a U.S. embassy abroad. He died during a terrorist bombing. Trevor was six when his father died. After the attack, life became difficult for Trevor and his mother. Edward's wife, Suzann, struggled with the loss of her husband and subsequently suffered a miscarriage caused by the extreme stress of losing her husband. She sank into a deep depression, and within a year of Edward's murder, she committed suicide leaving Trevor a true orphan.

Although Trevor was about eight when Ty was born, he had been living with Tom and Dawn for over a year. They had finalized the legal adoption of him, and for all intents and purposes, he was their son. Trevor and Ty had been close from day one. Ty had missed him horribly, first when he went off to college and then when he joined the Army to go fight what he described as the monsters who had murdered his father.

My father had once explained to me when we were discussing Ty's dad that Edward's death had awakened something in Tom. Before his brother died, Tom had been a carefree, fun-loving guy. After the terrorist attack that killed his brother, the doomsday prepping had begun. Then the 9-11 attack occurred, and things got even worse. Tom had taken his knowledge and beliefs and turned them into a very lucrative career. He had been careful to raise his sons with caution and an understanding that things could go very wrong at any time. Trevor had taken that belief and knowledge, as well as a hatred for the terrorists who had killed his father and a love of country, and made a career in the military. Ty had also always talked about going into the military. He'd wanted to be a Seal, but it seemed that the doomsday that his father had worried about had come before he could fulfill that goal.

I pulled myself from my reverie, jumped out of the truck and took off running. Ty and Trevor were embracing in the middle of the road ahead of me. I could see the soldiers waiting at the barricade, watching the brother's reunion unfold with looks of extreme confusion on their faces.

"Elli," I heard Trevor exclaim. He picked me up in a big, tight hug. "Well, I'll be damned. Look at you! You went and grew up into a beautiful young lady while I was off playing soldier. I can't believe you two are here. I've been hoping and praying."

He sat me gently back on my feet before turning back to Ty. "So what exactly are you two doing out here in the mountains of North Carolina?"

"We were on our way for a post-graduation beach trip."

"Man, I am so sorry I missed your graduation. I couldn't get leave. You know we just got back from deployment a few days ago."

"I know, and it's alright. I know you would have been there if there was any way that you possibly could have been. Anyway, we spent last night camping at Pilot Mountain. We were there when the news broke. I was able to get a call out to dad, and we are supposed to meet him, mom and Elli's family at the cabin. Well, that is if you all let us through. You know how bad things are going to go soon. How much information do you have?"

"Not as much as you would think," Trevor replied, his voice laced with annoyance. "Probably not much more than you do really, perhaps even less. We know that a giant rock hit the west coast. It was centralized somewhere around Los Angeles. We've lost contact with everything west of the Mississippi River. Initially, they were sending troops west for civilian support. However, now we are getting orders to ensure that civilians are sheltering in place and if they try to move west we are to escort them to shelters that have been established by the government. I'm glad you've talked to the folks. Do you know for sure that they got out of the city?"

"The last word we had came from mom, and she said that they were heading south. I hope that indicates that they got out of the city."

"Probably, I think that she would have said something about the city if they hadn't. Dad would know how hard it would be to get out of the city after the order to shelter in place was issued. So what is he saying? How bad is it really?"

"It's really bad. Other than radiation, I think we should expect to experience everything Dad always described would happen after a major impact event. The earthquakes have already happened, and, if you haven't noticed, it's becoming very overcast. I don't think we have much time before the sunlight can't get through the haze at all."

Trevor looked up and examined the hazy skies then completed Ty's thoughts. "Temperatures will begin to drop rapidly. The grid will go down and stay down. People won't have food, heat or any of the basic necessities of life. All of my men have families at home. We were supposed to be on leave starting today. Just twelve more hours and we would have been off base."

"So what are you going to do?" I asked him. I couldn't believe that the military would just leave them out here. Someone in power had to know what was really going on.

"I have some higher ranking contacts. I need to make some calls. Before I do, tell me who your companions are."

Ty explained to Trevor how Bonita, Trent, Sarah, and Brandon had come to join us, also mentioning that Jules was in the truck. "Ben was with us, but during one of the earthquakes, there was a landslide. He didn't make it."

"Damn, I'm sorry. Ken?"

"Ken and his girlfriend were supposed to meet us at the beach house. I talked to him right after I talked to dad this morning. I told him to meet us at the cabin if he could."

Trevor nodded solemnly. "Well, you go back up and bring the trucks down here. I'll have my guys let you through. I know that time is of the essence but give me just a bit of it, alright? Pull your trucks to the other side of the barricade and wait. There are other squads out on these roads too, and I need to figure out a way to get you to the cabin without further military interference."

We headed to the trucks and saw that everyone except for Jules was standing outside waiting. Sarah was playing with the dog again, while Bonita stood nearby keeping a close eye on her. I could hear Sarah's childish, singsong voice lecturing the dog about being good and not wandering away. Brandon and Trent were whispering, but when we walked up, they looked at us expectantly.

"So, that's my older brother," Ty explained. The surprise in his voice was unmistakable.

"Finally, a little bit of good luck it seems," I added. We went on to explain that Trevor wanted us to drive down and through the barricade, but that we were to wait there for further information. "Trevor thinks we will have issues getting through the mountains to where we need to go without running into more troops."

Everyone climbed back in the trucks, except Bonita and Sarah, who said they would rather walk down with the dog. We made our way to the barricade, and when we got close enough, the soldiers pulled the barrier aside so we could pull through. One of the trucks blocking the road was moved so that we could also make our way to the other side of their vehicles. The soldiers all watched us curiously as we parked and hopped back out of our trucks. It all felt very awkward, and I was anxious to be back on our way. I was ecstatic to have come across Trevor, but delays could be costly it seemed. I knew that Ty and Trevor understood this, probably better than any of us, but I really just wanted to get to the cabin before anything else went wrong or before someone else got hurt.

I could hear Sarah's voice singing a happy tune as she and Bonita approached. All of the soldiers milling around seemed to stop what they were doing and watch her as she happily made her way past them. She ran to her father, who lifted her into the air and spun her around and around. Her giggle was like sunlight breaking through clouds after days filled with nothing but unrelenting rain. It gave me a little bit of hope for the future in a moment when I had very little hope or optimism left for anything. Sarah's smile was radiant as she spun, experiencing nothing but pure joy in the moment. She wasn't afraid because she was leaving her home, or because some stranger had tried to kidnap her, she was just happy to be alive and spinning. I was mesmerized by the sight. It was the sound of Bonita's voice that pulled me back to reality.

"It's a beautiful thing to see isn't it?" I looked at her inquisitively. "Childish innocence. It's a shame that we don't get to keep it in some form. The world is falling apart around her, and she is euphoric to just spin in the cool air with her daddy. I could use a little bit of that feeling and joy about right now."

"Me too," I said looking at her. I heard Sarah squeal in delight as the dog danced around Trent's feet barking. "Me too."

∞ ∞ ∞

We had waited longer than I was comfortable with by the time Trevor came and found us. Everyone else just seemed to be casually waiting, but I was sitting on a rock, chewing on my fingernails. Ty and Brandon were in a conversation with some of the soldiers. Sarah, Trent, and Bonita were sitting on the ground playing with the dog. It was good to be out of the car, but I knew how urgently we needed to move on, and I couldn't get past that.

I jumped up when I saw Trevor coming. My sudden action must have caught Ty's attention because he turned to where I looked to see Trevor as well. Everyone's conversations seemed to stop as Trevor made his way to where we had all gathered.

"I was able to make contact with my commanding officer. You just got yourself a military escort. I need to address my squad, and then we can saddle up and be on our way." Trevor's second in command had gathered all the soldiers except for the two who were left to man the barricade, and they all stood looking raptly at Trevor. It was strange to me to see him in such a commanding position.

"At ease. I spoke with Major Rosney, and the situation is dire. Normally this information would be classified, but our choices at this point can make the difference between life and death. The west coast is presumed to be a total loss at this point. This is a catastrophic event unlike any that our government has planned for, and they believe that the effects of this event will be experienced on a global level. As far as the Major knows our government has had no contact with other countries at this point. The grid will go down, probably very soon. On top of that, we will start experiencing atmospheric changes. All of these particles in the air are going to block the sunlight. It's going to get cold, and that's going to happen quickly. I want you all to understand this perfectly. They are not planning to widely share this information, but the major and I go way back. He knows my background, so he knows that I understand the situation better than most. The government doesn't want to start hysteria, so this information is considered classified. As of right now, this unit is on leave. I am sure you all know that public communication systems are down. They will not be brought back up. If you want to go home to your families, please do so with the utmost haste. I would recommend that everyone do so. On a personal note, get your families and then find someplace warm and safe. Gather as much food as you can and make sure that where ever you are you can keep it warm while the grid is down. The grid will be down for a long time. Once the civilian population figures out how bad it is, and that the government cannot save or help them, things are going to get really bad very quickly. Having a way to protect yourself will be another major concern. I will be going with my brother, Ty, and if anyone does not have a family to go home to you are welcome to join us. Time is of the essence, so you are dismissed. It has been my honor to serve with you all."

Most of the men headed to the transport vehicles and climbed in, ready to be on their way as quickly as possible. A few of the soldiers stepped forward to shake Trevor's hand and thank him. Within just a few minutes, when the dust had settled, we were left with a Humvee and three soldiers. Introductions were swiftly made, and I tried to assign to memory that Brian was short with dark hair. He appeared young and a bit less confident than the other soldiers. Jeff was a ginger with a very light complexion. He looked somewhat rough around the edges. Jim was Trevor's second in command. He was taller than the other two, but not nearly as tall as Ty and Trevor. He had dark hair that looked like it would curl if it were allowed to grow at all.

"Alright, we'll lead the way in the Humvee so I can get us through any other roadblocks that we might come across. Hopefully, we can make quick work of this drive. I don't like the look of the sky. It's gotten much worse in just this short period of time. Saddle up!"

Once again we were on our way, this time with another truck and four more people. Trevor joining our group would take some of the responsibility from Ty's shoulders, and I hoped that he would be able to get some relief from all of the pressure that he had been feeling. I couldn't even begin to imagine what was going through his mind and how much worry and stress he was dealing with trying to figure out how to get us safely to the shelter.

I wondered if we would be an entire caravan by the time we got to the shelter. The Humvee led as we wove our way into even higher mountains. I could see beauty in the mountain scenery, despite the ever darkening skies. Neither the fires or their smoke were visible anymore and wondered if they had, in fact, been centralized to the area where we had happened to be at the time.

Jules was still out cold. Brandon and Ty were talking about Trevor, which gave my mind time to wander. I tried to avoid the thought of everything that we were going to be losing and focus instead on the blessings that we had compared to others. I tried really hard to not think about the peppermint hot chocolate that I wouldn't be able to run down to the coffee shop to pick up on those days when I felt like I had earned a treat. I remembered all the caramels I had grabbed at the little market, and it made me smile. I couldn't believe that I had been happily watching an eagle soar such a short time ago. It felt like days had passed not just hours. I had been utterly unaware that anything could possibly happen to change our world in such a drastic way. We had lost so much since then, but we had gained some things as well.

The miles passed quickly with the Humvee in the lead and an hour on the road flew by. The streets we traveled on were paved and well maintained, but they were obviously not main streets. We had to be making progress, and I wondered how close we were getting to the cabin. I leaned forward and posed the question to Ty.

"Well, I don't know this route that Trevor is taking but judging from the map I would say that we are less than an hour from the cabin." He turned to show me about where we were on the map. "We should be going down into this valley soon and then we will weave back around and end up near Paint Rock, just a bit away from the French Broad River." He pointed to a spot up in the hills beyond the mountains. "We will be in this area."

The area looked remote, nestled in the mountains on the border of Tennessee. I sat back in my seat and tried to remember what Ty had told me about their family trips to the cabin throughout the years. He had mostly shared stories of hunting, fishing, and hiking, always talking about how it was his peaceful place. He had promised that he would take me there someday. I guess now he was, just not under the circumstances that either of us had ever imagined.

When the road that we were traveling on intersected with a state route, we came across another group of soldiers. Ty explained that we needed to travel on the state route as a part of the final leg of our journey. This group had their barricade set up the same as Trevor's had been. This squad seemed a bit bigger than Trevor's. There were more vehicles parked behind the obstacles and increased number of soldiers both manning the roadblock and standing around. When I mentioned this, Ty explained that the intersection was commonly used and probably required an increased military presence as a deterrent.

The Humvee in front of us came to a stop, and I saw Trevor get out and walk to the barricade. The soldiers standing there saluted and after a few words were exchanged one left, returning a few moments later with an officer. Trevor spoke to the other officer for a few moments before shaking his hand and returning to the Humvee. The barricades were parted, and we were all allowed to pull through. I saw the officer speaking to his men as we progressed through the area and, before they were out of my sight, I saw them all climbing into their transports. As quick as that, Trevor had given another group of men a fighting chance of survival.

Once through the barricade, Trevor picked up speed, flying down the road like a man on a mission. I guess in a way we were all on a mission, one to save our lives. We didn't see any other traffic on the road, and none of the houses that we passed showed any signs of life. Eventually, Trevor turned off the state route, and we were back to traveling side roads. Houses were sparse. The streets made their way through rolling hills and were lined with trees. I wondered what it had been like to live here before life as we knew it had stopped. With the hazy skies, I couldn't clearly see the landscape, but I was willing to bet money that it was inspiring.

After about another thirty minutes on the road conditions began to rapidly decline. Soon it was as dark as night. We were driving with our headlights on in the early afternoon. Our speeds had reduced, but we still seemed to be making good time. It was also becoming evident that the temperatures were beginning to drop. I was dressed comfortably, having changed into jeans and a tee before we left the campsite that morning, but I was suddenly getting chilly.

"It's getting colder," I commented.

Ty turned to look at me, worry on his face. "Babe, if you reach into the space behind you'll find one of my hoodies. Put that on. There is also a blanket, grab it and throw it over Jules. I was hoping we would have more time before it happened, but it seems like the temperature drop is going to be more rapid than I anticipated."

"I didn't pack any clothes for cold temperatures. I packed bikinis. I am so not prepared for this life."

Ty laughed a little. "I would love to see you in those bikinis babe, but you're right. We probably aren't going to have bikini weather for a while. Don't worry we have artic wear at the cabin. It'll keep you warm. When you aren't wearing the artic wear, I'll keep you warm."

I grabbed Ty's hoodie and pulled it over my head. It smelled like him, and that made me smile. Once I was ensconced comfortably in the hoodie, I covered Jules with the blanket that had also been tucked behind the seat. Ty was always prepared for everything, I thought. I was lucky to have him in my life, especially while the world was falling apart.

"So, in some parts of Alaska they go for more than two months without sunlight is that what life is going to be like for us now?" I asked.

"Well, kind of," Ty replied. "We aren't going to see sunlight for quite a while, probably longer than the two months that they have to wait. Then it will transition back to hazy. It's going to take some time to get all of that crap out of the atmosphere."

At this point, I could only distinguish the shadows of buildings and trees as we drove past them. Trevor led our caravan onto a gravel, country road and we began to wind our way up into the mountains again. I thought I caught a glimpse of the river that Ty had mentioned. We drove through a small village, and I could only describe the scene as eerie. It was like we had driven onto some alternate universe, horror movie set. The houses and businesses were all completely dark. There wasn't a burning candle or a light of any sort visible as far as the eye could see. The air all around us and the sky above were more than hazy now. They had turned into an ever darkening grey. If this were a horror movie, evil could be lurking around any corner, but then again I guess it could be in this new world I lived in as well.

"Where did the people go?" I wondered aloud.

"I'm not sure. Maybe they decided as a group to go to a shelter? They are pretty isolated out here. Perhaps they were forced to evacuate to a larger area. It does seem odd, but I'm not sure where everyone is. It could also be that someone around here has an underground shelter and a little bit of knowledge. They could be worried about radiation or something else and have sheltered. I hope that it's as simple as that."

Chapter Thirteen

We made it quickly through the small village without incident. After driving a few miles, Trevor slowed the Humvee to a stop. He got out and made his way back to our truck. I looked back and saw Trent get out and join Trevor at the window. When Brandon put the window down the colder air rushed into the truck.

"In the interest of getting there as quickly as possible, I'm going to make this short and sweet. We are getting very close. Something in this area seems off to me though. I would still expect to see some signs of life, but everyone seems to be gone. We are going to proceed from here on out by using the utmost caution. We need eyes everywhere so keep your eyes open for even the slightest anomaly."

Everyone quickly agreed, and we were rapidly back on our way. In about a mile we turned off the road onto a path that I would never have guessed was designed for motor vehicle travel. It was very bumpy and dark. I had no clue how Trevor could see where he needed to go, instinct perhaps. We seemed to climb up the mountain, and at some point, the path led us into a small valley. I saw the headlights reflect off the windows of a house and wondered if we had finally made it.

Trevor and the other soldiers stepped out of the Humvee, looking every inch ready for battle. I took off Ty's hoodie and gave it to him before he stepped out to join them. I could hear the trucks idling, but beyond that, the world was eerily silent. Once Ty and the others moved past the circle of light cast by the truck's headlights I was unable to see them. After a minute a single, small beam of light appeared. I watched it bounce around from here to there as the group made their way around the area, cautiously and relatively slowly. I understood the need to act prudently and tried to wait patiently. I was anxious to get out of the truck and be somewhere that felt somewhat normal, somewhere that made me feel safe if that was even possible in this world. Waiting was one of the most challenging things I had ever had to do. The light disappeared after a while, and I wondered where they had gone.

Finally, when I couldn't stand the quiet anymore, I started asking Brandon questions. "Where do you think they went? Do you think everything is alright or is something wrong? They've been gone so long."

"I know it feels like it has been forever, but in reality, it's been," Brandon looked at his watch, "ten minutes. Caution is necessary, and I am sure they are safe and simply making sure that the area is secure. This new world isn't safe, as I am sure you have realized in the past few hours. This type of shelter is at a premium right now, and it can be the difference between life and death. If anyone who knew about this shelter was in closer proximity to it than us, they could have come here trying to lay claim before we got here. So before everyone goes in, they are making sure it's safe."

"I understand," I replied. "If they really thought they might find something you and Trent should have gone with them. They'll need all the help they can get."

"Trent and I need to stay out here and make sure that you, Jules, Bonita, and Sarah are safe. We also need to make sure that no one sneaks up on Ty and the guys from behind because they weren't able to figure out how to get in." Brandon turned to look at me from the driver's seat. He had a knowing smirk on his face. "I'd say that they are okay and able to handle themselves well. Four of them are well-trained soldiers and your boyfriend is pretty proficient himself for whatever reason."

Talking to Brandon seemed to relieve some of my anxiety. "Trevor and Ty's dad is a prepper. He raised them both to believe that an apocalyptic or catastrophic event was inevitable. They both understand the ins and outs of possible scenarios and what they would need to do if one of them happened. They both trained with firearms from a young age. Their dad made sure that they were well prepared for any and every possible challenge that they might run in to."

"Well, thank God he prepared them. So have you been to this shelter before?"

"No. It was usually a guy trip or a family trip. His family would come up here for vacations a couple of times a year. Of course, their vacations mostly consisted of working on the shelter. It may look just like a cabin, not like we can see it now, but it's so much more than just a log cabin. At least that is what Ty has told me."

"Ty told us there was enough room for all of us, is that true?"

"I think so, and for the record, Ty is very truthful by nature. He told me that there are multiple cabins that are connected somehow and that they have stockpiled enough resources that we will be okay for quite a while."

"Good, considering its early afternoon and black as midnight out here. Worse, actually if you think about it. In the dark of night, you can see stars and the moon, but you can't see any of that now. Who knows when we will see them again."

"I think that the shelter even has something that simulates sunlight so we can grow some crops. Ty's dad made a living helping other people learn how to prep. He has the best of everything here, not to mention anything and everything that he thought they might possibly need."

"I, for one, am glad that he did," Brandon said with a big smile. "I am also eternally grateful that you and Ty decided to stop at Trent's gas station and were kind enough to invite my family to join you, even after we tricked you a little bit."

"Well, it wasn't entirely an altruistic gesture," I replied. "Don't get me wrong, if this place had the means to support everyone I would have brought everyone we could have along the way. Unfortunately, we couldn't. When we stopped at that gas station we really just wanted to see if we could get any more current information. Trent and Bonita have some valuable skills though."

"And I was just a bonus! I have valuable skills of my own I'll have you know," Brandon laughed.

I was trying to come up with a witty reply when all of the sudden light exploded from the direction of where I thought the cabin might be. My eyes had grown used to the darkness, and I found that I had to blink rapidly so I could focus and clear the white spots that were suddenly popping up in my field of vision. When I could finally see clearly, I saw a large, beautiful, log cabin directly in front of where we were parked. It was a sight for sore eyes. It looked like a home, with a sprawling front porch that featured multiple white rocking chairs.

When I saw Ty walked out onto the front porch, I released a giant sigh of relief. I wanted to get out and run to him but made myself wait until he came for me, just in case. I watched and waited for the others to follow him out but the door shut behind him. Ty walked up to the driver's side window, and Brandon rolled it down so Ty could lean in and talk.

"Everything appears as it should be. I'm going to get in the Humvee and lead everyone around to the other entrance. We'll all be able to pull the vehicles in there. Just follow me."

I wasn't sure what the temperature was, but it was colder than it had been last night as we sat around the campfire. I watched Ty jog up to the Humvee and jump in. Within a minute we were following him as he made his way off the very camouflaged trail, which circled away from the cabin. Ty slowly made his way behind and away from the cabin, appearing to head straight for the side of the mountain. I could not for the life of me figure out where he was going.

Brandon must have been wondering the same thing because he whispered under his breathe, "Where in the hell is this kid going?"

Ty appeared to pull the Humvee right up against the mountain. Once there he just waited. I had no idea what was going on. Didn't he say he was taking us to a different entrance to the cabin? I was about to say something when heard a growling sort of noise, followed by a glowing emanating from cracks that had appeared on the mountain. What in the, I thought. I didn't need to say it aloud, Brandon did it for me again.

It appeared as if a considerable portion of the mountainside was just disappearing, revealing a ginormous cavern. Ty pulled the Humvee inside, and we all followed suit. We were able to fit all the vehicles into the area without even making much of a dent in the amount of available space. Once we were all inside the door began to close, and I turned to watch. On the outside, it had just looked like a part of the hillside, but inside it looked like a giant garage door that just happened to open by sliding to the side rather than being pulled up.

Ty got out of the Humvee and made his way back to his truck where I still sat, in awe of the sheer size of this hidden cavern. He opened the passenger side door so I could get out. When I finally got my feet back on the ground, he grabbed me up into a big, tight hug.

"We did it," he whispered in my ear. "We finally made it here. Thank you for helping me, for having faith in me. There were a few times that I wasn't sure we would ever actually get here."

After a quick kiss, he released me from the hug. I took a moment to look around. The room, if that is what you would call it, was even bigger than I had initially thought. Multiple tunnels were leading out of the area, and I wondered where they might go. Boxes were piled here and there, not at all randomly, and there was an area to one side where Trevor and his soldiers had all gathered. As we walked towards them, I realized that Trevor was sitting at a desk and there were multiple monitors mounted on the wall around him. There was a laptop, and Trevor was typing away.

"So this," Trevor explained as we all walked up, "is the command center, so to speak. We have cameras set up in not so random locations, as well as at each cabin. From here we can access each camera so that we can have remote eyes on the entire area. We can also monitor all of the systems from here and make sure that everything is operating as it should be."

Trent seemed particularly interested in the systems, and Trevor happily explained them all. I half listened as he talked about water collection and delivery systems, a wide variety of power sources, communication systems, and security systems. It wasn't that I wasn't interested in the systems that would keep us safe and able to survive, rather that I just didn't really understand all of the technical details that Trevor was sharing.

"This is an amazing setup," Trent said as he looked at the controls and monitors.

"Thanks, Dad really knows what he's doing when it comes to preparing for the worst. He tested anything he might recommend to a client before he made a recommendation. If it worked well and was a quality product, we have it here. He made provisions for almost every possible catastrophic scenario. I'm sure there is something that couldn't be prepared for, but I don't know what it would be. We have the supplies to support ourselves at max capacity for years, and we won't be at max capacity. We have air filtration systems and the ability to simulate sunlight so we can grow crops for fresh food. By the end of the day, we will also have life stock safely ensconced in their indoor simulated environments. We are good to go here for quite a while."

"Do you have any type of medical facility set up?" Bonita asked.

"Yes well, we have a place set up for one. I don't know that it will have everything that you will need, but in the future, we will be able to go out on supply runs. Hopefully, we will be able to find anything else that you might need at abandoned clinics or hospitals. I'll be happy to show it to you a little bit later."

"Thank you, I would appreciate that. Once you do get out to do supply runs another good place to look for medical supplies are vet clinics. No one really thinks about going there in the movies or anything, but they have very similar supplies to what you would find elsewhere." Trevor nodded before turning his attention to Trent, who had begun to speak.

"Bonita was able to grab some of her own supplies. When we unload the truck, we can add them to what you have. Personally, I'd like to learn all I can about the systems," Trent added. "I'm going to need to make my being here worth it for you. You have saved my family by letting us take shelter with you. You are also providing my family with protection that I wasn't able to provide them. We will be forever in your debt."

"Your skills are invaluable, as are Bonita's. I'm glad my kid brother was convincing enough that you decided to come with them. There will be something for everyone to do here and, hopefully, soon we will have more company. Mom and Dad are on their way with Elli's family, and I believe there are more families that Dad had prior arrangements with. As far as I know, the plan is for him to meet them along the way. They should all arrive together. We have ten cabins connected by these tunnels. Also, there are underground bunkers that could hold more people if we needed them. They aren't the most luxurious accommodations, but they are certainly better than the alternative."

"So what do we do now," I asked the room at large.

"Well," Trevor replied, "for now I think we should all bunk in the main cabin. I pulled the shutters down after you guys pulled the trucks to the back. The house now looks no different than any of the other houses that are tucked away without power. Lights visible to the outside would make us stand out like a Christmas tree at this point. We definitely do not want to draw attention to ourselves at all. The boys and I will take turns monitoring the security cameras for now."

"I can help with that," Brandon volunteered. "Just show me what I need to do."

"We appreciate it. You can work shifts with me for a few days until you really understand the systems and the controls. You don't have to worry there will be plenty that we will need your help with. This shelter has enough work to keep everyone occupied."

I was still looking around the room as everyone else talked. I noticed that the room had actually been carved into the mountain. I scanned the stone walls looking for something that was comforting and homey rather than cold and hard. There was nothing. My eyes finally came back to rest on Ty's truck. I was shocked when I saw Jules standing beside it looking very confused. I wasn't sure if I should approach her after her last interaction with Ty and me.

I turned to where Bonita was standing and spoke to her quietly. "Jules is out of the truck. She looks calm enough, but I don't know if I should go talk to her or not."

Bonita turned, took my hand, and led me towards where Jules had sat down beside the truck. She looked lost and fragile. Her knees were pulled to her chest, and she seemed lost. As we made our way across the expansive room, Bonita whispered, "We just need to play it by ear here. If she is still volatile, we will need to approach her differently. She doesn't look like she is still aggressive, but we still need to use caution. Sometimes looks can be deceiving."

I approached Jules cautiously as Bonita had suggested. She looked up and saw me. She didn't begin yelling or ranting, and I took that as a good sign. Her eyes were filled with pain, and a single tear slid down her cheek. I saw her lip quiver as I approached and knew that she was trying as hard as she could to hold herself together. Bonita patted my arm, whispering, "I think you will be okay," before walking over to stand by her truck where she would be close enough to intervene if necessary but far enough away to allow us some privacy.

I sat down beside Jules, leaning against the truck. I reached over, took her hand in mine, and just sat quietly, waiting for her to speak. I just wanted to be there for her, to comfort her or provide whatever small amount of support that I could. After a moment she leaned her head against my shoulder and began to sob, silently. It was heartbreaking. I felt eyes on me and saw that Ty was watching intently, ready to come to intervene if she seemed to flip back into the angry, combative Jules that we had encountered earlier.

The right thing to do seemed to be to just sit quietly and be there for her, so that's what I did. Eventually, the guys all took off to do whatever it was that they needed to do, but Ty stayed, watching. Bonita also remained nearby in case she was needed. Finally, Jules took a deep breath.

"Ty got us here. I knew that he would. I wish, well, I wish Ben was here too. I cannot believe that he is gone. It just doesn't seem real. None of this seems like it could possibly be real."

"I wish he was here with us too," I replied. "I'm so sorry. I would give anything if we could go back and change things."

"I know you would, and I know Ty would too." Jules squared her shoulders and seemed to pull all of her emotions back into herself. I had seen her do this before when dealing with her mother and it made me sad that she was reverting back into self-protection mode. "So we're here. What do we need to do now? What can I do to help?"

Brandon had just walked back into the room and, ignoring looks from both Bonita and Ty, made his way to where Jules and I were sitting.

"Glad to see you up. How are you feeling?" Brandon kneeled down in front of Jules and spoke to her gently.

"I'm sorry. Do I know you?" She looked at me in confusion.

"Do you remember Brandon, Bonita or Trent?" I asked her.

"No, I... No, should I?"

"Bonita is a nurse practitioner. She talked to you a few hours ago. This is her brother Brandon, and Trent is her husband. Their daughter, Sarah, is with us too. Do you remember them at all?"

"No. I'm sorry, I don't really remember anything after... after you know."

"It's okay sweetie. It's not important."

Brandon spoke up again. "How about I take you and show you where your room is going to be for now? You can clean up or rest, whatever you need to do."

Jules looked at me, and I nodded encouragingly. It would be good for her to go somewhere comfortable, somewhere that had a homey feel and where she might feel even a little bit safe. The day had been eye-opening and traumatizing for all of us, but Jules had gotten the worst of it. I patted her hand and then stood, pulling her up to her feet.

"I should stay and help. Shouldn't I?" She looked to me for an answer.

"There'll be plenty of time for you to help later. Go now and rest, or clean up. I am here for you if you need anything." I knew she needed some time for herself. Now that she seemed to be thinking more clearly she would need to process what had happened.

"Is there anything particular that you would like to grab to take to your room? Anything that I can carry for you?" Brandon asked.

I helped Brandon find Jules's bags in the back of Ty's truck and then they were on their way. I watched them go and noticed that Brandon was speaking quietly to her as they walked, seeming to reassure her. Ty was at my side almost immediately after Brandon led Jules from the room. He pulled me into his arms and looked into my eyes. I could see the worry there, and I wasn't sure if he was worried about my conversation with Jules or something else.

"How is she," he asked almost immediately.

"She's sad, depressed, confused, hurting. She's going to need some time and her friends." Ty nodded in reply and looked back to the command center, as Trevor had titled it. "Is something wrong?"

"I thought we would have some contact from Dad, but we have been trying to get them and haven't gotten any reply. All of our delays made our trip much longer than it should have been. Unless something happened on their end, they should be close enough to hear us by now."

"Isn't it likely they are just delayed too? You know, little delays like we had. Well, not that all of our delays weren't serious but, nevermind, I understand why you are worried." My mind started scrambling to try to find reasons for their delay that weren't as worrisome. "Aren't they supposed to be meeting other people along the way as well?"

"Yes, they are, and it is likely that they just ran into some small issue. I just have a bad feeling. I'm sure that I'm just overreacting. We will get some news soon."

If Ty felt a reason to be worried, then I was worried as well. Mr. Robins would have left the city prepared for almost anything. I couldn't imagine anything that would have delayed them, at least nothing small and insignificant. Did they get forced to a shelter by the military? They had more mountains to go through than we did. Was it possible that they had gotten trapped by a landslide? My imagination started to run away with itself. I hated this world where I couldn't just pick up my cell phone and call someone to make sure that they were alright. Somehow Ty could tell that his comment had caused me stress.

"Hey, I'm sure that they're fine, just delayed somehow. They had much further to go than we did and we haven't been here that long. If the roads that they were traveling became blocked by landslides, they would have had to find a way around. Their route had more mountain travel, and they had more cities to avoid as well. They'll get here, don't worry. Okay?"

"I'll do my best. So what do we do now?"

"We wait, and we do what you are so good at babe. We stay optimistic. They will get here, and until they do, we need to make sure that this place is secure and operating as it should. If there are system issues or damages to anything now would be the time to fix the problems. That's what we focus on."

"Okay, so what do I need to do? I can't help you with systems, and I am not capable of repairing anything. There has to be something I can do."

"The first thing we are going to do is go to our room and clean up. I don't know about you, but I am tired of all of this caked on dust and dirt, not to mention blood. We can grab some of our bags and take them to the cabin. We'll wash up and put on some clean clothes. I don't know about you, but I will think much more clearly once I've taken a shower. Trevor is checking over the systems now to make sure that everything is working as it should. He needs a little bit of time to do that. After we've cleaned up, I'll show you around, and then we'll go from there."

∞ ∞ ∞

With a plan in place, we grabbed what we could carry from the back of the truck. Ty led me to one of the tunnels which led away from the mountain in a relatively straight line back towards where the house was. The tunnel appeared to be made of concrete. Lights lined the ceiling, creating an atmosphere that was not at all what I would expect from an underground tunnel. It wasn't at all small, dark, dreary, cold, or wet. It seemed to just be a nice extension of the cavern. Large enough for a golf cart or four wheeler to easily travel through, it was clean, dry, and even relatively warm.

As we walked through the tunnel, Ty talked about all the work that his father had done to ensure that all the cabins were connected by these tunnels. Apparently, golf carts were used to travel to the cabins that were further away from the main area. I wondered where those were kept. I hadn't seen them in the main cavern that we had just left. There was pride in Ty's voice as he told me about the many different security features of what he called the bunker. It didn't surprise me that Mr. Robins had left nothing to chance. There were others who should be joining us, in addition to our families. According to Ty, they were all well versed in specific methods of security that the shelter had in place. Each group had been briefed on how to approach the bunker to ensure that the command center would know that they were a friend, not a threat.

"Sounds like a lot of work went into the building and preparation of this place. I am amazed, in awe even. I mean, yes we jokingly and affectionately referred to your dad as a doomsday prepper, but I never even could have imagined that you guys had all of this here. Obviously, I knew that your family spent vacations and long weekends here, but this is a lot of work. Ben and Ken had been here with you, they never mentioned the sheer magnitude of all that you guys have done to prepare. You're like the ants in the story about the ants and the grasshoppers. You all prepared while the rest of us played."

Ty chuckled at my analogy.

"You hate ants," he joked. "Much of the time we spent here was work, but it was always fun. Dad made sure of it. We always had time for recreation as well. A lot of the work was done when I wasn't here. Many of the business trips Dad took were to here. I mean this was his business and if he was going to advise others on how to prep for catastrophe than he had to be prepared as well."

Chapter Fourteen

Our trip down the tunnel didn't take very long, and soon we arrived at a wooden door that looked, surprisingly, very similar to any of the interior doors of my house. Ty opened the door, and we walked into a beautiful family room. There was a large flatscreen television, a billiard table, and a wide variety of other options for entertainment strategically placed throughout the expansive room. Ty closed the door behind us, and I realized that from the inside of the room the door just looked like it would hide a closet, not a secret passageway.

"Impressive," I commented.

Ty nodded. "He thought of everything. Normally the door would be locked, and no one would be the wiser about what was behind it. Come on, I'll show you my, well our, room and we can get cleaned up."

"That's rather presumptuous of you, isn't it?"

"Perhaps," he replied, "but in this world, I am not going to spend a night away from you without a good reason. I don't think you can give me a good reason. There is also the fact that, for now, we will all be staying in this cabin which means that we have to share accommodations. I'm just doing my part."

His wink made me smile, and for just a moment it felt like maybe things would be okay. That perhaps someday I would be able to pick up my cell phone, call my friends, and head to the mall. I would be able to go to college and follow my dreams. His smile had the power to make me forget that that world as we knew it was gone. When the truth came rushing back, it wasn't quite as devastating as it had been before. Against all the odds, we had made it here. For now, at least, we were safe and warm. We had plenty of supplies, and there were security measures in place to keep us safe. With Trevor and his soldiers here, we even had our own security team, in a manner of speaking. While I mourned the loss of what was I did know how lucky we were to be in the situation that we were.

My face must have shown the many mixed emotions that I was feeling. Ty pulled me into an embrace. He tilted my chin so that he could look directly into my eyes. "Don't worry babe. I am not going to pressure you to do anything that you aren't ready to do. I just really want you right beside me, day and night."

I flashed him a smile and pulled his lips to me for a kiss. "I'm not worried, and there is nowhere else that I would rather be. Now, show me where the room is so that we can clean up."

Ty quickly led me up two flights of stairs. I really wasn't able to take much time to get a good impression of the house, just a quick glimpse as we made our way to Ty's room. When we finally got to the upstairs hallway, Ty gave me a quick overview of the layout. His bedroom was at one end of the hallway and Trevor's was at the other. In between the two were three other closed doors. Ty explained that there were two additional bedrooms on this floor and a guest bathroom. Both his and Ty's bedrooms had attached bathrooms, and his parent's bedroom was on the main floor. There were additional bedrooms in the basement, which is where Brandon and the soldiers would likely bunk for now according to Ty.

We turned towards Ty's room, and I heard one of the doors open behind us. I looked back to see Brandon emerging from one of the guest rooms. He was smiling, and I heard him tell someone that they should get some rest. He added that he would stop by to check on the person a little bit later before lightly closing the door. I assumed that he was talking to Jules, and felt guilty because I should be the one taking care of her. I should be ensuring that she was alright and getting settled. I stopped and sat down the bags I was carrying. I turned and walked back to where Brandon stood.

"Thank you for bringing her up here, and for taking the time to get her settled. I should be the one taking care of all of that. Is there anything she needs, anything that I can take care of for her?" Brandon shook his head no at the question. "I should just peek in at her to make sure she's okay and knows where we are."

"You can if you want and if it will make you feel better, but she's okay for now. She's just settling in, and I think trying to feel normal. And you're welcome. I don't mind at all. She's just a little bit of a thing, and she's been through a bunch today. If I can help her in any way, I am more than willing to do so."

"You're a good man," Ty said from behind me. Apparently, he had followed me when I walked over to talk to Brandon. "If she tells you of anything that she needs just let me know. I'll see that she gets it. Elli, why don't you go in and check on her quickly? Let her know that we will be just down the hall if she needs anything. There was something I wanted to talk to Brandon about and could use a few minutes alone with him."

I knocked lightly on the door to Jules temporary room and heard her call out quietly from the other side. I slowly opened the door and walked into the room, closing the door behind me. Jules was sitting in a chair with her legs curled beneath her. She was looking at something which was held tightly in her hand. When I got closer, I saw that it was her cell phone. The lit screen showed a picture of her and Ben mugging for the camera in happier times. I sat on the edge of the bed, just across from where she sat.

"Is there anything I can get you? Anything that I can do for you?"

"That guy, what was his name?"

"Brandon?"

"Yes. Brandon brought my things up. I was just taking a minute to... Well, he showed me where the restroom is. I'm just going to go clean up. I feel dirty and ... Maybe I'll feel better after a shower. I think I'm okay. Well, I think I will be okay. I'm not okay now, but I'm okay. I'm sorry, that's confusing."

I patted her knee. "I understand. I'm here if you need anything. Ty and I will be staying in the room just down at the end of the hall. We are both here for you, no matter what. Do you understand?"

Jules got up and came to sit beside me on the bed. She gave me a hug, crying a few more tears. When she pulled away, her eyes were red and puffy but clear with their usual glint of intelligence.

"I understand. You two are good friends, the best. Some people would have just left me somewhere along the way. Especially if some of the things I kind of remember truly happened. I love you. Thank you," she said in an almost normal voice. "I just need some time alone for now, but if I need something, I will find you."

I nodded in reply giving her another quick hug before heading to the door. I put my hand on the knob and looked back to where Jules sat, once again in the chair curled up with her legs beneath her. The phone was clutched in her hand, and she stared down at it. I could see a lone tear rolling down her cheek. Grief was evident in every aspect that she presented to the world. I knew how Jules dealt with anything negative. She needed time alone, just like she had asked for. She needed to process what had happened and come to grips with it on her own terms. If she needed me, she would come to me. When I left, I quietly closed the door behind me.

Neither Brandon or Ty were anywhere to be seen when I emerged into the hallway. The bags that I had been carrying were missing as well. Ty had apparently taken all of the bags into his room. I didn't see him but the door to his room was open, and I made my way there. My bags were all neatly piled in one corner. Ty must have been in the attached restroom because I could hear the water running.

I took a moment to look around the room. It really reflected Ty, rather than just any typical teenage boy. It didn't have posters of women in bikinis or cars all over the walls. There were mementos of family trips, pictures of his family in addition to ones of he and I together all spread here and there throughout the room. The bedroom itself had subdued décor, most of the colors were those that would be found if you walked through the woods on a fall day. I noticed a shelf full of books and walked over to see what he had been reading. The books were all either how-to or survival guides. He wouldn't have had these in his room back home, I thought. His friends would have given him too much crap about being a prepper if he had. This room actually suited him more than the one at his house in Columbus. It was simplistic, providing just what he needed, while the one in Columbus was full of trophies from years of participating in, and winning, football and baseball. This room was the real Ty, the one he shared with me.

I was looking for clothes to change into when Ty emerged from the restroom. My breath caught in my throat at the sight of him. His hair was wet and had a sexy, tousled appearance. He'd apparently taken the quickest shower on record. The dirt and dust were gone. There were still cuts and abrasions, but the dried blood had been washed away. He had put on clean jeans but had obviously forgotten his shirt. I must have been mesmerized by the sight of him because his chuckle pulled me from my thoughts. Tearing my eyes up to his face I found him looking at me like he knew exactly what I had been thinking. I felt myself begin to blush.

"See something you like babe?"

I must have been feeling brave. I strolled to where he was standing and put one hand on his naked chest. The other hand reached up to caress his cheek before pulling his head down to mine for a long, lingering kiss. His eyes were smoldering when I finally pulled away from him.

"Yes, yes I do," I replied flippantly over my shoulder, grabbing my clothes and walking into the restroom. I heard him release a low groan behind me. I smiled as I closed the door, took a deep breath and tried to calm my racing heart. I looked in the mirror and saw that my blush was visible beneath the layer of grime and dust. I look horrible, I told myself. I'm surprised he even kissed me. I quickly stripped out of my clothes and jumped into the shower. It would be great to wash away the remnants of this trip and feel clean again. The hot water felt heavenly, and I closed my eyes, focusing on the feel of each warm drop as it hit my body. For just a few minutes, I wanted to forget all of the struggles that would face us in the future.

After a quick shower, I felt so much better. Perhaps even a bit more optimistic. I knew our families would overcome whatever had delayed them and arrive soon. I couldn't wait to see my parents. I really wanted to give Lucy a hug and apologize for our stupid fight yesterday. Everything that had happened had given me a new understanding of what was really important as well as a better appreciation of what I had compared to others. I hadn't realized how much I took for granted until today.

Once I had dried and dressed, Ty took me on a quick tour of the house. Temporarily Trent, Bonita, and Sarah would be staying in the fourth bedroom on our floor. Ty said they would probably be given one of the other cabins once everyone had arrived and things had been all sorted out. The main floor had an open concept design. It featured a spacious kitchen, a dining area with an enormous table that looked as if it could seat twenty, and a living room that was filled with overstuffed furniture, which looked comfortable enough to live in. An entire wall was filled with books, and I quietly hoped that there were diverse genres represented.

Ty knew me too well because he chose that moment to interject into my pondering, "Don't worry there are hundreds of books here that you will enjoy. Mom made sure that we had a wide variety of reading material. Not to mention, entertainment that does not require internet connectivity or even electricity."

I smiled up at him, and he continued the tour. Off to the side of this large open space were the master bedroom suite and Mr. Robins' office. I could see Ty's mom's influence in the comfortable and welcoming décor. It was evident that she had put a lot of thought and love into making sure that this would be more than just a safe house. It would be home.

We headed back into the basement, and I took a better look at what Ty called the game room. In addition to the billiard table, there was a card table, foosball, and Ping-Pong. Ty explained that the closets were filled with board games as well. Other than closets, there were a total of four doors in the room. One led back to the tunnel, two were more bedrooms, and the last led to another restroom. Ty explained that this, the main cabin, had been designed to be a sort of clubhouse/entertainment center for people who would be living in the other cabins. While all the cabins were fully functional homes and furnished comfortably, they weren't all set up as lavishly as the main house.

After touring the main house, we headed back through the tunnel to the mountain bunker. Ty wanted to check in with Trevor, and we needed to start unloading trucks and putting away the supplies that we had brought with us. We walked to where Trevor was still sitting at the command center pushing buttons and looking at screens.

"So how are things looking?"

"All systems seem to be operating properly. There might be some damage to one of the cabins from landslides, or it could just be an issue with the camera. Won't know until we get out to the cabin and check it out. It's not the top priority right now."

They started talking numbers and looking at different programs on the computer. The screen seemed to be displaying data from the life-supporting systems that kept the bunker operating and able to provide a completely safe and functional shelter. The two-way radio had been kept on and seemed to be working perfectly, Trevor shared, except for the fact that there had been no contact. After Ty was content that he had all the information that he needed about the current status he turned his focus to unloading his truck and getting things put in their proper places.

After a few minutes, Brandon and Trent appeared, and a joint venture began to move supplies to designated storage areas. Ty showed me where the clinic that Bonita would use was, and I was put in charge of running all medical supplies there while Bonita spent some time watching over Sarah while she rested.

The room that would house the clinic was big and bright. It had actual walls, and everything was white and sterile looking. I thought that Bonita would love it. There were multiple beds in the room where I supposed that Bonita would be able to care for anyone who needed more than patch up and go care. I carried all the boxes in that Ty and the others set aside for me. I was staring at the pile, contemplating whether or not I should try to put them away or wait and let Bonita organize them in a way that was logical to her, when she and Sarah bounced through the door.

Sarah immediately wandered off to explore while Bonita paused just inside the threshold to give the room a thorough once over. She seemed pleased by what she saw, a smile forming on her beautiful face.

"This is just wonderful," she said to me. "This will work very well. Thank you for bringing all of the supplies here for me. I'll take time to organize them and put them away, so I'll know just where everything is. I need to familiarize myself with everything that is already here anyway."

"Oh, you're welcome. It was no big deal. I need to keep busy and these things needed to be brought here. How is your room?"

"It is wonderful. This place is amazing. I have to thank you again for allowing my family to come here with you. You truly have saved our lives. We will never be able to repay you for this. How could we ever repay you?"

Bonita walked to me and pulled me into a firm hug. She held me for a moment or two until Sarah came up and pulled on her pants leg.

"Mommy? What wrong Mommy? Why you cry?"

Bonita released me and picked up her daughter. "I'm just happy to be here sweetie. I'm glad that our new friends, Elli and Ty, let us come with them."

Sarah looked at me and gave me a big smile. She took her small hand and placed it ever so gently on my cheek. "Elli my new friend."

I returned Sarah's smile and gave them both a quick hug. "We are glad you are here with us. I need to go see if Ty needs help with anything else. Enjoy exploring!"

I quickly made my way back to the main room. When I walked in, I immediately saw that Ty and Trevor were together at the command center again. I could hear a loud static coming from somewhere, and I walked over to see what was going on. I had just about reached them when I heard Mr. Robins's voice come across what I now realized was the two-way radio. The connection wasn't good, and we only heard maybe half of what he was saying.

"... unavoidable... delay. Watch out... unexpected dangers. ...separated."

Ty grabbed the radio and called out, "Dad? Dad! Can you hear us? When will you be here?"

His response, the last few words we heard over the radio, was almost crystal clear. "Trust no one. Stay safe. We are coming."

And then there was nothing but static.

Epilogue

May 23rd, Ten Years Later

The sight of the bright golden rays of sunlight breaking through clouds that were floating here and there in the beautiful blue sky still brought me a feeling of unimaginable joy. When we first arrived at the compound ten years ago, darkness descended, and it had lasted longer than any of us had ever imagined it would. Countless days passed while the sun stayed buried behind tons of dust and debris that had settled into the earth's atmosphere after a giant bolide struck the west coast. The longer the sun stayed hidden, the more desperate society had become. When the government didn't arrive to save its citizens, the people turned against it. Eventually, the structure of the government completely crumbled.

Once the military and police presence disappeared, complete chaos reigned. The population quickly dwindled. The lack of food, clean water, and warmth killed off much of humanity. However, the biggest killer of humanity was itself. Some men and women became predatory animals, preying on those weaker than themselves. They killed indiscriminately and took whatever they wanted. Inevitably the majority of the predators died as well. Eventually, small pockets of survivors were the only who remained. They had found shelter and methods for getting or keeping supplies to see them through the catastrophe.

We were one of those small pockets of survivors. There had been ups and downs for our group throughout the years. We'd lost people we loved, but we had also gained new family along the way. We collected people in the months that followed the event, and by the time things had gone completely bad, we had more than ten families living with us in the mountain cabins. With the systems to support life in place, our group was able to maintain a comfortable life while the world fell to pieces around us. Others had come to try to take the safety away from us, as we knew they would.

The sound of childish laughter pulled me from my reverie. I pushed myself out of the rocking chair where I had been sitting with my feet elevated. Getting up was starting to be quite a task, I thought. Swollen ankles were one of the joys of pregnancy that I could have done without. I made my way to the front porch and looked out to the green lawn that stretched from the house to the surrounding forest. I could see two small, rambunctious toddlers darting from tree to tree, joyously laughing as the sunlight warmed their skin. We had suffered through a long, cold winter this year and the children were happy to get out of the cabin to feel grass under their feet and sun on their skin. The young, dark-haired girl watching them play waved at me from her spot under a tree. Her action caught the attention of the small boy, who immediately looked in my direction.

"Mommy!" Two small pairs of feet immediately turned in my direction, running to me with the utmost haste. Luci, my youngest, stopped to pick a dandelion for me along the way. At her young age, she already looked so much my like my mother and sister that no one would have ever guessed her to be my child. Trev, my son, slid to a stop beside me. His big eyes looked up to mine. They were filled with questions, as he always was. So much like his father, even at four, he immediately tried to take control of the situation. He knew that I was not supposed to be on my feet. Bonita had wanted to put me on bed rest after all of the complications that I had experienced when delivering Luci, but in this world bed rest wasn't something that a person had the luxury of doing.

"Mommy, you know that you are not supposed to play. Miss Bonita said we have to let you rest. You go back inside and rest, or I will tell Miss Bonita!"

I smiled down at Trev and ruffled his hair. It felt so soft, still baby-like under my hand. He was definitely his father's son, always ultra-aware of his surroundings and the current situation. I tried to make sure that he spent time merely playing and having fun, but sometimes it was a challenge. He felt a sense of responsibility for everyone else's well-being, especially when his father wasn't home to keep everyone safe.

"It's okay Trev," I tried to reassure him. "I wish I could play with you, but I know that I can't. I just wanted to feel the warm sunshine and smell the fresh air. Are you having fun?"

"Yes Mommy, we are. When will Daddy be home?"

"Hopefully soon buddy." I felt a tug on my pants leg and looked down into big brown eyes. Luci's face was pudgy, and her hair was an unruly mess of curls that surrounded her head like a light brown cloud. Her chubby hand stretched up to me, holding a hastily picked bundle of blooming weeds and spring wildflowers. I wanted to pick her up and give her a huge hug, but I knew in my current condition that wasn't possible. Instead, I smiled down at her.

"Those are beautiful flowers sweetie. I love them so much. They are so special because you picked them for me. Maybe if we ask Trev very nicely, he would take these inside and put them in some water for me so I can see them while I rest."

"Sure I will Mommy!" Trev reached over to take the flowers from his sister. "At least I will if you go lay down like you are supposed to."

Trev smiled up at me impishly, waiting for my reply. "Yes, I will go lay back down, so you don't have to tell on me. Luci will help me inside, won't you sweetie?"

Luci grabbed my hand and headed towards the front door. It was wonderful to be able to feel the pure joy found in holding my young daughter's hand on a bright, sunny spring morning after spending such a long time in darkness. Each day had been a struggle to survive, and we had it better than most. Luci's pudgy fingers were warm against my hand, and her voice was filled with the kind of excitement only found in a small child as she chattered on about flowers and bumble bees.

I rubbed my hand over my swollen belly as the baby there kicked. My body was telling me, in its subtle way, that the baby would be joining us soon. While I was anxious to meet the newest member of our family, I was afraid that something would go wrong during delivery again. Bonita had tried to reassure us that it was unlikely for me to have complications again. However, there was a part of me that was sure that something was going to go wrong, something even worse than last time.

I turned to walk back into the house with Luci. From the corner of my eye, I saw Sarah standup under the tree and bend down to gather her things. As I twisted at the waist to turn back to her, I felt a gush of warm liquid and a sharp pain in my abdomen. I released a cry of pain and surprise at about the same moment that Luci squealed at the sudden splash of liquid at her feet. Sarah dropped the things in her arms and sprinted to me. I also heard the sound of Trev's feet hitting the hardwood floor as he ran back to the porch from the kitchen. Trev reached me first.

"Mom! What's wrong? Sarah! Something is wrong!" His voice had a note of panic, but I could tell that he was trying to sound brave and in charge.

I tried to keep my composure as I reached down to pat his shoulder. "I'm okay Trev. Everything is going to be okay." Sarah reached the porch and took my hand from Luci to help me inside. "Trev, go get Bonita. Tell her it's time."

Trev took off like a rocket, and I let Sarah lead me into the house and to the downstairs bedroom. In between contractions, which seemed to be coming all too quickly, I changed into a comfortable, dry nightgown. Once I had changed, Sarah helped me settle into the big bed. She fluffed pillows to place behind my head and covered me with a cool cotton sheet.

Luci was playing quietly in the corner with the dolls her daddy had brought her when he returned from his last supply run. New toys were not a priority, so the kids loved any little present that was found and brought back to them. Each new toy was a glimpse into a world that was gone. They made me sad, but my children's joy made up for the sadness. I felt the corner of the bed shift as Luci crawled up to curl up beside me.

"Mommy okay?"

Her sweet voice, filled with concern brought tears to my eyes. I had gone through so much to bring her into this world, and she was such pure joy. I loved Trev, but he had been born when we were still struggling to survive in this new world. He knew that this world we lived in was tough and hard. People weren't always nice, but Luci had come into our lives when the world had calmed down. Survivors had found their niches and had, for the most part, stopped attacking other groups of survivors to take what they had. People had learned to be self-sufficient, and as a result, our world had become a safer place. Recently they had begun having regional organized areas where people could meet monthly to trade and barter. Families joined together and socialized. The last event had even included a picnic where children were able to meet and play with other children. The air of danger around every corner was gone, although everyone still always kept an awareness that danger could present itself at any time.

Another contraction hit and I tried not to wince in pain as Luci curled in more closely to my side. Sarah walked back into the room with a cool cloth to put on my forehead, and it was apparent from her expression that I wasn't doing a good job hiding my pain. She rushed to my side and took my hand, which I couldn't help but squeeze when the next contraction hit.

"Please take Luci to play in her room," I whispered in a low voice laced with pain. Sarah nodded and playfully picked Luci up from my side.

"Come on cutie patootie," Sarah said as she scooped Luci up.

"But I wanna stay with Mommy," I heard Luci cry as Sarah took her away. I could hear Sarah talking to her and a low, calm voice and knew that she was trying to soothe Luci so she would go to her room and play without stressing me any more than I already was. I didn't want the kids to see me in pain, but I didn't want to go through this alone.

Where was my husband, I wondered before another contraction hit me. I didn't want to cry out and upset Luci, so I tried to do the Lamaze breathing that Bonita had taught me. I focused solely on breathing in and out, slowly and calmly. It seemed to help with the pain and by the time Trev got back to the cabin with Bonita I was a little more relaxed.

With difficulty, Sarah was able to get Trev to go watch over Luci, and soon I was surrounded by the calm comfort that was Bonita. She went into motion immediately, ordering Sarah to the kitchen to boil water and gather things that we would need. After accessing the situation, she told me to try to relax, explaining how it would make things progress more efficiently, and said that we would have a baby soon. Labor did seem to progress quickly, and the world turned into a blur of pain and movement, whispering and pain. I vaguely heard Bonita tell Sarah to take the kids to the main house and to send back someone. The only thought I could hold on to was where is he. Soon I wasn't sure that I was capable of any actual thought, the pain was too extreme.

"Bonita, somethings wrong," I panted through clenched teeth. "It's never hurt this bad before. What's wrong? And where is he? Why isn't he here? He should be back by now. This is all wrong!"

"Listen to me! You need to calm down. Everything is going fine. Every labor is different, and you are just progressing slower than the last two times. You are fine. The baby is fine." Bonita tried to calm me in her firm, yet soothing, voice.

As Bonita patted my hand, the worst pain I had ever felt ripped through my abdomen. I couldn't help myself, I screamed. Bonita jumped up into action, checking my stomach and then checking to see if it was time to push. "Okay, it's time to push. This baby wants to see you."

"But he's not here," I cried.

She ignored me. "Push!"

I pushed with all my might, but nothing seemed to happen. The contraction stopped, and I was barely able to take a breath before the next one started. "Push!"

The pain was so intense, and I was so focused on pushing that I only vaguely heard the sound of the front door slamming against the wall as it was thrown open. His voice, sounding anxious and frightened as I had only heard it once before, echoed throughout the house.

"He's here," I whispered. Bonita ignored the entire commotion and firmly told me to push again. As much as I wanted to focus on his voice, I knew that I needed to push so I refocused and did as Bonita told me too. I pushed with every bit of energy I had left. In the back of my mind, I could hear him calling for me, but I couldn't reply. I focused all my energy on that final push and with a scream our tiny son found his way into the world. With the baby's first cry he rushed into the room, a look of dread on his face. At the sight of me smiling up at him and our son kicking on the changing table, I saw him visibly relax.

He walked to the bed, and I scooted over so he would have room to sit beside me. Reaching out, he smoothed my sweat-dampened hair from my forehead and leaned down to place a kiss there. "I'm sorry El... we had a..."

At just that moment, Bonita put our swaddled and now happy son in my arms. I looked into his eyes and knew that all was right with the world. Nothing could ever be better than this moment and, if the world hadn't changed, nothing that would have happened in that life would have been as significant as this moment. And just like that ... the days began again.

Made in United States
Orlando, FL
10 May 2022

17713005R00096